Charles Morris

Historical Tales

Vol. 3

Charles Morris

Historical Tales
Vol. 3

ISBN/EAN: 9783337348380

Printed in Europe, USA, Canada, Australia, Japan

Cover: Foto ©Andreas Hilbeck / pixelio.de

More available books at **www.hansebooks.com**

HISTORICAL TALES

The Romance of Reality

BY

CHARLES MORRIS

AUTHOR OF "HALF-HOURS WITH THE BEST AMERICAN
AUTHORS," "TALES FROM THE DRAMATISTS," "KING
ARTHUR AND THE KNIGHTS OF THE ROUND-TABLE," ETC.

SPANISH

PHILADELPHIA

J. B. LIPPINCOTT COMPANY

1899

CONTENTS.

CONTENTS.

LIST OF ILLUSTRATIONS.

SPAIN.

THE GOOD KING WAMBA.

Long had the Goths been lords of Spain. Chief after chief had they chosen, king after king had they served; and, though it was young in time, Gothic Spain was growing old in years. It reached its golden age in the time of "Good King Wamba," a king of fancy as much as of fact, under whom Spain became a land of Arcady, everybody was happy, all things prospered, and the tide of evil events for a space ceased to flow.

In those days, when a king died and left no son, the Goths elected a new one, seeking their best and worthiest, and holding the election in the place where the old king had passed away. It was in the little village of Gerticos, some eight miles from the city of Valladolid, that King Recesuinto had sought health and found death. Hither came the electors, —the great nobles, the bishops, and the generals,— and here they debated who should be king, finally settling on a venerable Goth named Wamba, the one man of note in all the kingdom who throughout his life had declined to accept rank and station.

The story goes that their choice was aided by miracle. In those days miracles were "as plentiful as blackberries"; but the essence of many of them seems to have been what we call common sense or political shrewdness. St. Leo told them to seek a husbandman named Wamba, whose lands lay somewhere in the west. The worthy saint said he had received this order from Heaven,—for which we may take his saintly word if we choose. However that be, scouts were sent through the land in search of Wamba, whom they found at length in his fields, driving his plough through the soil and asking for no higher lot. He was like Cincinnatus, the famous Roman, who was called from the plough to the sceptre.

"Leave your plough in the furrow," they said to him; "nobler work awaits you. You have been elected king of Spain."

"There is no nobler work," answered Wamba. "Seek elsewhere your monarch. I prefer to rule over my fields."

The astonished heralds knew not what to make of this. To them the man who would not be king must be a saint—or an idiot. They reasoned, begged, implored, until Wamba, anxious to get rid of them, said,—

"I will accept the crown when the dry rod in my hand grows green again,—and not till then."

The good old husbandman fancied that he had fairly settled the question, but miracle defeated his purpose. To his utter surprise and their deep astonishment the dry stick which he thrust into the ground at once became a green plant, fresh leaves breaking out on its upper end. What was the old man fond of his plough to do in such a case? He had appealed to Heaven, and here was Heaven's reply. He went with the heralds to the electoral congress, but there, in spite of the green branch, he again refused to be king. He knew what it meant to try and govern men like those around him, and preferred not to undertake the task. But one of the chiefs sprang up, drew his sword, and advanced to the old man.

"If you are still obstinate in refusing the position we offer you," he sternly said, "you shall lose your head as well as your crown."

His fierce eyes and brandished sword gave weight to his words, and Wamba, concluding that he would rather be a king than a corpse, accepted the trust. He was then escorted by the council and the army to Toledo, feeling more like a captive than a monarch. There he was anointed and crowned, and, from being lord of his fields, the wise old husbandman became king of Spain.

Such a king as Wamba proved to be the Goths had never known. Age had brought him wisdom, but it had not robbed him of energy. He knew what he had to expect and showed himself master of the situation. Revolts broke out, conspiracies threatened the throne, but one after another he put them down. Yet he was as merciful as he was prompt. His enemies were set free and bidden to behave themselves better in the future. One ambitious noble named Paul, who thought it would be an easy thing to take the throne from an old man who had shown so plainly that he did not want it, rose in rebellion. He soon learned his mistake. Wamba met him in battle, routed his army, and took him prisoner. Paul expected nothing less than to have his head stricken off, but Wamba simply ordered that it should be shaved.

To shave the crown of the head in those days was no trifling matter. It formed what is known as the tonsure, and was the mark of the priesthood. A man condemned to the tonsure could not serve as king or chieftain, but must spend the remainder of his days in seclusion as a monk. So Paul was disposed of without losing his life.

Wamba, however, did not spend all his time in fighting with conspirators. He was so just a king that all the historians praise him to the stars,— though none of them tell us what just deeds he did. He was one of those famous monarchs around whom legend loves to grow, as the green leaves grew around his dry rod, and who become kings of fancy in the absence of facts. About all we know is that he was "Good King Wamba," a just and merciful man under whom Spain reached its age of gold.

He made a great and beautiful city of Toledo, his capital. It had a wall, but he gave it another, stronger and loftier. And within the city he built a noble palace and other splendid buildings, all of which time has swept away. But over the great gate of Toledo the inscription still remains: *Erexit fautore Deo Rex inclytus urbem Wamba.* "To God and King Wamba the city owes its walls."

Alas! the end was what might be expected of such goodness in so evil an age. A traitor arose among those he most favored. There was a youth named Ervigio, in whose veins ran the blood of former kings, and whom Wamba so loved and honored as to raise him to great authority in the kingdom. Ervigio was one of those who must be king or slave. Ambition made him forget all favors, and he determined to cast his royal benefactor from the throne. But he was not base enough to murder the good old man to whom he owed his greatness. It was enough if he could make him incapable of reigning,—as Wamba had done with Paul.

To accomplish this he gave the king a sleeping potion, and while he was under its influence had him tonsured,—that is, had the crown of his head shaved. He then proclaimed that this had been done at the wish of the king, who was weary of the throne. But whether or not, the law was strict. No matter how or why it was done, no man who had received the tonsure could ever again sit upon the Gothic throne. Fortunately for Ervigio, Wamba cared no more for the crown now than he had done at first, and when he came back to his senses he made little question of the base trick of his favorite, but cheerfully enough became a monk. The remaining seven years of his life he passed happily in withdrawal from a world into which he had been forced against his will.

But the people loved him, the good old man, and were not willing to accept the scheming Ervigio as their king unless he could prove his right to the throne. So, in the year 681, he called together a council of lords and bishops at Toledo, before whom he appeared with a great show of humility, bringing testimony to prove that Wamba had become monk at his own wish, when in peril of death. To this he added a document signed by Wamba, in which he

abdicated the throne, and another in which he rec-
ommended Ervigio as his successor. For eight days
the council considered the question. The documents
might be false, but Wamba was a monk, and Ervigio
was in power; so they chose him as king. The holy
oil of consecration was poured upon his unholy head.

Thus it was that Wamba the husbandman first became king and afterwards monk. In all his stations
—farmer, king, and monk—he acquitted himself well
and worthily, and his name has come down to us
from the mists of time as one of those rare men of
whom we know little, but all that little good.

THE GREEK KING'S DAUGHTER.

HISTORY wears a double face,—one face fancy, the other fact. The worst of it is that we cannot always tell which face is turned towards us, and we mistake one for the other far oftener than we know. In truth, fancy works in among the facts of the most sober history, while in that primitive form of history known as legend or tradition fancy has much the best of it, though it may often be founded upon fact. In the present tale we have to do with legend pure and simple, with hardly a thread of fact to give substance to its web.

There was a certain Grecian king of Cadiz whose daughter was of such peerless beauty that her hand was sought in marriage by many of the other kings of Andalusia. In those days "that country was ruled by several kings, each having estates not extending over more than one or two cities." What to do with the crowd of suitors the father was puzzled to decide. Had a single one asked for his daughter's hand he might have settled it with a word, but among so many, equally brave, handsome, and distinguished, answer was not so easy; and the worthy king of Cadiz was sorely troubled and perplexed.

Luckily for him, the fair damsel was as wise as she was beautiful, and took the matter into her own hands, making an announcement that quickly cut down the number of her admirers. She said that she would have no husband but one who could prove himself "a wise king." In our days, when every king and nearly every man thinks himself wise, such a decision would not have deterred suitors, and she would have been compelled, in the end, to choose among the few unwise. But wisdom, in those times of fable and necromancy, had a wider meaning than we give it. A wise king was one who had control of the powers of earth and air, who could call the genii to his aid by incantations, and perform supernatural deeds. Hence it was that the suitors fell off from the maiden like leaves from an autumn bough, leaving but two who deemed themselves fitting aspirants to her hand.

To test the wisdom of these two she gave them the following tasks: One was bidden to construct on the mainland an aqueduct and a water-wheel to bring water from the mountains into Cadiz. The other was to produce a talisman which should save the island of Cadiz from invasion by Berbers or any other of the fierce tribes of Africa, by whom it was frequently threatened.

"The one of you," said the princess, "who first and best performs his task, shall win my hand by his work."

The two suitors were warmly in love with the beautiful maiden, and both ardently entered upon their duties. The first to get to work was the aqueduct builder, whose task called for hard labor rather than magical aid. Cadiz stands on a long, narrow peninsula, opposite which, on the mainland, the king built a hydraulic machine, to which the water was brought by pipes or canals from springs in a near-by mountain. This stream of cool, refreshing water poured upon a wheel, by which it was driven into an aqueduct crossing the bay into Cadiz.

Here comes the fact behind the legend. Such an aqueduct stood long in evidence, and as late as the eighteenth century traces of it could be seen. We have an account of it by the Arab writer, Al Makkari. "It consisted," he says, "of a long line of arches, and the way it was done was this: whenever they came to high ground or to a mountain they cut a passage through it; when the ground was lower, they built a bridge over arches; if they met with a porous soil, they laid a bed of gravel for the passage of the water; when the building reached the sea-shore, the water was made to pass underground, and in this way it reached Cadiz." So it was built, and "wise" was the king who built it, even if he did not call upon the genii for assistance.

The other king could not perform his labor so simply. He had a talisman to construct, so powerful that it would keep out of Spain those fierce African tribes whose boats swept the seas. What talisman could he produce that would be proof against ships and swords? The king thought much and deeply, and then went diligently to work. On the border of the strait that lay between Spain and Africa he built a lofty marble column, a square, white shaft based on a solid foundation. On its summit he erected a colossal statue of iron and copper, melted and cast into the human form. The figure was that of a Berber, like whom it wore a full and flowing beard, while a tuft of hair hung over its forehead in Berber fashion. The dress was that of the African tribes. The extended right arm of the figure pointed across the strait towards the opposite shores. In its hand were a padlock and keys. Though it spoke not, it seemed to say, "No one must pass this way." It bore the aspect of a Berber captive, chained to the tower's top, and warning his brethren to keep away from Spain.

Rapidly wrought the rival kings, each seeking to finish his work the first. In this the aqueduct builder succeeded. The water began to flow, the wheel to revolve, and the refreshing liquid to pour into the public fountains of Cadiz. The multitude were overjoyed as the glad torrent flowed into their streets, and hailed with loud acclamations the successful builder.

The sound of the people's shouts of joy reached the ears of the statue builder as he was putting the last touches to his great work of art and magic. Despair filled his heart. Despite his labors, his rival had won the prize. In bitterness of spirit he threw himself from the top of the column and was dashed to pieces at its foot. "By which means," says the chronicle, "the other prince, freed from his rival, became the master of the lady, of the wheel, and of the charm."

The talisman was really a watch-tower, from which the news of an African invasion could be signalled through the land. In this cold age we can give its builder credit for no higher magic than that of wisdom and vigilance.

NEAR the city of Toledo, the capital of Spain when that country was a kingdom of the Goths, was a great palace of the olden time, or, as some say, a vast cave, which had been deepened and widened and made into many rooms. Still others say that it was a mighty tower, built by Hercules. Whatever it was, —palace, tower, or cavern,—a spell lay upon it from far past days, which none had dared to break. There was an ancient prophecy that Spain would in time be invaded by barbarians from Africa, and to prevent this a wise king, who knew the arts of magic, had placed a secret talisman in one of the rooms. While this remained undisturbed the country was safe from invasion. If once the secret of the talisman should be divulged, swift ruin would descend upon the kingdom of the Goths. It must be guarded strongly and well, for in it lay the destinies of Spain.

A huge iron gate closed the entrance to the enchanted palace, and upon this each king of the Goths, on coming to the throne, placed a strong lock, so that in time huge padlocks covered much of its front and its secrecy seemed amply assured. When Roderic, the last king of the Goths, came to the throne, twenty-seven of such locks hung upon the gate. As for the keys, some writers tell us that they remained in the locks, others say that they had been hidden and lost; but it is certain that no one had dared to open a single one of the locks; prudence and fear guarded the secret better than gates and locks.

At length the time came when the cherished secret was to be divulged. Don Roderic, who had seized the throne by violence, and bore in his heart the fatal bane of curiosity, determined to learn what had lain for centuries behind those locks. The whole affair, he declared, was the jest of an ancient king, which did very well when superstition ruled the world, but which was far behind the age in which he lived. Two things moved the epoch-breaking king,—curiosity, that vice which has led thousands to ruin, and avarice, which has brought destruction upon thousands more. "It is a treasure-house, not a talisman," he told himself. "Gold, silver, and jewels lie hidden in its mouldy depths. My treasury is empty, and I should be a fool to let a cluster of rusty locks keep me from filling it from this ancient store."

When it became known what Roderic proposed a shudder of horror ran through the land. Nobles and bishops hastened to the audience chamber and sought to hinder the fateful purpose of the rash monarch. Their hearts were filled with dread of the perils that would follow any meddling with the magic spell, and they earnestly implored him not to bring the foretold disaster upon the land.

"The kings who reigned before you have religiously obeyed the injunction," they said. "Each of them has fixed his lock to the gate. It will be wise and prudent in you to follow their example. If it is gold and jewels you look for, tell us how much you think the cavern holds, even all your fancy hopes to find, and so much we will give you. Even if it beggars us, we will collect and bring you this sum without fail. We pray and implore you, then, do not break a custom which our old kings have all held sacred. They knew well what they did when they commanded that none after them should seek to disclose the fatal secret of the hidden chamber."

Earnest as was their appeal, it was wasted upon Roderic. Their offer of gold did not reach his deepest motive; curiosity with him was stronger than greed, and he laughed in his beard at the fears and tremblings of his lords.

"It shall not be said that Don Roderic, the king of the Goths, fears the devil or his agents," he loudly declared, and orders were given that the locks should be forced.

One by one the rusty safeguards yielded to key or sledge, and the gates shrieked disapproval when at length they reluctantly turned on their stiff hinges, that had not moved for centuries. Into the cavern strode the king, followed by his fearful but curious train. The rooms, as tradition had said, were many, and from room to room he hurried with rapid feet. He sought in vain. No gold appeared, no jewels glittered on his sight. The rooms were drear and empty, their hollow floors mocking his footsteps with long-silent echoes. One treasure only he found, the jewelled table of Solomon, a famous ancient work of art which had long remained hidden from human sight. Of this wonderful relic we shall say no more here, for it has a history of its own, to be told in a future tale.

On and on went the disappointed king, with nothing to satisfy his avarice or his curiosity. At length he entered the chamber of the spell, the magic room which had so long been locked from human vision, and looked with eyes of wonder on the secret which had been so carefully preserved.

What he saw was simple but threatening. On the wall of the room was a rude painting, which represented a group of strangely dressed horsemen, some wearing turbans, some bareheaded, with locks of coarse black hair hanging over their foreheads. The skins of animals covered their limbs; they carried scimitars and lances and bore fluttering pennons; their horses were small, but of purest breed.

Turning in doubt and dread from this enigmatical drawing, the daring intruder saw in the centre of the apartment a pedestal bearing a marble urn, in which lay a scroll of parchment. From this one of his scribes read the following words:

"Whenever this asylum is violated and the spell contained in this urn broken, the people shown in the picture shall invade the land and overturn the throne of its kings. The rule of the Goths shall end and the whole country fall into the hands of heathen strangers."

King Roderic looked again with eyes of alarm on the pictured forms. Well he knew their meaning. The turban-wearers were Arabians, their horses the famous steeds of the desert; the bare-headed barbarians were Berbers or Moors. Already they threatened the land from Africa's shores; he had broken the spell which held them back; the time for the fulfilment of the prophecy was at hand.

Filled with sudden terror, the rash invader hurried from the chamber of the talisman, his courtiers flying with wild haste to the open air. The brazen gates were closed with a clang which rang dismally through the empty rooms, and the lock of the king was fixed upon them. But it was too late. The voice of destiny had spoken and the fate of the kingdom been revealed, and all the people looked upon Don Roderic as a doomed man.

We have given this legend in its mildest form. Some Arab writers surround it with magical incidents until it becomes a tale worthy of the "Arabian Nights' Entertainments." They speak of two ancient men with snowy beards who kept the keys of the gate and opened the locks only at Roderic's stern command. When the locks were removed no one could stir the gates until the hand of the king touched them, when they sprang open of themselves. Inside stood a huge bronze giant with a club of steel, with which he dealt resounding blows on the floor to right and left. He desisted at the king's command, and the train entered unharmed. In the magic chamber they found a golden casket containing a linen cloth between tablets of brass. On this were painted figures of Arabs in armor. As they gazed these began to move, sounds of war were heard, and the vision of a battle between Arab and Christian warriors passed before the affrighted eyes of the intruders. The Christian army was defeated, and Roderic saw the image of himself in flight, and finally of his horse without a rider. As he rushed in terror from the fatal room the bronze giant was no longer to be seen and the ancient guardians of the gate lay dead upon their posts. In the end the tower was burned by magic fire, and its very ashes were scattered by the wings of an innumerable flight of birds.

THE BATTLE OF THE GUADA-LETE.

THE legends just given are full of the pith of facts. Dread of Africa lay deep in the Spanish heart and gave point to these and other magical and romantic tales. The story of how the great conqueror, Mohammed, had come out from the deserts of Arabia and sent his generals, sword and Koran in hand, to conquer the world, had spread far to the east and the west, and brought terror wherever it came. From Arabia the Moslem hordes had swept through Egypt and along the African coast to the extremity of Morocco. They now faced Spain and coveted that rich and populous land. Well might the degenerate sons of the Goths fear their coming and strive to keep them out with talismans and spells.

Years before, in the days of good King Wamba, a great Mohammedan fleet had ravaged the Andalusian coast. Others came, not for conquest, but for spoil. But at length all North Africa lay under the Moslem yoke, and Musa Ibn Nasseyr, the conqueror of the African tribes, cast eyes of greed upon Spain and laid plans for the subjugation to Arab rule of that far-spreading Christian land.

Africa, he was told, was rich, but Spain was richer. Its soil was as fertile as that of Syria, its climate as mild and sweet as that of Araby the Blest. The far-famed mines of distant Cathay did not equal it in wealth of minerals and gems; nowhere else were such harbors, nowhere such highlands and plains. The mountain-ranges, beautiful to see, enclosed valleys of inexhaustible fertility. It was a land "plentiful in waters, renowned for their sweetness and clearness,"—Andalusia's noble streams. Famous monuments graced its towns: the statue of Hercules at Cadiz, the idol of Galicia, the stately ruins of Merida and Tarragona. It was a realm the conquest of which would bring wealth and fame,—great glory to the sons of Allah and great treasure to the successors of the Prophet. Musa determined upon its invasion.

A traitor came to his aid. Count Julian was governor of Ceuta, a Spanish city on the African coast. His daughter Florinda was maid of honor to the queen of Don Roderic. But word from the daughter came to the father that she had suffered grievous injury at the hands of the king, and Count Julian, thirsting for revenge upon Roderic, offered to deliver Ceuta into the hands of the Arabian warrior and aid him in the conquest of Spain. To test the good faith of Julian, Musa demanded that he should first invade Andalusia himself. This he did, taking over a small force in two vessels, overrunning the coast country, killing many of its people, and returning with a large booty in slaves and plunder.

In the summer of 710 a Berber named Tarif was sent over to spy out the land, and in the spring of 711 the army of invasion was led over by Tarik Ibn

Zeyad, a valiant chief, who had gained great glory in the wars with the Berber tribes. Who Tarik was cannot be told. He was of humble origin, probably of Persian birth, but possessed of a daring spirit that was to bring him the highest fame. He is described as a tall man, with red hair and a white complexion, blind of one eye, and with a mole on his hand. The Spanish historians call him Tarik el Tuerto, meaning either "one-eyed" or "squint-eyed." Such was the man whom Musa sent to begin the conquest of Spain.

The army of invasion consisted of seven thousand men,—a handful to conquer a kingdom. They were nearly all Moorish and Berber cavalry, there being only three hundred Arabians of pure blood, most of whom were officers. Landing in Spain, for a time they found no one to meet them. Roderic was busy with his army in the north and knew naught of this invasion of his kingdom, and for two months Tarik ravaged the land at his will. But at length the Gothic king, warned of his danger, began a hasty march southward, sending orders in advance to levy troops in all parts of the kingdom, the rallying place being Cordova.

It was a large army which he thus got together, but they were ill-trained, ill-disciplined, and ill-disposed to their king. Ninety thousand there were, as Arab historians tell us, while Tarik had but twelve thousand, Musa having sent him five thousand more. But the large army was a mob, half-armed, and lacking courage and discipline; the small army was a compact and valorous body, used to victory, fearless, and impetuous.

It was on Sunday, the 19th of July, 711, that the two armies came face to face on the banks of the Guadalete, a river whose waters traverse the plain of Sidonia, in which the battle was fought. It was one of the decisive battles in the world's history, for it gave the peninsula of Spain for eight centuries to Arab dominion. The story of how this battle was fought is, therefore, among the most important of the historical tales of Spain.

Roderic's army consisted of two bodies of men,—a smaller force of cavaliers, clad in mail armor and armed with swords and battle-axes, and the main body, which was a motley crew, without armor, and carrying bows, lances, axes, clubs, scythes, and slings. Of the Moslem army the greater number wore mail, some carrying lances and scimitars of Damascus steel, others being armed with light long-bows. Their horses were Arabian or Barbary steeds, such as Roderic had seen on the walls of the secret chamber.

It was in the early morning of a bright spring day that the Spanish clarions sounded defiance to the enemy, and the Moorish horns and kettle-drums rang back the challenge to battle. Nearer and nearer together came the hosts, the shouts of the Goths met by the shrill *lelies* of the Moslems.

"By the faith of the Messiah," Roderic is reported to have said, "these are the very men I saw painted on the walls of the chamber of the spell at Toledo." From that moment, say the chroniclers, "fear entered his heart." And yet the story goes that he fought long and well and showed no signs of fear.

On his journey to the south Roderic had travelled in a chariot of ivory, lined with cloth of gold, and drawn by three white mules harnessed abreast. On the silken awning of the chariot pearls, rubies, and other rich jewels were profusely sprinkled. He sat with a crown of gold on his head, and was dressed in a robe made of strings of pearls interwoven with silk. This splendor of display, however, was not empty ostentation, but the state and dignity which was customary with the Gothic kings.

In his chariot of ivory Roderic passed through the ranks, exhorting the men to valor, and telling them that the enemy was a low rabble of heathens, abhorred of God and men. "Remember," he said, "the valor of your ancestors and the holy Christian faith, for whose defence we are fighting." Then he sprang from his chariot, put on his horned helmet, mounted his war-horse Orelia, and took his station in the field, prepared to fight like a soldier and a king.

For two days the battle consisted of a series of skirmishes. At the end of that time the Christians had the advantage. Their numbers had told, and new courage came to their hearts. Tarik saw that defeat would be his lot if this continued, and on the morning of the third day he made a fiery appeal to his men, rousing their fanaticism and picturing the treasures and delights which victory would bring them. He ended with his war-cry of "Guala! Guala! Follow me, my warriors! I shall not stop until I reach the tyrant in the midst of his steel-clad warriors, and either kill him or he kill me!"

At the head of his men the dusky one-eyed warrior rushed with fiery energy upon the Gothic lines, cleaving his way through the ranks towards a general whose rich armor seemed to him that of the king. His impetuous charge carried him deep into their midst. The seeming king was before him. One blow and he fell dead; while the Moslems, crying that the king of the Goths was killed, followed their leader with resistless ardor into the hostile ranks. The Christians heard and believed the story, and lost heart as their enemy gained new energy.

At this critical moment, as we are told, Bishop Oppas, brother-in-law of the traitor Julian, drew off and joined the Moslem ranks. Whether this was the case or not, the charge of Tarik led the way to victory. He had pierced the Christian centre. The wings gave way before the onset of his chiefs. Resistance was at an end. In utter panic the soldiers flung away their arms and took to flight, heedless of the stores and treasures of their camp, thinking of nothing but safety, flying in all directions through the country, while the Moslems, following on their flying steeds, cut them down without mercy.

Roderic, the king, had disappeared. If slain in the battle, his body was never found. Wounded and despairing, he may have been slain in flight or been drowned in the stream. It was afterwards said that his war-horse, its golden saddle rich with rubies, was found riderless beside the stream, and that near by lay a royal crown and mantle, and a sandal embroidered with pearls and emeralds. But all we can safely say is that Roderic had vanished, his army was dispersed, and Spain was the prize of Tarik and the Moors, for resistance was quickly at an end, and they went on from victory to victory until the country was nearly all in their hands.

WE have told how King Roderic, when he invaded the enchanted palace of Toledo, found in its empty chambers a single treasure,—the famous table of Solomon. But this was a treasure worth a king's ransom, a marvellous talisman, so splendid, so beautiful, so brilliant that the chroniclers can scarce find words fitly to describe its richness and value. Some say that it was made of pure gold, richly inlaid with precious stones. Others say that it was a mosaic of gold and silver, burnished yellow and gleaming white, ornamented with three rows of priceless jewels, one being of large pearls, one of costly rubies, and a third of gleaming emeralds. Other writers say that its top was made of a single emerald, a talisman revealing the fates in its lucid depths. Most writers say that it stood upon three hundred and sixty-five feet, each made of a single emerald, though still another writer declares that it had not a foot to stand upon.

Evidently none of these worthy chroniclers had seen the jewelled table except in the eye of fancy, which gave it what shape and form best fitted its far-famed splendor. They varied equally in their history of the talisman. A mildly drawn story says that it first came from Jerusalem to Rome, that it fell into the hands of the Goths when they sacked the city of the Cæsars, and that some of them brought it into Spain. But there was a story more in accordance with the Arabian love of the marvellous which stated that the table was the work of the Djinn, or Genii, the mighty spirits of the air, whom the wise king Solomon had subdued and who obeyed his commands. After Solomon's time it was kept among the holy treasures of the temple, and became one of the richest spoils of the Romans when they captured and sacked Jerusalem. It afterwards became the prize of a king of Spain, perhaps in the way stated above.

Thus fancy has adorned the rich and beautiful work of art which Don Roderic is said to have found in the enchanted palace, and which he placed as the noblest of the treasures of Spain in the splendid church of Toledo, the Gothic capital. This city fell into the hands of Tarik el Tuerto in his conquering progress through the realm of Spain, and the emerald table, whose fame had reached the shores of Africa, was sought by him far and near.

It had disappeared from the church, perhaps carried off by the bishop in his flight. But fast as the fugitives fled, faster rode the Arab horsemen on their track, one swift troop riding to Medina Celi, on the high road to Saragossa. On this route they came to a city named by them Medinatu-l-Mayidah (city of the table), in which they found the famous talisman. They brought it to Tarik as one of the choicest spoils of Spain.

Its later history is as curious and much more authentic than its earlier. Tarik, as we have told in the previous tale, had been sent to Andalusia by Musa, the caliph's viceroy in Africa, simply that he might gain a footing in the land, whose conquest Musa reserved for himself. But the impetuous Tarik was not to be restrained. No sooner was Roderic slain and his army dispersed than the Arab cavaliers spread far and wide through Spain, city after city falling into their hands, until it seemed as if nothing would be left for Musa to conquer.

This state of affairs was far from agreeable to the jealous and ambitious viceroy. He sent messengers to the caliph at Damascus, in which he claimed the conquest of Spain as his own, and barely mentioned the name of the real conqueror. He severely blamed Tarik for presuming to conquer a kingdom without direct orders, and, gathering an army, he crossed to Spain, that he might rightfully claim a share in the glory of the conquest.

Tarik was not ignorant of what Musa had done. He expected to be called sharply to account by his jealous superior, and knew well that his brilliant deeds had been overlooked in the viceroy's despatches to Damascus, then the capital of the Arab empire. The daring soldier was therefore full of joy when the table of Solomon fell into his hands. He hoped to win favor from Al-Walid, the caliph, by presenting him this splendid prize. Yet how was he to accomplish this? Would not Musa, who was well aware of the existence and value of the table, claim it as his own and send it to Al-Walid with the false story that he had won it by the power of his arms?

To defeat this probable act Tarik devised a shrewd stratagem. The table, as has been stated, was abundantly provided with feet, but of these four were larger than the rest. One of the latter Tarik took off and concealed, to be used in the future if what he feared should come to pass.

As it proved, he had not misjudged his jealous lord. In due time Musa came to Toledo and rode in state through the gate-way of that city, Tarik following like a humble servitor in his train. As soon as he reached the palace he haughtily demanded a strict account of the spoils. These were at hand, and were at once delivered up. Their number and value should have satisfied his avarice, but the wonderful table of Solomon, of which he had heard such marvellous accounts, was not among them, and he demanded that this, too, should be brought forward. As Tarik had foreseen, he designed to send it to the caliph, as an acceptable present and an evidence of his victorious career.

The table was produced, and Musa gazed upon it with eyes of delight. His quick glance, however, soon discovered that one of the emerald feet was missing.

"It is imperfect," he said. "Where is the missing foot?"

"That I cannot tell you," replied Tarik; "you have the table as it was brought to me."

Musa, accepting this answer without suspicion, gave orders that the lost foot should be replaced with one of gold. Then, after thanking the other leading officers for their zeal and valor, he turned upon Tarik and accused him in severe tones of disobedience. He ended by depriving him of his command and putting him under arrest, while he sent the caliph a report in which Tarik was sharply blamed and the merit of his exploits made light of. He would have gone farther and put him to death, but this he dared not do without the caliph's orders.

As it proved, Al-Walid, the Commander of the Faithful, knew something of the truth. Far distant as Damascus was from Toledo, a report of Tarik's exploits had reached his august ears, and Musa received orders to replace him in his command, since it would not do "to render useless one of the best swords of Islam." Musa dared not disobey; and thus, for the time being, Tarik triumphed.

And now, for the end of the trouble between Musa and Tarik, we must go forward in time. They were left in Spain until they had completed the conquest of that kingdom, then both were ordered to appear before the caliph's judgment seat. This they did in different methods. Tarik, who had no thirst for spoil, made haste, with empty hands, to Damascus, where, though he had no rich presents for the commander of the faithful, he delighted him with the story of his brilliant deeds. Musa came more slowly and with more ostentation. Leaving his sons in command in Spain and Africa, he journeyed slowly to Syria, with all the display of a triumphal march. With him were one hundred of his principal officers, as many sons of the highest Berber chiefs, and the kings of the Balearic Islands in all their barbaric state. In his train rode four hundred captive nobles, each wearing a crown and girdle of gold, and thirty thousand captives of lower rank. At intervals in the train were camels and wagons, richly laden with gold, jewels, and other spoils. He brought to the East the novelties of the West, hawks, mules, and Barbary horses, and the curious fruits of Africa and Spain, "treasures," we are told, "the like of which no hearer ever heard of before, and no beholder ever saw before his eyes."

Thus the proud conqueror came, by slow marches, with frequent halts. He left Spain in August, 713. It was February, 715, when he reached the vicinity of Damascus, having spent a year and a half on the way.

Meanwhile, changes had taken place in Syria. Al-Walid, the caliph, was sick unto death, suffering from a mortal disease. Soliman, his brother and heir, wrote to Musa when at Tiberias, on the Sea of Galilee, asking him to halt there, as his brother could live but a few days. He, as the new caliph, would receive him. Al-Walid in turn ordered him to hasten his march. Musa was in a quandary. If Al-Walid should live, delay might be fatal. If he should die, haste might be fatal. He took what seemed to him the safest course, hastened to Damascus, and met with a brilliant reception. But a change soon came; in forty days Al-Walid died; Soliman, whom he had disobeyed, was caliph of the empire. Musa's sun was near its setting.

It was not long before the conqueror found himself treated as a criminal. He was charged with rapacity, injustice to Tarik, and the purpose of throwing all power into the hands of his sons. He was even accused of "disobedience" for making a triumphal entry into Damascus before the death of Al-Walid. These and other charges were brought, Soliman being bent on the ruin of the man who had added Africa to the Arabian empire.

When Musa was brought before the caliph for a final hearing Tarik and many other soldiers from Spain were present, and there stood before the monarch's throne the splendid table of Solomon, one of the presents which Musa had made to Al-Walid, declaring it to be the most magnificent of all the prizes of his valor.

"Tell me," said the caliph to Tarik, "if you know whence this table came."

"It was found by me," answered Tarik. "If you would have evidence of the truth of my words, O caliph, have it examined and see if it be perfect."

Soliman gave orders, the table was closely examined, and it was soon discovered that one of its emerald feet was gone and that a foot of gold occupied its place.

"Ask Musa," said Tarik, "if this was the condition of the table when he found it."

"Yes," answered Musa, "it was as you see it now."

Tarik answered by taking from under his mantle the foot of emerald which he had removed, and which just matched the others.

"You may learn now," he said to the caliph, "which of us is the truth-teller. Here is the lost leg of the table. I found the table and kept this for evidence. It is the same with most of the treasures Musa has shown you. It was I who won them and captured the cities in which they were found. Ask any of these soldiers if I speak the truth or not."

These words were ruinous to Musa. The table had revenged its finder. If Musa had lied in this case, he had lied in all. So held the angry caliph, who turned upon him with bitter abuse, calling him thief and liar, and swearing by Allah that he would crucify him. In the end he ordered the old man, fourscore years of age, corpulent and asthmatic, to be exposed to the fierce sun of Syria for a whole summer's day, and bade his brother Omar to see that the cruel sentence was executed.

Until high noon had passed the old warrior stood under the scorching solar rays, his blood at length seeming to boil in his veins, while he sank suffocated to the earth. Death would soon have ended his suffering had not Omar, declaring "that he had never passed a worse day in his life," prevailed upon the caliph to abridge his punishment.

Bent upon his utter ruin, the vindictive Soliman laid upon him the enormous fine of four million and thirty thousand dinars, equal to about ten million dollars. His sons were left in power in Spain that they might aid him in paying the fine. Great as the sum was, Musa, by giving up his own fortune, by the aid of his sons in Africa and Spain, and by assistance from his friends, succeeded in obtaining it. But even this did not satisfy the caliph, who now banished him to his birthplace, that his early friends might see and despise him in his ruin. He even determined to destroy his sons, that the whole family might be rooted out and none be left in whose veins the blood of Musa ran.

The ablest of these sons, Abdul-Aziz, had been left in chief command over Spain. Thither the caliph sent orders for his death. Much as the young ruler was esteemed, wisely as he had ruled, no one thought of questioning an order of the Commander of the Faithful, the mighty autocrat of the great Arabian empire, and the innocent Abdul was assassinated by some who had been among his chief friends. His head was then cut off, embalmed, and sent to Soliman, before whom it was laid, enclosed in a casket of precious wood.

Sending for Musa, the vindictive caliph had the casket opened in his presence, saying, as the death-like features appeared, "Do you know whose head that is?"

The answer of Musa was a pathetic one. Never was there a Moslem, he said, who less deserved such a fate; never a man of milder heart, braver soul, or more pious and obedient disposition. In the end the poor old man broke down, and he could only murmur,—

"Grant me his head, O Commander of the Faithful, that I may shut the lids of his eyes."

"Thou mayest take it," was Soliman's reply.

And so Musa left the caliph's presence, heartbroken and disconsolate. It is said that before he died he was forced to beg his bread. Of Tarik we hear no more. He had fully repaid Musa for his injustice, but the caliph, who perhaps feared to let any one become too great, failed to restore him to his command, and he disappeared from history. The cruel Soliman lived only a year after the death of the victim of his rage. He died in 717, of remorse for his injustice to Musa, say some, but the record of history is that he was defeated before Constantinople and died of grief.

Thus ends our story of the table of Solomon. It brought good to none who had to do with it, and utter disaster to him who had made it an agent of falsehood and avarice. Injustice cannot hope to hide itself behind a talisman.

WHEN Roderic overthrew the ancient dynasty of
Spain and made himself king, he had the defences
of the cities thrown down that they might not give
shelter to his enemies. Only the walls of the frontier
cities were left, and among these was the ancient
city of Denia, on the Mediterranean shores. Dread
of the Moorish pirates was felt in this stronghold,
and a strong castle was built on a high rock that
overlooked the sea. To the old alcaide who served
as governor of Denia word was brought, at the end
of a day of fierce tempest, that a Moorish ship was
approaching the shore. Instantly the bells were
rung to rouse the people, and signal fires were
kindled on the tower that they might flash from
peak to peak the news of an invasion by the Moors.

But as the ship came closer it was seen that alarm
had been taken too soon. The vessel was alone and
had evidently been in the grip of the tempest. It
was seen to be a bark rich in carving and gilding,
adorned with silken banderoles, and driven through
the water by banks of crimson oars; a vessel of state
and ceremony, not a ship of war. As it came nearer
it was perceived to have suffered severely in the
ruthless grasp of the storm. Broken were its masts
and shattered its oars, while there fluttered in the
wind the torn remnants of its banners and sails.

40

When at length it grounded on the sands below the castle the proud bark was little better than a shattered wreck.

It was with deep curiosity that the Spaniards saw on the deck of the stranded bark a group of high-born Moors, men and maidens dressed in robes of silk rich with jewels, and their features bearing the stamp of lofty rank. In their midst stood a young lady of striking beauty, sumptuously attired, and evidently of the highest station, for all paid her reverence, and a guard of armed Moors stood around her, scimitar in hand.

On landing, a venerable Moor approached the alcaide, who had descended to meet the strangers, and said, in such words of the Gothic language as he could command,—

"Worthy sir, we beg your protection and compassion. The princess under our care is the only daughter of the king of Algiers, on her way to the court of the king of Tunis, to whom she is betrothed. The tempest has driven us to your shores. Be not, we implore you, more cruel than the storm, which has spared us and our precious charge."

The alcaide returned a courteous answer, offering the princess and her train the shelter of the castle, but saying that he had not the power to release them. They must hold themselves the captives of Roderic, the king of the Goths, to whom his duty required him to send them. The fate of a royal captive, he said, could be decided only by the royal voice.

Some days afterwards Elyata, the Moorish princess, entered Toledo in a procession more like that of a triumphant heroine than of a captive. A band of Christian horsemen preceded the train. The Moorish guard, richly attired, followed. In the midst rode the princess, surrounded by her maidens and dressed in her bridal robes, which were resplendent with pearls, diamonds, and other gems. Roderic advanced in state from his palace to receive her, and was so struck with her beauty and dignity of aspect that at first sight warm emotions filled his heart.

Elyata was sadly downcast at her captivity, but Roderic, though not releasing her, did all he could to make her lot a pleasant one. A royal palace was set aside for her residence, in whose spacious apartments and charming groves and gardens the grief of the princess gradually softened and passed away. Roderic, moved by a growing passion, frequently visited her, and in time soft sentiments woke in her heart for the handsome and courteous king. When, in the end, he begged her to become his bride her blushes and soft looks spoke consent.

One thing was wanting. Roderic's bride should be a Christian. Taught the doctrines of the new faith by learned bishops, love as much as conviction won Elyata's consent, and the Moorish princess was baptized as a Christian maiden under the new name of Exilona. The marriage was celebrated with the greatest magnificence, and was followed by tourneys and banquets and all the gayeties of the time. Some of the companions of the princess accepted the new faith and remained with her. Those who clung to their old belief were sent back to Africa with rich presents from the king, an embassy going with them

TOLEDO, WITH THE ALCAZAR.

to inform the monarch of Algiers of his daughter's marriage, and to offer him the alliance and friendship of Roderic the Gothic king.

Queen Exilona passed a happy life as the bride of the Gothic monarch, but many were the vicissitudes which lay before her, for the Arab conquest was near at hand and its effects could not but bear heavily upon her destiny. After the defeat and death of Roderic a considerable number of noble Goths sought shelter in the city of Merida, among them the widowed queen. Thither came Musa with a large army and besieged the city. It was strongly and bravely defended, and the gallant garrison only yielded when famine came to the aid of their foes.

A deputation from the city sought the Arab camp and was conducted to the splendid pavilion of Musa, whom the deputies found to be an old man with long white beard and streaming white hair. He received them kindly, praised them for their valor, and offered them favorable terms. They returned the next day to complete the conditions. On this day the Mohammedan fast of Ramadhan ended, and the Arabs, who had worn their meanest garb, were now in their richest attire, and joy had everywhere succeeded penitent gloom. As for Musa, he seemed transformed. The meanly dressed and hoary ancient of the previous visit now appeared a man in the prime of life, his beard dark-red in hue, and his robes rich with gold and jewels. The Goths, to whom the art of dyeing the hair was unknown, looked on the transformation as a miracle.

"We have seen," they said on their return, "their

king, who was an old man, become a young one. We
have to do with a nation of prophets who can change
their appearance at will and transform themselves
into any shape they like. Our advice is that we
should grant Musa his demands, for men like these
we cannot resist."

The stratagem of the Arab was successful, the
gates were opened, and Merida became a captive city.
The people were left their private wealth and were
free to come and go as they would, with the exception of some of their noblest, who were to be held as
hostages. Among these was the widowed Queen
Exilona.

She was still young and beautiful. By paying
tribute she was allowed to live unmolested, and in this
way she passed to the second phase of her romantic
career. Arab fancy has surrounded her history with
many surprising incidents, and Lope de Vega, the
Spanish dramatist, has made her the heroine of a
romantic play, but her actual history is so full of
interest that we need not draw contributions from
fable or invention.

When Musa went to Syria at the command of the
caliph he left his son Abdul-Aziz as emir or governor
of Spain. The new emir was a young, handsome,
and gallant man. He had won fame in Africa, and
gained new repute for wisdom and courage in Spain.
The Moorish princess who had become a Gothic queen
was now a hostage in his hands, and her charms
moved his susceptible heart. His persuasive tongue
and attractive person were not without their effect
upon the fair captive, who a second time lost her

heart to her captor, and agreed once more to become a bride. Her first husband had been the king of Gothic Spain. Her second was the ruler of Moorish Spain. She declined to yield her Christian creed, but she became his wife and the queen of his heart, called by him Ummi-Assam, a name of endearment common in Arab households.

Exilona was ambitious, and sought to induce her new husband to assume the style of a king. She made him a crown of gold and precious stones which her soft persuasion induced him to wear. She bowed in his presence as if to a royal potentate, and to oblige the nobles to do the same she induced him to have the door-way of his audience chamber made so low that no one could enter it without making an involuntary bow. She even tried to convert him to Christianity, and built a low door to her oratory, so that any one entering would seem to bow to the cross.

These arts of the queen proved fatal to the prince whom she desired to exalt, for this and other stories were told to the caliph, who was seeking some excuse to proceed against the sons of Musa, whose ruin he had sworn. It was told him that Abdul-Aziz was seeking to make Spain independent and was bowing before strange gods. Soliman asked no more, but sent the order for his death.

It was to friends of the emir that the fatal mandate was sent. They loved the mild Abdul, but they were true sons of Islam, and did not dare to question the order of the Commander of the Faithful. The emir was then at a villa near Seville, whither he was accustomed to withdraw from the cares of state to the society of his beloved wife. Near by he had built a mosque, and here, on the morning of his death, he entered and began to read the Koran.

A noise at the door disturbed him, and in a moment a throng burst into the building. At their head was Habib, his trusted friend, who rushed upon him and struck him with a dagger. The emir was unhurt, and sought to escape, but the others were quickly upon him, and in a moment his body was rent with dagger strokes and he had fallen dead. His head was at once cut off, embalmed, and sent to the caliph. The cruel use made of it we have told.

A wild commotion followed when the people learned of this murder, but it was soon quelled. The power of the caliph was yet too strong to be questioned, even in far-off Spain. What became of Exilona we do not know. Some say that she was slain with her husband; some that she survived him and died in privacy. However it be, her life was one of singular romance.

As for the kindly and unfortunate emir, his memory was long fondly cherished in Spain, and his name still exists in the title of a valley in the suburbs of Antequera, which was named Abdelaxis in his honor.

PELISTES, THE DEFENDER OF CORDOVA.

No sooner had Tarik defeated the Christian army on the fatal field of Sidonia than he sent out detachments of horsemen in all directions, hoping to win the leading cities of Spain before the people should recover from their terror. One of these detachments, composed of seven hundred horse, was sent against Cordova, an ancient city which was to become the capital of Moslem Spain. This force was led by a brave soldier named Magued, a Roman or Greek by birth, who had been taken prisoner when a child and reared in the Arab faith. He now ranked next to Tarik in the arts and stratagems of war, and as a horseman and warrior was the model and admiration of his followers.

Among the Christian leaders who had fled from the field of the Guadalete was an old and valiant Gothic noble, Pelistes by name, who had fought in the battle front until his son sank in death and most of his followers had fallen around him. Then, with the small band left him, he rode in all haste to Cordova, which he hoped to hold as a stronghold of the Goths. But he found himself almost alone in the town, most of whose inhabitants had fled with their valuables, so that, including the invalids and old soldiers found there, he had but four hundred men with whom to defend the city.

A river ran south of the city and formed one of its defences. To its banks came Magued,—led, say some of the chronicles, by the traitor, Count Julian, . —and encamped in a forest of pines. He sent heralds to the town, demanding its surrender, and threatening its defenders with death if they resisted. But Pelistes defied him to do his worst.

What Magued might have found difficult to do by force he accomplished by stratagem. A shepherd whom he had captured told him of the weakness of the garrison, and acquainted him with a method by which the city might be entered. Forcing the rustic to act as guide, Magued crossed the river on a stormy night, swimming the stream with his horses, each cavalier having a footman mounted behind him. By the time they reached the opposite shore the rain had changed to hail, whose loud pattering drowned the noise of the horses' hoofs as the assailants rode to a weak place in the wall of which the shepherd had told them. Here the battlements were broken and part of the wall had fallen, and near by grew a fig-tree whose branches stretched towards the breach. Up this climbed a nimble soldier, and by hard effort reached the broken wall. He had taken with him Magued's turban, whose long folds of linen were unfolded and let down as a rope, by whose aid others soon climbed to the summit. The storm had caused the sentries to leave their posts, and this part of the wall was left unguarded.

In a short time a considerable number of the assailants had gained the top of the wall. Leaping from the parapet, they entered the city and ran to the nearest gate, which they flung open to Magued and his force. The city was theirs; the alarm was taken too late, and all who resisted were cut down. By day-dawn Cordova was lost to Spain with the exception of the church of St. George, a large and strong edifice, in which Pelistes had taken refuge with the remnant of his men. Here he found an ample supply of food and obtained water from some secret source, so that he was enabled to hold out against the enemy.

For three long months the brave garrison defied its foes, though Magued made every effort to take the church. How they obtained water was what most puzzled him, but he finally discovered the secret through the aid of a negro whom the Christians had captured and who escaped from their hands. The prisoner had learned during his captivity that the church communicated by an underground channel with a spring somewhere without. This was sought for with diligence and at length found, whereupon the water supply of the garrison was cut off at its source, and a new summons to surrender was made.

There are two stories of what afterwards took place. One is that the garrison refused to surrender, and that Magued, deeply exasperated, ordered the church to be set on fire, most of its defenders perishing in the flames. The other story is a far more romantic one, and perhaps as likely to be true. This tells us that Pelistes, weary of long waiting for assistance from without, determined to leave the church in search of aid, promising, in case of failure, to return and die with his friends.

Mounted on the good steed that he had kept alive in the church, and armed with lance, sword, and shield, the valiant warrior set forth before the dawn, and rode through the silent streets, unseen by sentinel or early wayfarer. The vision of a Christian knight on horseback was not likely to attract much attention, as there were many renegade Christians with the Moors, brought thither in the train of Count Julian. Therefore, when the armed warrior presented himself at a gate of the city just as a foraging party was entering, he rode forth unnoticed in the confusion and galloped briskly away towards the neighboring mountains.

Having reached there he stopped to rest, but to his alarm he noticed a horseman in hot pursuit upon his trail. Spurring his steed onward, Pelistes now made his way into the rough intricacies of the mountain paths; but, unluckily, as he was passing along the edge of a declivity, his horse stumbled and rolled down into the ravine below, so bruising and cutting him in the fall that, when he struggled to his feet, his face was covered with blood.

While he was in this condition the pursuer rode up. It proved to be Magued himself, who had seen him leave the city and had followed in haste. To his sharp summons for surrender the good knight responded by drawing his sword, and, wounded and bleeding as he was, put himself in posture for defence.

The fight that followed was as fierce as some of those told of King Arthur's knights. Long and sturdily the two champions fought, foot to foot, sword to scimitar, until their shields and armor were rent and hacked and the ground was red with their blood. Never had those hills seen so furious a fight by so well-matched champions, and during their breathing spells the two knights gazed upon each other with wonder and admiration. Magued had never met so able an antagonist before, nor Pelistes encountered so skilfully wielded a blade.

But the Gothic warrior had been hurt by his fall. This gave Magued the advantage, and he sought to take his noble adversary alive. Finally, weak from loss of blood, the gallant Goth gave a last blow and fell prostrate. In a moment Magued's point was at his throat, and he was bidden to ask for his life or die. No answer came. Unlacing the helmet of the fallen knight, Magued found him insensible. As he debated with himself how he would get the captive of his sword to the city, a group of Moorish cavaliers rode up and gazed with astonishment on the marks of the terrible fight. The Christian knight was placed by them on a spare horse and carried to Cordova's streets.

As the train passed the beleaguered church its garrison, seeing their late leader a captive in Moorish hands, sallied fiercely out to his rescue, and for some minutes the street rang sharply with the sounds of war. But numbers gathered to the defence, the assailants were driven back, and the church was entered by their foes, the clash of arms resounding within its sacred precincts. In the end most of the garrison were killed and the rest made prisoners.

The wounded knight was tenderly cared for by his captor, soon regaining his senses, and in time recovering his health. Magued, who had come to esteem him highly, celebrated his return to health by a magnificent banquet, at which every honor was done the noble knight. The Arabs knew well how to reward valor, even in a foe.

In the midst of the banquet Pelistes spoke of a noble Christian knight he once had known, his brother in arms and the cherished friend of his heart, one whom he had most admired and loved of all the Gothic host,—his old and dear comrade, Count Julian.

"He is here!" cried some of the Arabs, enthusiastically, pointing to a knight who had recently entered. "Here is your old friend and comrade, Count Julian."

"That Julian!" cried Pelistes, in tones of scorn; "that traitor and renegade my friend and comrade! No, no; this is not Julian, but a fiend from hell who has entered his body to bring him dishonor and ruin."

Turning scornfully away he strode proudly from the room, leaving the traitor knight, overwhelmed with shame and confusion, the centre of a circle of scornful looks, for the Arabs loved not the traitor, however they might have profited by his treason.

The fate of Pelistes, as given in the Arab chronicles, was a tragic one. Magued, who had never before met his equal at sword play, proposed to send him to Damascus, thinking that so brave a man would be a fitting present to the caliph and a living testimony to his own knightly prowess. But others valued the prize of valor as well as Magued, Tarik demanding that the valiant prisoner should be delivered to him, and Musa afterwards claiming possession. The controversy ended in a manner suitable to the temper of the times, Magued slaying the captive with his own hand rather than deliver to others the prize of his sword and shield.

THE STRATAGEM OF THEO-DOMIR.

THE defeat of the Guadalete seemed for the time to have robbed the Goths of all their ancient courage. East and west, north and south, rode the Arab horsemen, and stronghold after stronghold fell almost without resistance into their hands, until nearly the whole of Spain had surrendered to the scimitar. History has but a few stories to tell of valiant defence by the Gothic warriors. One was that of Pelistes, at Cordova, which we have just told. The other was that of the wise and valorous Theodomir, which we have next to relate.

Abdul-Aziz, Musa's noble son, whose sad fate we have chronicled, had been given the control of Southern Spain, with his head-quarters in Seville. Here, after subduing the Comarca, he decided on an invasion of far-off Murcia, the garden-land of the south, a realm of tropic heat, yet richly fertile and productive. There ruled a valiant Goth named Theodomir, who had resisted Tarik on his landing, had fought in the fatal battle in which Roderic fell, and had afterwards, with a bare remnant of his followers, sought his own territory, which after him was called the land of Tadmir.

Hither marched Abdul-Aziz, eager to meet in battle

a warrior of such renown, and to add to his dominions a country so famed for beauty and fertility.
He was to find Theodomir an adversary worthy of
his utmost powers. So small was the force of the
Gothic lord that he dared not meet the formidable
Arab horsemen in open contest, but he checked their
advance by all the arts known in war, occupying the
mountain defiles and gorges through which his
country must be reached, cutting off detachments,
and making the approach of the Arabs difficult and
dangerous.

His defence was not confined to the hills. At
times he would charge fiercely on detached parties
of Arabs in the valleys or plains, and be off again to
cover before the main force could come up. Long he
defeated every effort of the Arab leader to bring on
an open battle, but at length found himself cornered
at Lorca, in a small valley at a mountain's foot.
Here, though the Goths fought bravely, they found
themselves too greatly outnumbered, and in the end
were put to panic-flight, numbers of them being left
dead on the hotly contested field.

The handful of fugitives, sharply pursued by the
Moorish cavalry, rode in all haste to the fortified
town of Orihuela, a place of such strength that with
sufficient force they might have defied there the
powerful enemy. But such had been their losses in
battle and in flight that Theodomir found himself
far too weak to face the Moslem host, whose advance cavalry had followed so keenly on his track as
to reach the outer walls by the time he had fairly
closed the gates.

Defence was impossible. He had not half enough men to guard the walls and repel assaults. It would have been folly to stand a siege, yet Theodomir did not care to surrender except on favorable terms, and therefore adopted a shrewd stratagem to deceive the enemy in regard to his strength.

To the surprise of the Arab leader the walls of the town, which he had thought half garrisoned, seemed to swarm with armed and bearded warriors, far too great a force to be overcome by a sudden dash. In the face of so warlike an array, caution awoke in the hearts of the assailants. They had looked for an easy victory, but against such numbers as these assault might lead to severe bloodshed and eventual defeat. They felt that it would be necessary to proceed by the slow and deliberate methods of a regular siege.

While Abdul-Aziz was disposing his forces and making heedful preparations for the task he saw before him, he was surprised to see the principal gate of the city thrown open and a single Gothic horseman ride forth, bearing a flag of truce and making signals for a parley. A safe-conduct was given him, and he was led to the tent of the Moslem chief.

"Theodomir has sent me to negotiate with you," he said, "and I have full power to conclude terms of surrender. We are abundantly able to hold out, as you may see by the forces on our walls, but as we wish to avoid bloodshed we are willing to submit on honorable terms. Otherwise we will defend ourselves to the bitter end."

The boldness and assurance with which he spoke deeply impressed the Arab chief. This was not a fearful foe seeking for mercy, but a daring antagonist as ready to fight as to yield.

"What terms do you demand?" asked Abdul-Aziz.

"My lord," answered the herald, "will only surrender on such conditions as a generous enemy should grant and a valiant people receive. He demands peace and security for the province and its people and such authority for himself as the strength of his walls and the numbers of his garrison justify him in demanding."

The wise and clement Arab saw the strength of the argument, and, glad to obtain so rich a province without further loss of life, he assented to the terms proposed, bidding the envoy to return and present them to his chief. The Gothic knight replied that there was no need of this, he having full power to sign the treaty. The terms were therefore drawn up and signed by the Arab general, after which the envoy took the pen and, to the astonishment of the victor, signed the name of Theodomir at the foot of the document. It was the Gothic chief himself.

Pleased alike with his confidence and his cleverness, Abdul-Aziz treated the Gothic knight with the highest honor and distinction. At the dawn of the next day the gates of the city were thrown open for surrender, and Abdul-Aziz entered at the head of a suitable force. But when the garrison was drawn up in the centre of the city for surrender, the surprise of the Moslem became deep amazement. What he saw before him was a mere handful of stalwart soldiers, eked out with feeble old men and boys. But the main body before him was composed of women, whom the astute Goth had bidden to dress like men and to tie their long hair under their chins to represent beards; when, with casques on their heads and spears in their hands, they had been ranged along the walls, looking at a distance like a line of sturdy warriors.

Theodomir waited with some anxiety, not knowing how the victor would regard this stratagem. Abdul might well have viewed with anger the capitulation of an army of women and dotards, but he had a sense of humor and a generous heart, and the smile of amusement on his face told the Gothic chief that he was fully forgiven for his shrewd stratagem. Admiration was stronger than mortification in the Moslem's heart. He praised Theodomir for his witty and successful expedient, and for the three days that he remained at Orihuela banquets and fêtes marked his stay, he occupying the position of a guest rather than an enemy. No injury was done to people or town, and the Arabs soon left the province to continue their career of conquest, satisfied with the arrangements for tribute which they had made.

By a strange chance the treaty of surrender of the land of Tadmir still exists. It is drawn up in Latin and in Arabic, and is of much interest as showing the mode in which such things were managed at that remote date. It stipulates that war shall not be waged against Theodomir, son of the Goths, and his people; that he shall not be deprived of his kingdom; that the Christians shall not be separated from their wives and children, or hindered in the services of their religion; and that their temples shall not be burned. Theodomir was left lord of seven cities,—Orihuela, Valencia, Alicante, Mula, Biscaret, Aspis, and Lorca,—in which he was to harbor no enemies of the Arabs.

The tribute demanded of him and his nobles was a dinar (a gold coin) yearly from each, also four measures each of wheat, barley, must, vinegar, honey, and oil. Vassals and taxable people were to pay half this amount.

These conditions were liberal in the extreme. The tribute demanded was by no means heavy for a country so fertile, in which light culture yields abundant harvests; the delightful valley between Orihuela and Murcia, in particular, being the garden spot of Spain. The inhabitants for a long period escaped the evils of war felt in other parts of the conquered territory, their province being occupied by only small garrisons of the enemy, while its distance from the chief seat of war removed it from danger.

After the murder of Abdul-Aziz, Theodomir sent an embassy to the Caliph Soliman, begging that the treaty should be respected. The caliph in reply sent orders that its stipulations should be faithfully observed. In this the land of Tadmir almost stood alone in that day, when treaties were usually made only to be set at naught.

Tarik landed in Spain in April, 711. So rapid were the Arabs in conquest that in two years from that date nearly the whole peninsula was in their hands. Not quite all, or history might have another story to relate. In a remote province of the once proud kingdom—a rugged northwest corner—a few of its fugitive sons remained in freedom, left alone by the Arabs partly through scorn, partly on account of the rude and difficult character of their place of refuge. The conquerors despised them, yet this slender group was to form the basis of the Spain we know to-day, and to expand and spread until the conquerors would be driven from Spanish soil.

The Goths had fled in all directions from their conquerors, taking with them such of their valuables as they could carry, some crossing the Pyrenees to France, some hiding in the mountain valleys, some seeking a place of refuge in the Asturias, a rough hill country cut up in all directions by steep, scarped rocks, narrow defiles, deep ravines, and tangled thickets. Here the formidable Moslem cavalry could not pursue them; here no army could deploy; here ten men might defy a hundred. The place was far from inviting to the conquerors, but in it was sown the seed of modern Spain.

A motley crew it was that gathered in this rugged

region, a medley of fugitives of all ranks and stations,—soldiers, farmers, and artisans; nobles and vassals; bishops and monks; men, women, and children,—brought together by a terror that banished all distinctions of rank and avocation. For a number of years this small band of fugitive Christians, gathered between the mountains and the sea in northwestern Spain, remained quiet, desiring only to be overlooked or disregarded by the conquerors. But in the year 717 a leader came to them, and Spain once more lifted her head in defiance of her invaders.

Pelayo, the leader named, is a hero shrouded in mist. Fable surrounds him; a circle of romantic stories have budded from his name. He is to us like his modern namesake, the one battle-ship of Spain, which, during the recent war, wandered up and down the Mediterranean with no object in view that any foreigner could discover. Of the original Pelayo, some who profess to know say that he was of the highest rank,—young, handsome, and heroic, one who had fought under Roderic at the Guadalete, had been held by the Arabs as a hostage at Cordova, and had escaped to his native hills, there to infuse new life and hope into the hearts of the fugitive group.

Ibun Hayyan, an Arabian chronicler, gives the following fanciful account of Pelayo and his feeble band. "The commencement of the rebellion happened thus: there remained no city, town, or village in Galicia but what was in the hands of the Moslems with the exception of a steep mountain, on which this Pelayo took refuge with a handful of men. There his followers went on dying through hunger until he saw their numbers reduced to about thirty men and ten women, having no other food for support than the honey which they gathered in the crevices of the rock, which they themselves inhabited like so many bees. However, Pelayo and his men fortified themselves by degrees in the passes of the mountain until the Moslems were made acquainted with their preparations; but, perceiving how few they were, they heeded not the advice given to them, but allowed them to gather strength, saying, 'What are thirty barbarians perched upon a rock? They must inevitably die.'"

Die they did not, that feeble relic of Spain on the mountain-side, though long their only care was for shelter and safety. Here Pelayo cheered them, doing his utmost to implant new courage in their fearful hearts. At length the day came when Spain could again assume a defiant attitude, and in the mountain valley of Caggas de Onis Pelayo raised the old Gothic standard and ordered the beating of the drums. Beyond the sound of the long roll went his messengers seeking warriors in valley and glen, and soon his little band had grown to a thousand stalwart men, filled with his spirit and breathing defiance to the Moslem conquerors. That was an eventful day for Spain, in which her crushed people again lifted their heads.

It was a varied throng that gathered around Pelayo's banner. Sons of the Goths and the Romans were mingled with descendants of the more ancient

Celts and Iberians. Representatives of all the races that had overrun Spain were there gathered, speaking a dozen dialects, yet instinct with a single spirit. From them the modern Spaniard was to come, no longer Gothic or Roman, but a descendant of all the tribes and races that had peopled Spain. Some of them carried the swords and shields they had wielded in the battle of the Guadalete, others brought the rude weapons of the mountaineers. But among them were strong hands and stout hearts, summoned by the drums of Pelayo to the reconquest of Spain.

Word soon came to Al Horr, the new emir of Spain, that a handful of Christians were in arms in the mountains of the northwest, and he took instant steps to crush this presumptuous gathering, sending his trusty general Al Kamah with a force that seemed abundant to destroy Pelayo and his rebel band.

Warning of the approach of the Moslem foe was quickly brought to the Spanish leader, who at once left his place of assembly for the cave of Covadonga, a natural fortress in Eastern Asturia, some five miles from Caggas de Onis, which he had selected as a place strikingly adapted to a defensive stand. Here rise three mountain-peaks to a height of nearly four thousand feet, enclosing a small circular valley, across which rushes the swift Diva, a stream issuing from Mount Orandi. At the base of Mount Auseva, the western peak, rises a detached rock, one hundred and seventy feet high, projecting from the mountain in the form of an arch. At a short distance above its foot is visible the celebrated cave or grotto of

Covadonga, an opening forty feet wide, twelve feet high, and extending twenty-five feet into the rock.

The river sweeps out through a narrow and rocky defile, at whose narrowest part the banks rise in precipitous walls. Down this ravine the stream rushes in rapids and cascades, at one point forming a picturesque waterfall seventy-five feet in height. Only through this straitened path can the cave be reached, and this narrow ravine and the valley within Pelayo proposed to hold with his slender and ill-armed force.

Proudly onward came the Moslem captain, full of confidence in his powerful force and despising his handful of opponents. Pelayo drew him on into the narrow river passage by a clever stratagem. He had posted a small force at the mouth of the pass, bidding them to take to flight after a discharge of arrows. His plan worked well, the seeming retreat giving assurance to the Moslems, who rushed forward in pursuit along the narrow ledge that borders the Diva, and soon emerged into the broader path that opens into the valley of Covadonga.

They had incautiously entered a *cul-de-sac*, in which their numbers were of no avail, and where a handful of men could hold an army at bay. A small body of the best armed of the Spaniards occupied the cave, the others being placed in ambush among the chestnut-trees that covered the heights above the Diva. All kept silent until the Moslem advance had emerged into the valley. Then the battle began, one of the most famous conflicts in the whole history of Spain, famous not for the numbers engaged, but for the issue involved. The future of Spain dwelt in the hands of that group of patriots. The fight in the valley was sharp, but one-sided. The Moslem arrows rebounded harmlessly from the rocky sides of the cave, whose entrance could be reached only by a ladder, while the Christians, hurling their missiles from their point of vantage into the crowded mass below, punished them so severely that the advance was forced back upon those that crowded the defile in the rear. Al Kamah, finding his army recoiling in dismay and confusion, and discovering too late his error, ordered a retreat; but no sooner had a reverse movement been instituted than the ambushed Christians on the heights began their deadly work, hurling huge stones and fallen trees into the defile, killing the Moslems by hundreds, and choking up the pass until flight became impossible.

The panic was complete. From every side the Christians rushed upon the foe. Pelayo, bearing a cross of oak and crying that the Lord was fighting for his people, leaped downward from the cave, followed by his men, who fell with irresistible fury on the foe, forcing them backward under the brow of Mount Auseva, where Al Kamah strove to make a stand.

The elements now came to the aid of the Christians, a furious storm arising whose thunders reverberated among the rocks, while lightnings flashed luridly in the eyes of the terrified troops. The rain poured in blinding torrents, and soon the Diva, swollen with the sudden fall, rose into a flood, and swept away many of those who were crowded on its slippery banks. The heavens seemed leagued with the Christians against the Moslem host, whose destruction was so thorough that, if we can credit the chronicles, not a man of the proud army escaped.

This is doubtless an exaggeration, but the victory of Pelayo was complete and the first great step in the reconquest of Spain was taken. The year was 717, six years after the landing of the Arabs and the defeat of the Goths.

Thus ended perhaps the most decisive battle in the history of Spain. With it new Spain began. The cave of Covadonga is still a place of pilgrimage for the Spanish patriot, a stairway of marble replacing the ladder used by Pelayo and his men. We may tell what followed in a few words. Their terrible defeat cleared the territory of the Austurias of Moslem soldiers. From every side fugitive Christians left their mountain retreats to seek the standard of Pelayo. Soon the patriotic and daring leader had an army under his command, by whom he was chosen king of Christian Spain.

The Moslems made no further attack. They were discouraged by their defeat and were engaged in a project for the invasion of Gaul that required their utmost force. Pelayo slowly and cautiously extended his dominions, descending from the mountains into the plains and valleys, and organizing his new kingdom in civil as well as in military affairs. All the men under his control were taught to bear arms, fortifications were built, the ground was planted, and industry revived. Territory which the Moslems had abandoned was occupied, and from a group of sol-

BARONIAL CASTLE IN OLD CASTILE.

diers in a mountain cavern a new nation began to emerge.

Pelayo died at Caggas de Onis in the year 737, twenty years after his great victory. After his death the work he had begun was carried forward, until by the year 800 the Spanish dominion had extended over much of Old Castile,—so called from its numerous castles. In a hundred years more it had extended to the borders of New Castile. The work of reconquest was slowly but surely under way.

THE ADVENTURES OF A FUGI-TIVE PRINCE.

A NEW dynasty came to the throne of the caliphs of Damascus in 750. The line of the Ommeyades, who had held the throne since the days of the Prophet Mohammed, was overthrown, and the line of the Abbassides began. Abdullah, the new caliph, bent on destroying every remnant of the old dynasty, invited ninety of its principal adherents to a banquet, where they were set upon and brutally murdered. There followed a scene worthy of a savage. The tables were removed, carpets were spread over the bleeding corpses, and on these the viands were placed, the guests eating their dinner to the dismal music of the groans of the dying victims beneath.

The whole country was now scoured for all who were connected with the fallen dynasty, and wherever found they were brutally slain; yet despite the vigilance of the murderers a scion of the family of the Ommeyades escaped. Abdurrahman, the princely youth in question, was fortunately absent from Damascus when the order for his assassination was given. Warned of his proposed fate, he gathered what money and jewels he could and fled for his life, following little-used paths until he reached the banks of the Euphrates. But spies were on his track and descriptions of him had been sent to all provinces. He was just twenty years old, and, unlike the Arabians in general, had a fair complexion and blue eyes, so that he could easily be recognized, and it seemed impossible that he could escape.

His retreat on the Euphrates was quickly discovered, and the agents of murder were so hot upon his track that he was forced to spring into the river and seek for safety by swimming. The pursuers reached the banks when the fugitives were nearly half-way across, Abdurrahman supporting his son, four years of age, and Bedr, a servant, aiding his thirteen-year-old brother. The agents of the caliph called them back, saying that they would not harm them, and the boy, whose strength was giving out, turned back in spite of his brother's warning. When Abdurrahman reached the opposite bank, it was with a shudder of horror that he saw the murder of the boy, whose head was at once cut off. That gruesome spectacle decided the question of his trusting himself to the mercy of the caliph or his agents.

The life of the fugitive prince now became one of unceasing adventure. He made his way by covert paths towards Egypt, wandering through the desert in company with bands of Bedouins, living on their scanty fare, and constantly on the alert against surprise. Light sleep and hasty flittings were the rule with him and his few attendants as they made their way slowly westward over the barren sands, finally reaching Egypt. Here he was too near the caliph for safety, and he kept on westward to Barca, where he hoped for protection from the governor, who owed his fortunes to the favor of the late caliph.

He was mistaken. Ibn Habib, the governor of Barca, put self-interest above gratitude, and made vigorous efforts to seize the fugitive, whom he hoped to send as a welcome gift to the cruel Abdullah. The life of the fugitive was now one of hair-breadth escapes. For five years he remained in Barca, disguised and under a false name, yet in almost daily peril of his life. On one occasion a band of pursuers surrounded the tent in which he was and advanced to search it. His life was saved by Tekfah, the wife of the chief, who hid him under her clothes. When, in later years, he came to power, he rewarded the chief and his wife richly for their kindly aid.

On another occasion a body of horse rode into the village of tents in which he dwelt as a guest and demanded that he should be given up. The handsome aspect and gentle manner of the fugitive had made the tribesmen suspect that they were the hosts of a disguised prince; he had gained a sure place in their hearts, and they set the pursuers on a false scent. Such a person was with them, they said, but he had gone with a number of young men on a lion hunt in a neighboring mountain valley and would not return until the next evening. The pursuers at once set off for the place mentioned, and the fugitive, who had been hidden in one of the tents, rode away in the opposite direction with his slender train.

Leaving Barca, he journeyed farther westward

over the desert, which at that point comes down to the Mediterranean. Finally Tahart was reached, a town within the modern Algeria, the seat of the Beni Rustam, a tribe which gave him the kindliest welcome. To them, as to the Barcans, he seemed a prince in disguise. Near by was a tribe of Arabs named the Nefezah, to which his mother had belonged, and from which he hoped for protection and assistance. Reaching this, he told his rank and name, and was welcomed almost as a king, the tribesmen, his mother's kindred, paying him homage, and offering their aid to the extent of their ability in the ambitious scheme which he disclosed.

This was an invasion of Spain, which at that time was a scene of confusion and turmoil, distracted by rival leaders, the people exhausted by wars and quarrels, many of their towns burned or ruined, and the country ravaged by famine. What could be better than for the heir of the illustrious house of Ommeyades, flying from persecution by the Abbassides, and miraculously preserved, to seek the throne of Spain, bring peace to that distracted land, and found an independent kingdom in that western section of the vast Arabian empire?

His servant, Bedr, who had kept with him through all his varied career and was now his chief officer, was sent to Spain on a secret mission to the friends of the late dynasty of caliphs, of whom there were many in that land. Bedr was highly successful in his mission. Yusuf, the Abbasside emir, was absent from Cordova and ignorant of his danger, and all promised well. Not waiting for the assistance promised him in Africa, the prince put to sea almost alone. As he was about to step on board his boat a number of Berbers gathered round and showed an intention to prevent his departure. They were quieted by a handful of dinars and he hastened on board,—none too soon, for another band, greedy for gold, rushed to the beach, some of them wading out and seizing the boat and the camel's-hair cable that held it to the anchor. These fellows got blows instead of dinars, one, who would not let go, having his hand cut off by a sword stroke. The edge of a scimitar cut the cable, the sail was set, and the lonely exile set forth upon the sea to the conquest of a kingdom. It was evening of a spring day of the year 756 that the fugitive prince landed near Malaga, in the land of Andalusia, where some prominent chiefs were in waiting to receive him with the homage due to a king.

Hundreds soon flocked to the standard of the adventurer, whose manly and handsome presence, his beaming blue eyes, sweet smile, and gracious manner won him the friendship of all whom he met. With steadily growing forces he marched to Seville. Here were many of his partisans, and the people flung open the gates with wild shouts of welcome. It was in the month of May that the fortunes of Abdurrahman were put to the test, Yusuf having hastily gathered a powerful force and advanced to the plain of Musarah, near Cordova, on which field the fate of the kingdom was to be decided.

It was under a strange banner that Abdurrahman advanced to meet the army of the emir,—a turban attached to a lance-head. This standard afterwards became sacred, the turban, as it grew ragged, being covered by a new one. At length the hallowed old rags were removed by an irreverent hand, "and from that time the empire of the Beni Ummeyah began to decline."

We may briefly conclude our tale. The battle was fierce, but Abdurrahman's boldness and courage prevailed, and the army of Yusuf in the end gave way, Cordova becoming the victor's prize. The generous conqueror gave liberty and distinction to the defeated emir, and was repaid in two years by a rebellion in which he had an army of twenty thousand men to meet. Yusuf was again defeated, and now lost his life.

Thus it was that the fugitive prince, who had saved his life by swimming the Euphrates under the eyes of an assassin band, became the Caliph of the West, for under him Spain was cut loose from the dominion of the Abbassides and made an independent kingdom, its conqueror becoming its first monarch under the title of Abdurrahman I.

Almansur, then the Caliph of the East, sought to recover the lost domain, sending a large army from Africa; but this was defeated with terrible slaughter by the impetuous young prince, who revenged himself by sending the heads of the general and many of his officers to the caliph in bags borne by merchants, which were deposited at the door of Almansur's tent during the darkness of the night. The finder was cautioned to be careful, as the bags contained treasure. So they were brought in to the

caliph, who opened them with his own hand. Great
was his fury and chagrin when he saw what a
ghastly treasure they contained. "This man is the
foul fiend in human form," he exclaimed. "Praised
be Allah that he has placed a sea between him and
me."

BERNARDO DEL CARPIO.

SPAIN, like France, had its hero of legend. The great French hero was Roland, whose mighty deeds in the pass of Roncesvalles have been widely commemorated in song and story. In Spanish legend the gallant opponent of the champion of France was Bernardo del Carpio, a hero who perhaps never lived, except on paper, but about whose name a stirring cycle of story has grown. The tale of his life is a tragedy, as that of heroes is apt to be. It may be briefly told.

When Charlemagne was on the throne of France Alfonso II. was king of Christian Spain. A hundred years had passed since all that was left to Spain was the cave of Covadonga, and in that time a small kingdom had grown up with Oviedo for its capital city. This kingdom had spread from the Asturias over Leon, which gave its name to the new realm, and the slow work of driving back the Moslem conquerors had well begun.

Alfonso never married and had no children. People called him Alfonso the Chaste. He went so far as to forbid any of his family to marry, so that the love affairs of his sister, the fair infanta Ximena, ran far from smooth. The beautiful princess loved and was loved again by the noble Sancho Diaz, Count of Saldaña, but the king would not listen to their union. The natural result followed; as they dared not marry in public they did so in private, and for a year or two lived happily together, none knowing of their marriage, and least of all the king.

But when a son was born to them the truth came out. It threw the tyrannical king into a violent rage. His sister was seized by his orders and shut up in a convent, and her husband was thrown into prison for life, some accounts saying that his eyes were put out by order of the cruel king. As for their infant son, he was sent into the mountains of the Asturias, to be brought up among peasants and mountaineers.

It was known that he had been sent there by Alfonso, and the people believed him to be the king's son and treated him as a prince. In the healthy out-door life of the hills he grew strong and handsome, while his native courage was shown in hunting adventures and the perils of mountain life. When old enough he learned the use of arms, and soon left his humble friends for the army, in which his boldness and bravery were shown in many encounters with the French and the Arabs. Those about him still supposed him to be the son of the king, though Alfonso, while furnishing him with all knightly arms and needs, neither acknowledged nor treated him as his son. But if not a king's son, he was a very valiant knight, and became the terror of all the foes of Spain.

All this time his unfortunate father languished in prison, where from time to time he was told by his keepers of the mighty deeds of the young prince

Bernardo del Carpio, by which name the youthful warrior was known. Count Sancho knew well that this was his son, and complained bitterly of the ingratitude of the youth who could leave his father perishing in a prison cell while he rode freely and joyously in the open air, engaged in battle and banquet, and was everywhere admired and praised. He knew not that the young warrior had been kept in ignorance of his birth.

During this period came that great event in the early history of Spain in which Charlemagne crossed the Pyrenees with a great army and marched upon the city of Saragossa. It was in the return from this expedition that the dreadful attack took place in which Roland and the rear guard of the army were slain in the pass of Roncesvalles. In Spanish story it was Bernardo del Carpio who led the victorious hosts, and to whose prowess was due the signal success.

This fierce fight in a mountain-pass, in which a valiant band of mountaineers overwhelmed and destroyed the flower of the French army, has been exalted by poetic legend into one of the most stupendous and romantic of events. Ponderous epic poems have made Roland their theme, numbers of ballads and romances tell of his exploits, and the far-off echoes of his ivory horn still sound through the centuries. One account tells that he blew his horn so loud and long that the veins of his neck burst in the strain. Others tell that he split a mountain in twain by a mighty stroke of his sword Durandal. The print of his horse's hoofs are shown on a mountain-peak where only a flying horse could ever have stood. In truth, Roland, whose name is barely mentioned in history, rose to be the greatest hero of romance, the choicest and best of the twelve paladins of Charlemagne.

Bernardo del Carpio was similarly celebrated in Spanish song, though he attained no such world-wide fame. History does not name him at all, but the ballads of Spain say much of his warlike deeds. It must suffice here to say that this doughty champion marched upon Roland and his men while they were winding through the narrow mountain-pass, and as they advanced the mountaineers swelled their ranks.

> "As through the glen his spears did gleam, the soldiers from
> the hills,
> They swelled his host, as mountain-stream receives the
> roaring rills;
> They round his banner flocked in scorn of haughty Charle-
> magne,
> And thus upon their swords are sworn the faithful sons of
> Spain."

Roland and his force lay silent in death when the valiant prince led back his army, flushed with victory, and hailed with the plaudits of all the people of the land. At this moment of his highest triumph the tragedy of his life began. His old nurse, who had feared before to tell the tale, now made him acquainted with the true story of his birth, telling him that he was the nephew, not the son, of the king; that his mother, whom he thought long dead, still lived, shut up for life in a convent; and that his father lay languishing in a dungeon cell, blind and in chains.

As may well be imagined, this story filled the soul of the young hero with righteous wrath. He strode into the presence of the king and asked, with little reverence, if the story were true. Alfonso surlily admitted it. Bernardo then demanded his father's freedom. This the king refused. Burning with anger, the valiant youth shut himself up in his castle, refusing to take part in the rejoicings that followed the victory, and still sternly demanding the release of his father.

"Is it well that I should be abroad fighting thy battles," he asked the king, "while my father lies fettered in thy dungeons? Set him free and I shall ask no further reward."

Alfonso, who was obstinate in his cruelty, refused, and the indignant prince took arms against him, joining the Moors, whom he aided to harry the king's dominions. Fortifying his castle, and gathering a bold and daring band from his late followers, he made incursions deep into the country of the king, plundering hamlet and city and fighting in the ranks of the Moslems.

This method of argument was too forcible even for the obstinacy of Alfonso. His counsellors, finding the kingdom itself in danger, urged him to grant Bernardo's request, and to yield him his father in return for his castle. The king at length consented, and Bernardo, as generous and trusting as he was brave, immediately accepted the proposed exchange, sought the king, handed him the keys of his castle, and asked him to fulfil his share of the contract.

Alfonso agreed to do so, and in a short time the

king and his nephew rode forth, Bernardo's heart full of joy at the thought of meeting the parent whom he had never yet seen. As they rode forward a train came from the opposite direction to meet them, in the midst a tall figure, clad in splendid attire and mounted on horseback. But there was something in his aspect that struck Bernardo's heart deep with dread.

"God help me!" he exclaimed, "is that sightless and corpse-like figure the noble Count of Saldaña, my father?"

"You wished to see him," coldly answered the king. "He is before you. Go and greet him."

Bernardo did so, and reverently took the cold hand of his father to kiss it. As he did so the body fell forward on the neck of the horse. It was only a corpse. Alfonso had killed the father before delivering him to his son.

Only his guards saved the ruthless tyrant at that moment from death. The infuriated knight swore a fearful oath of vengeance upon the king, and rode away, taking the revered corpse with him. Unfortunately, the story of Bernardo ends here. None of the ballads tell what he did for revenge. We may imagine that he joined his power to the Moors and harried the land of Leon during his after life, at length reaching Alfonso's heart with his vengeful blade. But of this neither ballad nor legend tells, and with the pathetic scene of the dead father's release our story ends.

RUY DIAZ, THE CID CAMPEADOR.

BERNARDO DEL CARPIO is not the chief Spanish hero of romance. To find the mate of Roland the paladin we must seek the incomparable Cid, the campeador or champion of Spain, the noblest figure in Spanish story or romance. *El Mio Cid*, " My Cid," as he is called, with his matchless horse Bavieca and his trenchant sword Tisona, towers in Spanish tale far above Christian king and Moslem caliph, as the pink of chivalry, the pearl of knighthood, the noblest and worthiest figure in all that stirring age.

Cid is an Arabic word, meaning "lord" or "chief." The man to whom it was applied was a real personage, not a figment of fancy, though it is to poetry and romance that he owes his fame, his story having been expanded and embellished in chronicles, epic poems, and ballads until it bears little semblance to actual history. Yet the deeds of the man himself probably lie at the basis of all the splendid fictions of romance.

The great poem in which his exploits were first celebrated, the famous " Poema del Cid," is thought to be the oldest, as it is one of the noblest in the Spanish language. Written probably not later than the year 1200, it is of about three thousand lines in length, and of such merit that its unknown author has been designated the " Homer of Spain." As it was written soon after the death of the Cid, it could not have deviated far from historic truth. Chief among the prose works is the "Chronicle of the Cid,"—*Chronica del famoso Cavallero Cid Ruy Diez,*—which, with additions from the poem, was charmingly rendered in English by the poet Southey, whose production is a prose poem in itself. Such are the chief sources of our knowledge of the Cid, an active, stirring figure, full of the spirit of mediævalism, whose story seems to bring back to us the living features of the age in which he flourished. A brave and daring knight, rousing the jealousy of nobles and kings by his valiant deeds, now banished and now recalled, now fighting against the Moslems, now with them, now for his own hand, and in the end winning himself a realm and dying a king without the name,—such is the man whose story we propose to tell.

This hero of romance was born about the year 1040 at Bivar, a little village near Burgos, his father being Diego Lainez, a man of gentle birth, his mother Teresa Rodriguez, daughter of the governor of the Asturias. He is often called Rodrigo de Bivar, from his birthplace, but usually Rodrigo Diaz, or Ruy Diez, as his name is given in the chronicle.

While still a boy the future prowess of the Cid was indicated. He was keen of intellect, active of frame, and showed such wonderful dexterity in manly exercises as to become unrivalled in the use of arms. Those were days of almost constant war. The kingdom of the Moors was beginning to fall to pieces; that of the Christians was growing steadily stronger;

not only did war rage between the two races, but Moor fought with Moor, Christian with Christian, and there was abundant work ready for the strong hand and sharp sword. This state of affairs was to the taste of the youthful Rodrigo, whose ambition was to become a hero of knighthood.

While gentle in manner and magnanimous in disposition, the young soldier had an exalted sense of honor and was sternly devoted to duty. While he was still a boy his father was bitterly insulted by Count Gomez, who struck him in the face. The old man brooded over his humiliation until he lost sleep and appetite, and withdrew from society into disconsolate seclusion.

Rodrigo, deeply moved by his father's grief, sought and killed the insulter, and brought the old man the bleeding head of his foe. At this the disconsolate Diego rose and embraced his son, and bade him sit above him at table, saying that "he who brought home that head should be the head of the house of Layn Calvo."

From that day on the fame of the young knight rapidly grew, until at length he defeated and captured five Moorish kings who had invaded Castile. This exploit won him the love of Ximena, the fair daughter of Count Gomez, whom he had slain. Foreseeing that he would become the greatest man in Spain, the damsel waited not to be wooed, but offered him her hand in marriage, an offer which he was glad to accept. And ever after, says the chronicle, she was his loving wife.

The young champion is said to have gained the

good-will of St. Lazarus and the Holy Virgin by sleeping with a leper who had been shunned by his knights. No evil consequences came from this example of Christian philanthropy,—if it ever happened,—while it added to the knight's high repute.

Fernando I., who had gathered a large Christian kingdom under his crown, died when Rodrigo was but fifteen years of age, and in his will foolishly cut up his kingdom between his three sons and two daughters, greatly weakening the Christian power, and quickly bringing his sons to sword's point. By the will Sancho was placed over Castile, Alfonso became king of Leon, Garcia ruled in Galicia; Urraca, one of the daughters, received the city of Toro, and Elvira was given that of Zamora.

Sancho was not satisfied with this division. Being the oldest, he thought he should have all, and prepared to seize the shares of his brothers and sisters. Looking for aid in this design, he was attracted by the growing fame of young Rodrigo, and gained his aid in the restoration of Zamora, which the Moors had destroyed. While thus engaged there came to Rodrigo messengers with tribute from the five Moorish kings whom he had captured and released. They hailed the young warrior as Sid, or Cid, and the king, struck by the title, said that Ruy Diez should thenceforth bear it; also that he should be known as campeador or champion.

King Sancho now knighted the young warrior with his own hand, and soon after made him *alferez*, or commander of his troops. As such he was despatched against Alfonso, who was soon driven from his kingdom of Leon and sought shelter in the Moorish city of Toledo. Leon being occupied, the Cid marched against Galicia, and drove out Garcia as he had done Alfonso. Then he deprived Urraca and Elvira of the cities left them by their father, and the whole kingdom was once more placed under a single ruler.

It did not long remain so. Sancho died in 1072, and at once Alfonso and Garcia hurried back from exile to recover their lost realms. But Alfonso's ambition equalled that of Sancho. All or none was his motto. Invading the kingdom of Galicia, he robbed Garcia of it and held him prisoner. Then he prepared to invade Castile, and offered the command of the army for this enterprise to the Cid.

The latter was ready for fighting in any form, so that he could fight with honor. But there was doubt in his mind if service under Alfonso was consistent with the honor of a knight. King Sancho had been assassinated while hunting, and it was whispered that Alfonso had some share in the murder. The high-minded Cid would not draw sword for him unless he swore that he had no lot or part in his brother's death. Twice the Cid gave him the oath, whereupon, says the chronicle, "My Cid repeated the oath to him a third time, and the king and the knights said 'Amen.' But the wrath of the king was exceeding great; and he said to the Cid, 'Ruy Diez, why dost thou press me so, man?' From that day forward there was no love towards My Cid in the heart of the king."

But the king had sworn, and the Cid entered his

service and soon conquered Castile, so that Alfonso became monarch of Castile, Leon, Galicia, and Portugal, and took the title of Emperor of Spain. As adelantado, or lord of the marches, Ruy Diez now occupied himself with the Moors,—fighting where hostility reigned, taking tribute for the king from Seville and other cities, and settling with the sword the disputes of the chiefs, or aiding them in their quarrels. Thus he took part with Seville in a war with Cordova, and was rewarded with so rich a present by the grateful king that Alfonso, inspired by his secret hatred for the Cid, grew jealous and envious.

During these events years passed on, and the Cid's two fair daughters grew to womanhood and were married, at the command of the king, to the two counts of Carrion. The Cid liked not his sons-in-law, and good reason he had, for they were a pair of base hounds despite their lordly title. The brides were shamefully treated by them, being stripped and beaten nearly to death on their wedding-journey.

When word of this outrage came to the Cid his wrath overflowed. Stalking with little reverence into the king's hall, he sternly demanded redress for the brutal act. He could not appeal to the law. The husband in those days was supreme lord and master of his wife. But there was an unwritten law, that of the sword, and the incensed father demanded that the brutal youths should appear in the lists and prove their honor, if they could, against his champion.

They dared not refuse. In those days, when the

sword was the measure of honor and justice, to refuse would have been to be disgraced. They came into the lists, where they were beaten like the hounds that they had shown themselves, and the noble girls were set free from their bonds. Better husbands soon sought the Cid's daughters, and they were happily married in the end.

The exploits of the Cid were far too many for us to tell. Wherever he went victory attended his sword. On one occasion the king marched to the aid of one of his Moorish allies, leaving the Cid behind him too sick to ride. Here was an opportunity for the Moors, a party of whom broke into Castile and by a rapid march made themselves masters of the fortress of Gomez. Up from his bed of sickness rose the Cid, mounted his steed (though he could barely sit in the saddle), charged and scattered the invaders, pursued them into the kingdom of Toledo, and returned with seven thousand prisoners and all the Moorish spoil.

This brilliant defence of the kingdom was the turning point in his career. The king of Toledo complained to Alfonso that his neutral territory had been invaded by the Cid and his troops, and King Alfonso, seeking revenge for the three oaths he had been compelled to take, banished the Cid from his dominions, on the charge of invading the territory of his allies.

Thus the champion went forth as a knight-errant, with few followers, but a great name. Tears came into his eyes as he looked back upon his home, its doors open, its hall deserted, no hawks upon the perches, no horses in the stalls. "My enemies have done this," he said. "God be praised for all things." He went to Burgos, but there the people would not receive him, having had strict orders from the king. Their houses were closed, the inn-keepers barred their doors, only a bold little maiden dared venture out to tell him of the decree. As there was no shelter for him there, he was forced to seek lodging in the sands near the town.

Needing money, he obtained it by a trick that was not very honorable, though in full accord with the ethics of those times. He pawned to the Jews two chests which he said were treasure chests, filled with gold. Six hundred marks were received, and when the chests were afterwards opened they proved to be filled with sand. This was merely a good joke to poet and chronicler. The Jews lay outside the pale of justice and fair-dealing.

Onward went the Cid, his followers growing in number as he marched. First to Barcelona, then to Saragossa, he went, seeking knightly adventures everywhere. In Saragossa he entered the service of the Moorish king, and for several years fought well and sturdily for his old enemies. But time brought a change. In 1081 Alfonso captured Toledo and made that city his capital, from which he prepared to push his way still deeper into the Moorish dominions. He now needed the Cid, whom he had banished five years before.

But it was easier to ask than to get. The Cid had grown too great to be at any king's beck and call. He would fight for Alfonso, but in his own way, holding himself free to attack whom he pleased and when he pleased, and to capture the cities of the Moslems and rule them as their lord. He had become a free lance, fighting for his own hand, while armies sprang, as it were, from the ground at his call to arms.

In those days of turmoil valor rarely had long to wait for opportunity. Ramon Berenguer, lord of Barcelona, had laid siege to Valencia, an important city on the Mediterranean coast. Thither marched the Cid with all speed, seven thousand men in his train, and forced Ramon to raise the siege. The Cid became governor of Valencia, under tribute to King Alfonso, and under honor to hold it against the Moors.

The famous champion was not done with his troubles with Alfonso. In the years that followed he was once more banished by the faithless king, and his wife and children were seized and imprisoned. At a later date he came to the king's aid in his wars, but found him again false to his word, and was obliged to flee for safety from the camp.

Valencia had passed from his control and had more than once since changed hands. At length the Moorish power grew so strong that the city refused to pay tribute to Spain and declared its independence. Here was work for the Cid—not for the benefit of Alfonso, but for his own honor and profit. He was weary of being made the foot-ball of a jealous and faithless monarch, and craved a kingdom of his own. Against Valencia he marched with an army of free swords at his back. He was fighting now for the

Cid, not for Moorish emir or Spanish monarch. For twenty months he beseiged the fair city, until starvation came to the aid of his sword. No relief reached the Moors; the elements fought against them, floods of rain destroying the roads and washing away the bridges; on June 15, 1094, the Cid Campeador marched into the city thenceforth to be associated with his name.

Ascending its highest tower, he gazed with joy upon the fair possession which he had won with his own good sword without aid from Spanish king or Moorish ally, and which he proposed to hold for his own while life remained. His city it was, and to-day it bears his name, being known as Valencia del Cid. But he had to hold it with the good sword by which he won it, for the Moors, who had failed to aid the beleaguered city, sought with all their strength to win it back.

During the next year thirty thousand of them came and encamped about the walls of the city. But fighting behind walls was not to the taste of the Cid Campeador. Out from the gates he sallied and drove them like sheep from their camp, killing fifteen thousand of them in the fight.

"Be it known," the chronicle tells us, "that this was a profitable day's work. Every foot-soldier shared a hundred marks of silver that day, and the Cid returned full honorably to Valencia. Great was the joy of the Christians in the Cid Ruy Diez, who was born in a happy hour. His beard was grown, and continued to grow, a great length. My Cid said of his chin, 'For the love of King Don Alfonso,

VALENCIA DEL CID.

who hath banished me from his land, no scissors shall come upon it, nor shall a hair be cut away, and Moors and Christians shall talk of it.'" And until he died his great beard grew on untouched.

Not many were the men with whom he had done his work, but they were soldiers of tried temper and daring hearts. "There were one thousand knights of lineage and five hundred and fifty other horsemen. There were four thousand foot-soldiers, besides boys and others. Thus many were the people of My Cid, him of Bivar. And his heart rejoiced, and he smiled and said, 'Thanks be to God and to Holy Mother Mary! We had a smaller company when we left the house of Bivar.'"

The next year King Yussef, leader of the Moors, came again to the siege of Valencia, this time with fifty thousand men. Small as was the force of the Cid as compared with this great army, he had no idea of fighting cooped up like a rat in a cage. Out once more he sallied, with but four thousand men at his back. His bishop, Hieronymo, absolved them, saying, "He who shall die, fighting full forward, I will take as mine his sins, and God shall have his soul."

A learned and wise man was the good bishop, but a valorous one as well, mighty in arms alike on horseback and on foot. "A boon, Cid don Rodrigo," he cried. "I have sung mass to you this morning. Let me have the giving of the first wounds in this battle."

"In God's name, do as you will," answered the Cid. That day the bishop had his will of the foe, fighting with both hands until no man knew how many of the infidels he slew. Indeed, they were all too busy to heed the bishop's blows, for, so the chronicle says, only fifteen thousand of the Moslems escaped. Yussef, sorely wounded, left to the Cid his famous sword Tisona, and barely escaped from the field with his life.

Bucar, the brother of Yussef, came to revenge him, but he knew not with whom he had to deal. Bishop Hieronymo led the right wing, and made havoc in the ranks of the foe. "The bishop pricked forward," we are told. "Two Moors he slew with the first two thrusts of his lance; the haft broke and he laid hold on his sword. God! how well the bishop fought. He slew two with the lance and five with the sword. The Moors fled."

"Turn this way, Bucar," cried the Cid, who rode close on the heels of the Moorish chief; "you who came from behind sea to see the Cid with the long beard. We must greet each other and cut out a friendship."

"God confound such friendships," cried Bucar, following his flying troops with nimble speed.

Hard behind him rode the Cid, but his horse Bavieca was weary with the day's hard work, and Bucar rode a fresh and swift steed. And thus they went, fugitive and pursuer, until the ships of the Moors were at hand, when the Cid, finding that he could not reach the Moorish king with his sword, flung the weapon fiercely at him, striking him between the shoulders. Bucar, with the mark of battle thus upon him, rode into the sea and was taken into a boat, while the Cid picked up his sword from the ground and sought his men again.

The Moorish host did not escape so well. Set upon fiercely by the Spaniards, they ran in a panic into the sea, where twice as many were drowned as were slain in the battle; and of these, seventeen thousand and more had fallen, while a vast host remained as prisoners. Of the twenty-nine kings who came with Bucar, seventeen were left dead upon the field.

The chronicler uses numbers with freedom. The Cid is his hero, and it is his task to exalt him. But the efforts of the Moors to regain Valencia and their failure to do so may be accepted as history. In due time, however, age began to tell upon the Cid, and death came to him as it does to all. He died in 1099, from grief, as the story goes, that his colleague, Alvar Fañez, had suffered a defeat. Whether from grief or age, at any rate he died, and his wife, Ximena, was left to hold the city, which for two years she gallantly did, against all the power of the Moors. Then Alfonso entered it, and, finding that he could not hold it, burned the principal buildings and left it to the Moors. A century and a quarter passed before the Christians won it again.

When Alfonso left the city of the Cid he brought with him the body of the campeador, mounted upon his steed Bavieca, and solemnly and slowly the train wound on until the corpse of the mighty dead was brought to the cloister of the monastery of Cardeña. Here the dead hero was seated on a throne, with his sword Tisona in his hand; and, the story goes, a caitiff Jew, perhaps wishing to revenge his brethren who had been given sand for gold, plucked the flowing beard of the Cid.   At this insult the hand of the corpse struck out and the insulter was hurled to the floor.

The Cid Campeador is a true hero of romance, and well are the Spaniards proud of him. Honor was the moving spring of his career. As a devoted son, he revenged the insult to his father; as a loving husband, he made Ximena the partner of his fame; as a tender father, he redressed his daughters' wrongs; as a loyal subject, he would not serve a king on whom doubt of treachery rested. In spite of the injustice of the king, he was true to his country, and came again and again to its aid. Though forced into the field as a free lance, he was throughout a Christian cavalier. And, though he cheated the Jews, the story goes that he repaid them their gold. Courage, courtesy, and honor were the jewels of his fame, and romance holds no nobler hero.

It will not be amiss to close our tale of the Cid with a quotation from the famous poem in which it is shown how even a lion quailed before his majesty:

" Peter Bermuez arose; somewhat he had to say;
    The words were strangled in his throat, they could not find
        their way;
    Till forth they came at once, without a stop or stay:
' Cid, I'll tell you what, this always is your way;
    You have always served me thus, whenever you have come
    To meet here in the Cortes, you call me Peter the Dumb.
    I cannot help my nature; I never talk nor rail;
    But when a thing is to be done, you know I never fail.

Fernando, you have lied, you have lied in every word;
You have been honored by the Cid and favored and preferred.
I know of all your tricks, and can tell them to your face :
Do you remember in Valencia the skirmish and the chase?
You asked leave of the Cid to make the first attack ;
You went to meet a Moor, but you soon came running back.
I met the Moor and killed him, or he would have killed you ;
I gave you up his arms, and all that was my due.
Up to this very hour, I never said a word ;
You praised yourself before the Cid and I stood by and heard
How you had killed the Moor, and done a valiant act ;
And they believed you all, but they never knew the fact.
You are tall enough and handsome, but cowardly and weak,
Thou tongue without a hand, how can you dare to speak?
There's the story of the lions should never be forgot ;
Now let us hear, Fernando, what answer you have got?
The Cid was sleeping in his chair, with all his knights around ;
The cry went forth along the hall that the lion was unbound.
What did you do, Fernando?   Like a coward as you were,
You shrunk behind the Cid, and crouched beneath his chair.
We pressed around the throne to shield our loved from harm,
Till the good Cid awoke.   He rose without alarm.
He went to meet the lion with his mantle on his arm.
The lion was abashed the noble Cid to meet ;
He bowed his mane to the earth, his muzzle at his feet.
The Cid by the neck and the mane drew him to his den,
He thrust him in at the hatch, and came to the hall again.
He found his knights, his vassals, and all his valiant men.
He asked for his sons-in-law, they were neither of them there.
I defy you for a coward and a traitor as you are.' "

LAS NAVAS DE TOLOSA.

On the 16th of July, 1212, was fought the great battle which broke the Moorish power in Spain. During the two centuries before fresh streams of invasion had flowed in from Africa to yield new life to the Moslem power. From time to time in the Mohammedan world reforms have sprung up, and been carried far and wide by fanaticism and the sword. One such body of reformers, the Almoravides, invaded Spain in the eleventh century and carried all before it. It was with these that the Cid Campeador had to deal. A century later a new reformer, calling himself El Mahdi, appeared in Africa, and set going a movement which overflowed the African states and made its way into Spain, where it subdued the Moslem kingdoms and threatened the Christian states. These invaders were known as the Almohades. They were pure Moors. The Arab movement had lost its strength, and from that time forward the Moslem dominions in Spain were peopled chiefly by Moors.

Spain was threatened now as France had been threatened centuries before when Charles Martel crushed the Arab hordes on the plains of Tours. All Christendom felt the danger and Pope Innocent III. preached a crusade for the defence of Spain against the infidel. In response, thousands of armed crusaders flocked into Spain, coming in corps, in bands, and as individuals, and gathered about Toledo, the capital of Alfonso VIII., King of Castile. From all the surrounding nations they came, and camped in the rich country about the capital, a host which Alfonso had much ado to feed.

Mohammed An-Nassir, the emperor of the Almohades, responded to the effort of the Pope by organizing a crusade in Moslem Africa. He proclaimed an *Algihed*, or Holy War, ordered a massacre of all the Christians in his dominions, and then led the fanatical murderers to Spain to join the forces there in arms. Christian Europe was pitted against Moslem Africa in a holy war, Spain the prize of victory, and the plains of Andalusia the arena of the coming desperate strife.

The decisive moment was at hand. Mohammed left Morocco and reached Seville in June. His new levies were pouring into Spain in hosts. On the 21st of June Alfonso began his advance, leading southward a splendid array. Archbishops and bishops headed the army. In the van marched a mighty force of fifty thousand men under Don Diego Lopez de Haro, ten thousand of them being cavalry. After them came the troops of the kings of Aragon and Castile, each a distinct army. Next came the knights of St. John of Calatrava and the knights of Santiago, their grand-masters leading, and after them many other bodies, including troops from Italy and Germany. Such a gallant host Spain had rarely seen. It was needed, for the peril was great. While one hundred thousand marched under the Christian banners, the green standard of the prophet, if we may credit the historians, rose before an army nearly four times as large.

Without dwelling on the events of the march, we may hasten forward to the 12th of July, when the host of Alfonso reached the vicinity of the Moorish army, and the Navas de Tolosa, the destined field of battle, lay near at hand. The word *navas* means "plains." Here, on a sloping spur of the Sierra Morena, in the upper valley of the Guadalquiver, about seventy miles east of Cordova, lies an extended table-land, a grand plateau whose somewhat sloping surface gave ample space for the vast hosts which met there on that far-off July day.

To reach the plateau was the problem before Alfonso. The Moslems held the ground, and occupied in force the pass of Losa, Nature's highway to the plain. What was to be done? The pass could be won, if at all, only at great cost in life. No other pass was known. To retire would be to inspirit the enemy and dispirit the Christian host. No easy way out of the quandary at first appeared, but a way was found,—by miracle, the writers of that time say; but it hardly seems a miracle that a shepherd of the region knew of another mountain-pass. This man, Martin Halaja, had grazed his flocks in that vicinity for years. He told the king of a pass unknown to the enemy, by which the army might reach the table-land, and to prove his words led Lopez de Haro and another through this little-known mountain by-way. It was difficult but passable, the army was put in motion and traversed it all night long, and on the morning of the 14th of July the astonished eyes of the Mohammedans gazed on the Christian host, holding in force the borders of the plateau, and momentarily increasing in numbers and strength. Ten miles before the eyes of Alfonso and his men stretched the plain, level in the centre, in the distance rising in gentle slopes to its border of hills, like a vast natural amphitheatre. The soldiers, filled with hope and enthusiasm, spread through their ranks the story that the shepherd who had led them was an angel, sent by the Almighty to lead his people to victory over the infidel.

Mohammed and his men had been told on the previous day by their scouts that the camp of the Christians was breaking up, and rejoiced in what seemed a victory without a blow. But when they saw these same Christians defiling in thousands before them on the plain, ranged in battle array under their various standards, their joy was changed to rage and consternation. Against the embattled front their wild riders rode, threatening the steady troops with brandished lances and taunting them with cowardice. But Alfonso held his mail-clad battalions firm, and the light-armed Moorish horsemen hesitated to attack. Word was brought to Mohammed that the Christians would not fight, and in hasty gratulation he sent off letters to cities in the rear to that effect. He little dreamed that he was soon to follow his messengers in swifter speed.

It was a splendid array upon which the Christians gazed,—one well calculated to make them tremble for the result,—for the hosts of Mohammed covered the

hill-sides and plain like "countless swarms of lo-
custs." On an eminence which gave an outlook over
the whole broad space stood the emperor's tent, of
three-ply crimson velvet flecked with gold, strings
of pearls depending from its purple fringes. To
guard it from assault rows of iron chains were
stretched, before which stood three thousand camels
in line. In front of these ten thousand negroes
formed a living wall, their front bristling with the
steel of their lances, whose butts were planted firmly
in the sand. In the centre of this powerful guard
stood the emperor, wearing the green dress and turban of his ancestral line. Grasping in one hand his
scimitar, in the other he held a Koran, from which
he read those passages of inspiration to the Moslems
which promised the delights of Paradise to those
who should fall in a holy war and the torments of
hell to the coward who should desert his ranks.

The next day was Sunday. The Moslems, eager
for battle, stood all day in line, but the Christians
declined to fight, occupying themselves in arranging
their different corps. Night descended without a
skirmish. But this could not continue with the two
armies so closely face to face. One side or the other
must surely attack on the following day. At midnight heralds called the Christians to mass and
prayer. Everywhere priests were busy confessing
and shriving the soldiers. The sound of the furbish-
ing of arms mingled with the strains of religious
service. At the dawn of the next day both hosts
were drawn up in battle array. The great struggle
was about to begin.

The army of the Moors, said to contain three hundred thousand regular troops and seventy-five thousand irregulars, was drawn up in crescent shape in front of the imperial tent,—in the centre the vast host of the Almohades, the tribes of the desert on the wings, in advance the light-armed troops. The Christian host was formed in four legions, King Alfonso occupying the centre, his banner bearing an effigy of the Virgin. With him were Rodrigo Ximenes, the archbishop of Toledo, and many other prelates. The force was less than one hundred thousand strong, some of the crusaders having left it in the march.

The sun was not high when the loud sound of the Christian trumpets and the Moorish *atabals* gave signal for the fray, and the two hosts surged forward to meet in fierce assault. Sternly and fiercely the battle went on, the struggling multitudes swaying in the ardor of the fight,—now the Christians, now the Moslems surging forward or driven back. With difficulty the thin ranks of the Christians bore the onsets of their densely grouped foes, and at length King Alfonso, in fear for the result, turned to the prelate Rodrigo and exclaimed,—

"Archbishop, you and I must die here."

"Not so," cried the bold churchman. "Here we must triumph over our enemies."

"Then let us to the van, where we are sorely needed, for, indeed, our lines are being bitterly pressed."

Nothing backward, the archbishop followed the king. Fernan Garcia, one of the king's cavaliers, urged him to wait for aid, but Alfonso, commending himself to God and the Virgin, spurred forward and plunged into the thick of the fight. And ever as he rode, by his side rode the archbishop, wearing his chasuble and bearing aloft the cross. The Moorish troops, who had been jeering at the king and the cross-bearing prelate, drew back before this impetuous assault, which was given force by the troops who crowded in to the rescue of the king. The Moors soon yielded to the desperate onset, and were driven back in wild disarray.

This was the beginning of the end. Treason in the Moorish ranks came to the Christian aid. Some of Mohammed's force, who hated him for having cruelly slain their chief, turned and fled. The breaking of their centre opened a way for the Spaniards to the living fortress which guarded the imperial tent, and on this dense line of sable lancers the Christian cavalry madly charged.

In vain they sought to break that serried line of steel. Some even turned their horses and tried to back them in, but without avail. Many fell in the attempt. The Moslem ranks seemed impervious. In the end one man did what a host had failed to perform. A single cavalier, Alvar Nuñez de Lara, stole in between the negroes and the camels, in some way passed the chains, and with a cheer of triumph raised his banner in the interior of the line. A second and a third followed in his track. The gap between the camels and the guard widened. Dozens, hundreds rushed to join their daring leader. The camels were loosened and dispersed; the negroes, attacked front and rear, perished or fled; the living wall that guarded the emperor was gone, and his sacred person was in peril.

Mohammed was dazed. His lips still repeated from the Koran, "God alone is true, and Satan is a betrayer," but terror was beginning to stir the roots of his hair. An Arab rode up on a swift mare, and, springing to the ground, cried,—

"Mount and flee, O king. Not thy steed but my mare. She comes of the noblest breed, and knows not how to fail her rider in his need. All is lost! Mount and flee!"

All was lost, indeed. Mohammed scrambled up and set off at the best speed of the Arabian steed, followed by his troops in a panic of terror. The rout was complete. While day continued the Christian horsemen followed and struck, until the bodies of slain Moors lay so thick upon the plain that there was scarce room for man or horse to pass. Then Archbishop Rodrigo, who had done so much towards the victory, stood before Mohammed's tent and in a loud voice intoned the *Te Deum laudamus*, the soldiers uniting in the sacred chant of victory.

The archbishop, who became the historian of this decisive battle, speaks of two hundred thousand Moslem slain. We cannot believe it so many, even on the word of an archbishop. Twenty-five Christians alone fell. This is as much too small as the other estimate is too large. But, whatever the losses, it was a great and glorious victory, and the spoils of war that fell to the victors were immense. Gold and silver were there in abundance; horses, camels, and wagons in profusion; arms of all kinds, commissary stores in quantities. So vast was the number of lances strewn on the ground that the conquering army used only these for firewood in their camp, and did not burn the half of them.

King Alfonso, with a wise and prudent liberality, divided the spoil among his troops and allies, keeping only the glory of the victory for himself. Mohammed's splendid tent was taken to Rome to adorn St. Peter's, and the captured banners were sent to the cities of Spain as evidences of the great victory. For himself, the king reserved a fine emerald, which he placed in the centre of his shield. Ever since that brilliant day in Spanish annals, the sixteenth of July has been kept as a holy festival, in which the captured banners are carried in grand procession, to celebrate the "Triumph of the Cross."

The supposed miracle of the shepherd was not the only one which the monkish writers saw in the victorious event. It was said that a red cross, like that of Calatrava, appeared in the sky, inspiriting the Christians and dismaying their foes; and that the sight of the Virgin banner borne by the king's standard-bearer struck the Moslems with torpor. It was a credulous age, one in which miracles could be woven out of the most homely and every-day material.

Death soon came to the leaders in the war. Mohammed, sullen with defeat, hurried to Morocco, where he shut himself up in gloomy seclusion, and died—or was poisoned—before the year's end. Alfonso died two years later. The Christians did not follow up their victory with much energy, and the Moslems still held a large section of Spain, but their power had culminated and with this signal defeat began its decline. Step by step they yielded before the Christian advance, though nearly three centuries more passed before they lost their final hold on Spain.

NEARLY eight hundred years had passed away after the landing of Tarik, the Arab, in Spain and the defeat and death of Don Roderic, the last king of the Goths. During those centuries the handful of warriors which in the mountains of the north had made a final stand against the invading hordes had grown and spread, pushing back the Arabs and Moors, until now the Christians held again nearly all the land, the sole remnant of Moslem dominion being the kingdom of Granada in the south. The map of Spain shows the present province of Granada as a narrow district bordering on the Mediterranean Sea, but the Moorish kingdom covered a wider space, spreading over the present provinces of Malaga and Almeria, and occupying one of the richest sections of Spain. It was a rock-bound region. In every direction ran sierras, or rugged mountain-chains, so rocky and steep as to make the kingdom almost impregnable. Yet within their sterile confines lay numbers of deep and rich valleys, prodigal in their fertility.

In the centre of the kingdom arose its famous capital, the populous and beautiful city of Granada, standing in the midst of a great vega or plain, one hundred miles and more in circumference and encompassed by the snowy mountains of the Sierra

Nevada. The seventy thousand houses of the city spread over two lofty hills and occupied the valley between them, through which ran the waters of the Douro. On one of these hills stood the Alcazaba, a strong fortress; on the other rose the famous Alhambra, a royal palace and castle, with space within its confines for forty thousand men, and so rare and charming in its halls and courts, its gardens and fountains, that it remains to-day a place of pilgrimage to the world for lovers of the beautiful in architecture. And from these hills the city between showed no less attractive, with its groves of citron, orange, and pomegranate trees, its leaping fountains, its airy minarets, its mingled aspect of crowded dwellings and verdant gardens.

High walls, three leagues in circuit, with twelve gates and a thousand and thirty towers, girded it round, beyond which extended the vega, a vast garden of delight, to be compared only with the famous plain of Damascus. Through it the Xenil wound in silvery curves, its waters spread over the plain in thousands of irrigating streams and rills. Blooming gardens and fields of waving grain lent beauty to the plain; orchards and vineyards clothed the slopes of the hills; in the orange and citron groves the voice of the nightingale made the nights musical. In short, all was so beautiful below and so soft and serene above that the Moors seemed not without warrant for their fond belief that Paradise lay in the skies overhanging this happy plain.

But, alas for Granada! war hung round its borders, and the blare of the trumpet and clash of the sword were ever familiar sounds within its confines. Christian kingdoms surrounded it, whose people envied the Moslems this final abiding-place on the soil of Spain. Hostilities were ceaseless on the borders; plundering forays were the delight of the Castilian cavaliers and the Moorish horsemen. Every town was a fortress, and on every peak stood a watch-tower, ready to give warning with a signal fire by night or a cloud of smoke by day of any movement of invasion. For many years such a state of affairs continued between Granada and its principal antagonist, the united kingdoms of Castile and Leon. Even when, in 1457, a Moorish king, disheartened by a foray into the vega itself, made a truce with Henry IV., king of Castile and Leon, and agreed to pay him an annual tribute, the right of warlike raids was kept open. It was only required that they must be conducted secretly, without sound of trumpet or show of banners, and must not continue more than three days. Such a state of affairs was desired alike by the Castilian and Moorish chivalry, who loved these displays of daring and gallantry, and enjoyed nothing more than a crossing of swords with their foes. In 1465 a Moorish prince, Muley Abul Hassan, a man who enjoyed war and hated the Christians, came to the throne, and at once the tribute ceased to be paid. For some years still the truce continued, for Ferdinand and Isabella, the new monarchs of Spain, had troubles at home to keep them engaged. But in 1481 the war reopened with more than its old fury, and was continued until Granada fell in 1492, the year in which the wise Isabella gave aid to Columbus for the discovery of an unknown world beyond the seas.

The war for the conquest of Granada was one full of stirring adventure and hair-breadth escapes, of forays and sieges, of the clash of swords and the brandishing of spears. It was no longer fought by Spain on the principle of the raid,—to dash in, kill, plunder, and speed away with clatter of hoofs and rattle of spurs. It was Ferdinand's policy to take and hold, capturing stronghold after stronghold until all Granada was his. In a memorable pun on the name of Granada, which signifies a pomegranate, he said, "I will pick out the seeds of this pomegranate one by one."

Muley Abul Hassan, the new Moorish king, began the work, foolishly breaking the truce which Ferdinand wished a pretext to bring to an end. On a dark night in 1481 he fell suddenly on Zahara, a mountain town on the Christian frontier, so strong in itself that it was carelessly guarded. It was taken by surprise, its inhabitants were carried off as slaves, and a strong Moorish garrison was left to hold it.

The Moors paid dearly for their daring assault. The Christians retaliated by an attack on the strong and rich city of Alhama, a stronghold within the centre of the kingdom, only a few leagues distant from the capital itself. Strongly situated on a rocky height, with a river nearly surrounding it and a fortress seated on a steep crag above it, and far within the border, no dream of danger to Alhama came to the mind of the Moors, who contented themselves with a small garrison and a negligent guard.

But the loss of Zahara had exasperated Ferdinand. His wars at home were over and he had time to attend to the Moors, and scouts had brought word of the careless security of the guard of Alhama. It could be reached by a difficult and little-travelled route through the defiles of the mountains, and there were possibilities that a secret and rapid march might lead to its surprise.

At the head of the enterprise was Don Rodrigo Ponce de Leon, Marquis of Cadiz, the most distinguished champion in the war that followed. With a select force of three thousand light cavalry and four thousand infantry, adherents of several nobles who attended the expedition, the mountains were traversed with the greatest secrecy and celerity, the marches being made mainly by night and the troops remaining quiet and concealed during the day. No fires were made and no noise was permitted, and midnight of the third day found the invaders in a small, deep valley not far from the fated town. Only now were the troops told what was in view. They had supposed that they were on an ordinary foray. The inspiring tidings filled them with ardor, and they demanded to be led at once to the assault.

Two hours before daybreak the army was placed in ambush close to Alhama, and a body of three hundred picked men set out on the difficult task of scaling the walls of the castle and surprising its garrison. The ascent was steep and very difficult, but they were guided by one who had carefully studied the situation on a previous secret visit and knew what paths to take. Following him they reached the foot of the castle walls without discovery.

Here, under the dark shadow of the towers, they halted and listened. There was not a sound to be heard, not a light to be seen; sleep seemed to brood over castle and town. The ladders were placed and the men noiselessly ascended, Ortega, the guide, going first. The parapet reached, they moved stealthily along its summit until they came upon a sleepy sentinel. Seizing him by the throat, Ortega flourished a dagger before his eyes and bade him point the way to the guard-room. The frightened Moor obeyed, and a dagger thrust ended all danger of his giving an alarm. In a minute more the small scaling party was in the guard-room, massacring the sleeping garrison, while the remainder of the three hundred were rapidly ascending to the battlements.

Some of the awakened Moors fought desperately for their lives, the clash of arms and cries of the combatants came loudly from the castle, and the ambushed army, finding that the surprise had been effective, rushed from their lurking-place with shouts and the sound of trumpets and drums, hoping thereby to increase the dismay of the garrison. Ortega at length fought his way to a postern, which he threw open, admitting the Marquis of Cadiz and a strong following, who quickly overcame all opposition, the citadel being soon in full possession of the Christians.

While this went on the town took the alarm. The

garrison had been destroyed in the citadel, but all the Moors, citizens and soldiers alike, were accustomed to weapons and warlike in spirit, and, looking for speedy aid from Granada, eight leagues away, the tradesmen manned the battlements and discharged showers of stones and arrows upon the Christians wherever visible. The streets leading to the citadel were barricaded, and a steady fire was maintained upon its gate, all who attempted to sally into the city being shot down.

It began to appear as if the Spaniards had taken too great a risk. Their peril was great. Unless they gained the town they must soon be starved out of the castle. Some of them declared that they could not hope to hold the town even if they took it, and proposed to sack and burn the castle and make good their retreat before the king of Granada could reach them with his forces.

This weak-hearted counsel was not to the taste of the valiant Ponce de Leon. "God has given us the castle," he said, "and He will aid us in holding it. We won it with bloodshed; it would be a stain upon our honor to abandon it through fear. We knew our peril before we came; let us face it boldly."

His words prevailed, and the army was led to the assault, planting their scaling-ladders against the walls and swarming up to attack the Moors upon the ramparts. The Marquis of Cadiz, finding that the gate of the castle was commanded by the artillery of the town, ordered a breach to be made in the wall; and through this, sword in hand, he led a body of troops into the town. At the same time an assault was made from every point, and the battle raged with the greatest fury at the ramparts and in the streets.

The Moors, who fought for life, liberty, and property, defended themselves with desperation, fighting in the streets and from the windows and roofs of their houses. From morning until night the contest continued; then, overpowered, the townsmen sought shelter in a large mosque near the walls, whence they kept up so hot a flight of arrows and lances that the assailants dared not approach. Finally, protected by bucklers and wooden shields, some of the soldiers succeeded in setting fire to the door of the mosque. As the flames rolled upward the Moors, deeming that all was lost, rushed desperately out. Many of them were killed in this final fight; the rest surrendered as prisoners.

The struggle was at an end; the town lay at the mercy of the Spaniards; it was given up to plunder, and immense was the booty taken. Gold and silver, rare jewels, rich silks, and costly goods were found in abundance; horses and cattle, grain, oil, and honey, all the productions of the kingdom, in fact, were there in quantities; for Alhama was the richest town in the Moorish territory, and from its strength and situation was called the Key of Granada. The soldiers were not content with plunder. Thinking that they could not hold the place, they destroyed all they could not carry away. Huge jars of oil were shattered, costly furniture was demolished, much material of the greatest value was destroyed. In the dungeons were found many of the Christian captives who had been taken at Zahara, and who gladly gained their freedom again.

The loss of Alhama was a terrible blow to the kingdom of Granada. Terror filled the citizens of the capital when the news reached that city. Sighs and lamentations came from all sides, the mournful ejaculation, "Woe is me, Alhama!" was in every mouth, and this afterwards became the burden of a plaintive ballad, "*Ay de mi, Alhama*," which remains among the gems of Spanish poetry.

Abul Hassan, full of wrath at the daring presumption of his foes, hastened at the head of more than fifty thousand men against the city, driving back a force that was marching to the aid of the Christians, attacking the walls with the fiercest fury, and cutting off the stream upon which the city depended for water, thus threatening the defenders with death by thirst. Yet, though in torments, they fought with unyielding desperation, and held their own until the duke of Medina Sidonia, a bitter enemy of the Marquis of Cadiz in peace, but his comrade in war, came with a large army to his aid. King Ferdinand was hastening thither with all speed, and the Moorish monarch, after a last fierce assault upon the city, broke up his camp and retreated in despair. From that time to the end of the contest the Christians held the "Key of Granada," a threatening stronghold in the heart of the land, from which they raided the vega at will, and exhausted the resources of the kingdom. "*Ay de mi, Alhama!*"

KING ABUL HASSAN AND THE ALCAIDE OF GIBRALTAR.

MULEY ABUL HASSAN, the warlike king of Granada, weary of having his lands raided and his towns taken, resolved to repay the Christians in kind. The Duke of Medina Sidonia had driven him from captured Alhama. He owed this mighty noble a grudge, and the opportunity to repay it seemed at hand. The duke had led his forces to the aid of King Ferdinand, who was making a foray into Moorish territory. He had left almost unguarded his far-spreading lands, wide pasture plains covered thickly with flocks and herds and offering a rare opportunity for a hasty foray.

"I will give this cavalier a lesson that will cure him of his love for campaigning," said the fierce old king.

Leaving his port of Malaga at the head of fifteen hundred horse and six thousand foot, the Moorish monarch followed the sea-shore route to the border of his dominions, entering Christian territory between Gibraltar and Castellar. There was only one man in this quarter of whom he had any fear. This was Pedro de Vargas, governor of Gibraltar, a shrewd and vigilant old soldier, whose daring Abul Hassan well knew, but knew also that his garrison was too small to serve for a successful sally.

The alert Moor, however, advanced with great caution, sending out parties to explore every pass where an ambush might await him, since, despite his secrecy, the news of his coming might have gone before. At length the broken country of Castellar was traversed and the plains were reached. Encamping on the banks of the Celemin, he sent four hundred lancers to the vicinity of Algeciras to keep a close watch upon Gibraltar across the bay, to attack Pedro if he sallied out, and to send word to the camp if any movement took place. This force was four times that said to be in Gibraltar. Remaining on the Celemin with his main body of troops, King Hassan sent two hundred horsemen to scour the plain of Tarifa, and as many more to the lands of Medina Sidonia, the whole district being a rich pasture land upon which thousands of animals grazed.

All went well. The parties of foragers came in, driving vast flocks and herds, enough to replace those which had been swept from the vega of Granada by the foragers of Spain. The troops on watch at Algeciras sent word that all was quiet at Gibraltar. Satisfied that for once Pedro de Vargas had been foiled, the old king called in his detachments and started back in triumph with his spoils.

He was mistaken. The vigilant governor had been advised of his movements, but was too weak in men to leave his post. Fortunately for him, a squadron of the armed galleys in the strait put into port, and, their commander agreeing to take charge of Gibraltar in his absence, Pedro sallied out at midnight with seventy of his men, bent upon giving the Moors what trouble he could.

Sending men to the mountain-tops, he had alarm fires kindled as a signal to the peasants that the Moors were out and their herds in peril. Couriers were also despatched at speed to rouse the country and bid all capable of bearing arms to rendezvous at Castellar, a stronghold which Abul Hassan would have to pass on his return. The Moorish king saw the fire signals and knew well what they meant. Striking his tents, he began as hasty a retreat as his slow-moving multitude of animals would permit. In advance rode two hundred and fifty of his bravest men. Then came the great drove of cattle. In the rear marched the main army, with Abul Hassan at its head. And thus they moved across the broken country towards Castellar.

Near that place De Vargas was on the watch, a thick and lofty cloud of dust revealing to him the position of the Moors. A half-league of hills and declivities separated the van and the rear of the raiding column, a long, dense forest rising between. De Vargas saw that they were in no position to aid each other quickly, and that something might come of a sudden and sharp attack. Selecting the best fifty of his small force, he made a circuit towards a place which he knew to be suitable for ambush. Here a narrow glen opened into a defile with high, steep sides. It was the only route open to the Moors, and he proposed to let the vanguard and the herds pass and fall upon the rear.

The Moors, however, were on the alert. While the

Spaniards lay hidden, six mounted scouts entered the defile and rode into the mouth of the glen, keenly looking to right and left for a concealed enemy. They came so near that a minute or two more must reveal to them the ambush.

"Let us kill these men and retreat to Gibraltar," said one of the Spaniards; "the infidels are far too many for us."

"I have come for larger game than this," answered De Vargas, "and, by the aid of God and Santiago, I will not go back without making my mark. I know these Moors, and will show you how they stand a sudden charge."

The scouts were riding deeper into the glen. The ambush could no longer be concealed. At a quick order from De Vargas ten horsemen rushed so suddenly upon them that four of their number were in an instant hurled to the ground. The other two wheeled and rode back at full speed, hotly pursued by the ten men. Their dashing pace soon brought them in sight of the vanguard of the Moors, from which about eighty horsemen rode out to the aid of their friends. The Spaniards turned and clattered back, with this force in sharp pursuit. In a minute or two both parties came at a furious rush into the glen.

This was what De Vargas had foreseen. Bidding his trumpeter to sound, he dashed from his concealment at the head of his men, drawn up in close array. They were upon the Moors almost before they were seen, their weapons making havoc in the disordered ranks. The skirmish was short and sharp.

The Moors, taken by surprise, and thrown into confusion, fell rapidly, their ranks being soon so thinned that scarce half of them turned in the retreat.

"After them!" cried De Vargas. "We will have a brush with the vanguard before the rear can come up."

Onward after the flying Moors rode the gallant fifty, coming with such force and fury on the advance-guard that many were overturned in the first shock. Those behind held their own with some firmness, but their leaders, the alcaides of Marabella and Casares, being slain, the line gave way and fled towards the rear-guard, passing through the droves of cattle, which they threw into utter confusion.

Nothing further could be done. The trampling cattle had filled the air with a blinding cloud of dust. De Vargas was badly wounded. A few minutes might bring up the Moorish king with an overwhelming force. Despoiling the slain, and taking with them some thirty horses, the victorious Spaniards rode in triumph back to Castellar.

The Moorish king, hearing the exaggerated report of the fugitives, feared that all Xeres was up and in arms.

"Our road is blocked," cried some of his officers. "We had better abandon the animals and seek another route for our return."

"Not so," cried the old king; "no true soldier gives up his booty without a blow. Follow me; we will have a brush with these dogs of Christians."

In hot haste he galloped onward, right through the centre of the herd, driving the cattle to right

and left. On reaching the field of battle he found
no Spaniard in sight, but dozens of his own men lay
dead and despoiled, among them the two alcaides.
The sight filled the warlike old king with rage.
Confident that his foes had taken refuge in Castellar, he rode on to that place, set fire to two houses
near its walls, and sent a shower of arrows into its
streets. Pedro de Vargas was past taking to horse,
but he ordered his men to make a sally, and a sharp
skirmish took place under the walls. In the end the
king drew off to the scene of the fight, buried the
dead except the alcaides, whose bodies were laid on
mules to be interred at Malaga, and, gathering the
scattered herds, drove them past the walls of Castellar by way of taunting the Christian foe.

Yet the stern old Moorish warrior could thoroughly
appreciate valor and daring even in an enemy.

"What are the revenues of the alcaide of Gibraltar?" he asked of two Christian captives he had
taken.

"We know not," they replied, "except that he is
entitled to one animal out of every drove of cattle
that passes his bounds."

"Then Allah forbid that so brave a cavalier should
be defrauded of his dues."

He gave orders to select twelve of the finest cattle
from the twelve droves that formed the herd of spoil,
and directed that they should be delivered to Pedro
de Vargas.

"Tell him," said the king, "that I beg his pardon
for not sending these cattle sooner, but have just
learned they are his dues, and hasten to satisfy

them in courtesy to so worthy a cavalier. Tell
him, at the same time, that I did not know the
alcaide of Gibraltar was so vigilant in collecting his
tolls."

The soldierly pleasantry of the old king was much
to the taste of the brave De Vargas, and called for
a worthy return. He bade his men deliver a rich
silken vest and a scarlet mantle to the messenger,
to be presented to the Moorish king.

"Tell his majesty," he said, "that I kiss his hands
for the honor he has done me, and regret that my
scanty force was not fitted to give him a more signal
reception. Had three hundred horsemen, whom I
have been promised from Xeres, arrived in time, I
might have served him up an entertainment more
befitting his station. They may arrive during the
night, in which case his majesty, the king, may look
for a royal service in the morning."

"Allah preserve us," cried the king, on receiving
this message, "from a brush with these hard riders
of Xeres! A handful of troops familiar with these
wild mountain-passes may destroy an army encumbered like ours with booty."

It was a relief to the king to find that De Vargas
was too sorely wounded to take the field in person.
A man like him at the head of an adequate force might
have given no end of trouble. During the day the
retreat was pushed with all speed, the herds being
driven with such haste that they were frequently
broken and scattered among the mountain defiles,
the result being that more than five thousand cattle
were lost, being gathered up again by the Christians.

The king returned triumphantly to Malaga with the remainder, rejoicing in his triumph over the Duke of Medina Sidonia, and having taught King Ferdinand that the game of ravaging an enemy's country was one at which two could play.

"In the hand of God is the destiny of princes. He alone giveth empire," piously says an old Arabian chronicler, and goes on with the following story: A Moorish horseman, mounted on a fleet Arabian steed, was one day traversing the mountains which extend between Granada and the frontier of Murcia. He galloped swiftly through the valleys, but paused and gazed cautiously from the summit of every height. A squadron of cavaliers followed warily at a distance. There were fifty lances. The richness of their armor and attire showed them to be warriors of noble rank, and their leader had a lofty and prince-like demeanor.

For two nights and a day the cavalcade made its way through that rugged country, avoiding settled places and choosing the most solitary passes of the mountains. Their hardships were severe, but campaigning was their trade and their horses were of generous spirit. It was midnight when they left the hills and rode through darkness and silence to the city of Granada, under the shadows of whose high walls they passed to the gate of the Albaycin. Here the leader ordered his followers to halt and remain concealed. Taking four or five with him, he advanced to the gate and struck upon it with the handle of his scimitar.

"Who is it knocks at this unseasonable hour of the night?" demanded the warder within.

"Your king," was the answer. "Open and admit him."

Opening a wicket, the warder held forth a light and looked at the man without. Recognizing him at a glance, he opened the gate, and the cavalier, who had feared a less favorable reception, rode in with his followers and galloped in haste to the hill of the Albaycin, where the new-comers knocked loudly at the doors of the principal dwellings, bidding their tenants to rise and take arms for their lawful sovereign. The summons was obeyed. Trumpets soon resounded in the streets; the gleam of torches lit the dark avenues and flashed upon naked steel. From right and left the Moors came hurrying to the rendezvous. By daybreak the whole force of the Albaycin was under arms, ready to meet in battle the hostile array on the opposite height of the Alhambra.

To tell what this midnight movement meant we must go back a space in history. The conquest of Granada was not due to Ferdinand and the Spaniards alone. It was greatly aided by the dissensions of the Moors, who were divided into two parties and fought bitterly with each other during their intervals of truce with the Christians. Ferdinand won in the game largely by a shrewd playing off of one of these factions against the other and by taking advantage of the weakness and vacillation of the young king, whose clandestine entrance to the city we have just seen.

Boabdil el Chico, or Boabdil the Young, as he was called, was the son of Muley Abul Hassan, against whom he had rebelled, and with such effect that, after a bloody battle in the streets of the city, the old king was driven without its walls. His tyranny had caused the people to gather round his son.

From that time forward there was dissension and civil war in Granada, and the quarrels of its kings paved the way for the downfall of the state. The country was divided into the two factions of the young and the old kings. In the city the hill of the Albaycin, with its fortress of the Alcazaba, was the stronghold of Boabdil, while the partisans of Abul Hassan dwelt on the height of the Alhambra, the lower town between being the battle-ground of the rival factions.

The succeeding events were many, but must be told in few words. King Boabdil, to show his prowess to the people, marched over the border to attack the city of Lucena. As a result he was himself assailed, his army put to the rout, and himself taken prisoner by the forces of Ferdinand of Aragon. To regain his liberty he acknowledged himself a vassal of the Spanish monarch, to whom he agreed to pay tribute. On his release he made his way to the city of Granada, but his adherents were so violently assailed by those of his father that the streets of the city ran blood, and Boabdil the Unlucky, as he was now called, found it advisable to leave the capital and fix his residence in Almeria, a large and splendid city whose people were devoted to him.

As the years went on Muley Abul Hassan became

sadly stricken with age. He grew nearly blind and was bed-ridden with paralysis. His brother Abdallah, known as El Zagal, or "The Valiant," commander-in-chief of the Moorish armies, assumed his duties as a sovereign, and zealously took up the quarrel with his son. He attempted to surprise the young king at Almeria, drove him out as a fugitive, and took possession of that city. At a later date he endeavored to remove him by poison. It was this attempt that spurred Boabdil to the enterprise we have just described. El Zagal was now full king in Granada, holding the Alhambra as his palace, and his nephew, who had been a wanderer since his flight from Almeria, was instigated to make a bold stroke for the throne.

On the day after the secret return of Boabdil battle raged in the streets of Granada, a fierce encounter taking place between the two kings in the square before the principal mosque. Hand to hand they fought with the greatest fury till separated by the charges of their followers.

For days the conflict went on, death and turmoil ruling in Granada, such hatred existing between the two factions that neither side gave quarter. Boabdil was the weaker in men. Fearing defeat in consequence, he sent a messenger to Don Fadrique de Toledo, the Christian commander on the border, asking for assistance. Don Fadrique had been instructed by Ferdinand to give what aid he could to the young king, the vassal of Spain, and responded to Boabdil's request by marching with a body of troops to the vicinity of Granada. No sooner had

KING CHARLES'S WELL, ALHAMBRA.

Boabdil seen their advancing banners than he sallied forth with a squadron to meet them. El Zagal, who was equally on the alert, sallied forth at the same time, and drew up his troops in battle array.

The wary Don Fadrique, in doubt as to the meaning of this double movement, and fearing treachery, halted at a safe distance, and drew off for the night to a secure situation. Early the next morning a Moorish cavalier approached the sentinels and asked for an audience with Don Fadrique, as an envoy from El Zagal. The Christian troops, he said on behalf of the old king, had come to aid his nephew, but he was ready to offer them an alliance on better terms than those of Boabdil. Don Fadrique listened courteously to the envoy, but for better assurance, determined to send a representative to El Zagal himself, under protection of a flag. For this purpose he selected Don Juan de Vera, one of the most intrepid and discreet of his cavaliers, who had in years before been sent by King Ferdinand on a mission to the Alhambra.

Don Juan, on reaching the palace, was well received by the old king, holding an interview with him which extended so far into the night that it was too late to return to camp, and he was lodged in a sumptuous apartment of the Alhambra. In the morning he was approached by one of the Moorish courtiers, a man given to jest and satire, who invited him to take part in a ceremony in the palace mosque. This invitation, given in jest, was received by the punctilious Catholic knight in earnest, and he replied, with stern displeasure,—

"The servants of Queen Isabella of Castile, who bear on their armor the cross of St. Iago, never enter the temples of Mohammed, except to level them to the earth and trample on them."

This discourteous reply was repeated by the courtier to a renegade, who, having newly adopted the Moorish faith, was eager to show his devotion to the Moslem creed, and proposed to engage the stiff-necked Catholic knight in argument. Seeking Don Juan, they found him playing chess with the alcaide of the palace, and the renegade at once began to comment on the Christian religion in uncomplimentary terms. Don Juan was quick to anger, but he restrained himself, and replied, with grave severity,—

"You would do well to cease talking about what you do not understand."

The renegade and his jesting companion replied in a series of remarks intended as wit, though full of insolence, Don Juan fuming inwardly as he continued to play. In the end they went too far, the courtier making an obscene comparison between the Virgin Mary and Amina, the mother of Mohammed. In an instant the old knight sprang up, white with rage, and dashing aside chess-board and chessmen. Drawing his sword, he dealt such a "*hermosa cuchillada*" ("handsome slash") across the head of the offending Moor as to stretch him bleeding on the floor. The renegade fled in terror, rousing the echoes of the palace with his outcries and stirring up guards and attendants, who rushed into the room where the irate Christian stood sword in hand defying Mohammed and his hosts. The alarm quickly reached the ears of the king, who hurried to the scene, his appearance at once restoring order. On hearing from the alcaide the cause of the affray, he acted with becoming dignity, ordering the guards from the room and directing that the renegade should be severely punished for daring to infringe the hospitality of the palace and insult an embassador.

Don Juan, his quick fury evaporated, sheathed his sword, thanked the king for his courtesy, and proposed a return to the camp. But this was not easy of accomplishment. A garbled report of the tumult in the palace had spread to the streets, where it was rumored that Christian spies had been introduced into the palace with treasonable intent. In a brief time hundreds of the populace were in arms and thronging about the gate of Justice of the Alhambra, where they loudly demanded the death of all Christians in the palace and of all who had introduced them.

It was impossible for Don Juan to leave the palace by the route he had followed on his arrival. The infuriated mob would have torn him to pieces. But it was important that he should depart at once. All that El Zagal could do was to furnish him with a disguise, a swift horse, and an escort, and to let him out of the Alhambra by a private gate. This secret mode of departure was not relished by the proud Spaniard, but life was just then of more value than dignity, as he appreciated when, in Moorish dress, he passed through crowds who were thirsting for his blood.   A gate of the city was at length reached, and Don Juan and his escort rode quietly out.   But he was no sooner on the open plain than he spurred his horse to its speed, and did not draw rein until the banners of Don Fadrique waved above his head.

Don Fadrique heard with much approval of the boldness of his envoy.   His opinion of Don Juan's discretion he kept to himself.   He rewarded him with a valuable horse, and wrote a letter of thanks to El Zagal for his protection to his emissary.   Queen Isabella, on learning how stoutly the knight had stood up for the supremacy of the Blessed Virgin, was highly delighted, and conferred several distinctions of honor upon the cavalier besides presenting him with three hundred thousand maravedis.

The outcome of the advances of the two kings was that Don Fadrique chose Boabdil as his ally, and sent him a reinforcement of foot-soldiers and arquebusiers.   This introduction of Christians into the city rekindled the flames of war, and it continued to rage in the streets for the space of fifty days.

The result of the struggle between the two kings may be briefly told.   While they contended for supremacy Ferdinand of Aragon invaded their kingdom with a large army and marched upon the great seaport of Malaga.   El Zagal sought an accommodation with Boabdil, that they might unite their forces against the common foe, but the short-sighted young man spurned his overtures with disdain.   El Zagal then, the better patriot of the two, marched himself against the Christian host, hoping to surprise them in the passes of the mountains and per-

haps capture King Ferdinand himself. Unluckily
for him, his well-laid plan was discovered by the
Christians, who attacked and defeated him, his
troops flying in uncontrollable disorder.

The news of this disaster reached Granada before
him and infuriated the people, who closed their gates
and threatened the defeated king from the walls.
Nothing remained to El Zagal but to march to Almeria and establish his court in that city in which
Boabdil had formerly reigned. Thus the positions
of the rival kings became reversed. From that time
forward the kingdom of Granada was divided into
two, and the work of conquest by the Christians
was correspondingly reduced.

THE dull monotony of sieges, of which there were many during the war with Granada, was little to the taste of the valorous Spanish cavaliers. They burned for adventure, and were ever ready for daring exploits, the more welcome the more dangerous they promised to be. One day during the siege of Baza, a strong city in El Zagal's dominions, two of these spirited young cavaliers, Francisco de Bazan and Antonio de Cueva, were seated on the ramparts of the siege works, bewailing the dull life to which they were confined. They were overheard by a veteran scout, who was familiar with the surrounding country.

"Señors," he said, "if you pine for peril and profit and are eager to pluck the beard of the fiery old Moorish king, I can lead you where you will have a fine opportunity to prove your valor. There are certain hamlets not far from the walls of El Zagal's city of Guadix where rich booty awaits the daring raider. I can lead you there by a way that will enable you to take them by surprise; and if you are as cool in the head as you are hot in the spur you may bear off spoils from under the very eyes of the king of the Moors."

He had struck the right vein. The youths were at once hot for the enterprise. To win booty from the very gates of Guadix was a stirring scheme, and they quickly found others of their age as eager as themselves for the daring adventure. In a short time they had enrolled a body of nearly three hundred horse and two hundred foot, well armed and equipped, and every man of them ready for the road.

The force obtained, the raiders left the camp early one evening, keeping their destination secret, and made their way by starlight through the mountain passes, led by the *adalid*, or guide. Pressing rapidly onward by day and night, they reached the hamlets one morning just before daybreak, and fell on them suddenly, making prisoners of the inhabitants, sacking the houses, and sweeping the fields of their grazing herds. Then, without taking a moment to rest, they set out with all speed for the mountains, which they hoped to reach before the country could be roused.

Several of the herdsmen had escaped and fled to Guadix, where they told El Zagal of the daring ravage. Wild with rage at the insult, the old king at once sent out six hundred of his choicest horse and foot, with orders for swift pursuit, bidding them to recover the booty and bring him as prisoners the insolent marauders. The Christians, weary with their two days and nights of hard marching, were driving the captured cattle and sheep up a mountainside, when, looking back, they saw a great cloud of dust upon their trail. Soon they discerned the turbaned host, evidently superior to them in number, and man and horse in fresh condition.

"They are too much for us," cried some of the

horsemen. "It would be madness in our worn-out state to face a fresh force of that number. We shall have to let the cattle go and seek safety in flight."

"What!" cried Antonio and Francisco, their leaders; "abandon our prey without a blow? Desert our foot-soldiers and leave them to the enemy? Did any of you think El Zagal would let us off without a brush? You do not give good Spanish counsel, for every soldier knows that there is less danger in presenting our faces than our backs to the foe, and fewer men are killed in a brave advance than in a cowardly retreat."

Some of the cavaliers were affected by these words, but the mass of the party were chance volunteers, who received no pay and had nothing to gain by risking their lives. Consequently, as the enemy came near, the diversity of opinions grew into a tumult, and confusion reigned. The captains ordered the standard-bearer to advance against the Moors, confident that any true soldiers would follow his banner. He hesitated to obey; the turmoil increased; in a moment more the horsemen might be in full flight.

At this critical juncture a horseman of the royal guards rode forward,—the good knight Hernan Perez del Pulgar, governor of the fortress of Salar. Taking off the handkerchief which, in the Andalusian fashion, he wore round his head, he tied it to a lance and raised it in the air.

"Comrades," he cried, "why do you load yourself with arms if you trust for safety to your feet? We shall see who among you are the brave men and who are the cowards. If it is a standard you want, here is mine. Let the man who has the heart to fight follow this handkerchief."

Waving his improvised banner, he spurred against the Moors. Many followed him. Those who at first held back soon joined the advance. With one accord the whole body rushed with shouts upon the enemy. The Moors, who were now close at hand, were seized with surprise and alarm at this sudden charge. The foremost files turned and fled in panic, followed by the others, and pursued by the Christians, who cut them down without a blow in return. Soon the whole body was in full flight. Several hundred of the Moors were killed and their bodies despoiled, many were taken prisoners, and the Christians returned in triumph to the army, driving their long array of cattle and sheep and of mules laden with booty, and bearing in their front the standard under which they had fought.

King Ferdinand was so delighted with this exploit, and in particular with the gallant action of Perez del Pulgar, that he conferred knighthood upon the latter with much ceremony, and authorized him to bear upon his escutcheon a golden lion in an azure field, showing a lance with a handkerchief at its point. Round its border were to be depicted the eleven alcaides defeated in the battle. This heroic deed was followed by so many others during the wars with the Moors that Perez del Pulgar became in time known by the flattering appellation of "He of the exploits."

The most famous exploit of this daring knight took place during the siege of Granada,—the final operation of the long war. Here single combats and minor skirmishes between Christian and Moorish cavaliers were of almost daily occurrence, until Ferdinand strictly forbade all such tilts, as he saw that they gave zeal and courage to the Moors, and were attended with considerable loss of life among his bravest followers.

This edict of the king was very distasteful to the fiery Moorish knights, who declared that the crafty Christian wished to destroy chivalry and put an end to heroic valor. They did their best to provoke the Spanish knights to combat, galloping on their fleet steeds close to the borders of the camp and hurling their lances over the barriers, each lance bearing the name of its owner with some defiant message. But despite the irritation caused by these insults to the Spanish knights, none of them ventured to disobey the mandate of the king.

Chief among these Moorish cavaliers was one named Tarfe, a man of fierce and daring spirit and a giant in size, who sought to surpass his fellows in acts of audacity. In one of his sallies towards the Christian camp this bold cavalier leaped his steed over the barrier, galloped inward close to the royal quarters, and launched his spear with such strength that it quivered in the earth close to the tents of the sovereigns. The royal guards rushed out, but Tarfe was already far away, scouring the plain on his swift Barbary steed. On examining the lance it was found to bear a label indicating that it was intended for the queen, who was present in the camp.

This bravado and the insult offered Queen Isabella

excited the highest indignation among the Christian warriors. "Shall we let this insolent fellow outdo us?" said Perez del Pulgar, who was present. "I propose to teach these insolent Moors a lesson. Who will stand by me in an enterprise of desperate peril?" The warriors knew Pulgar well enough to be sure that his promise of peril was likely to be kept, yet all who heard him were ready to volunteer. Out of them he chose fifteen,—men whom he knew he could trust for strength of arm and valor of heart.

His proposed enterprise was indeed a perilous one. A Moorish renegade had agreed to guide him into the city by a secret pass. Once within, they were to set fire to the Alcaiceria and others of the principal buildings, and then escape as best they could.

At dead of night they set out, provided with the necessary combustibles. Their guide led them up a channel of the river Darro, until they halted under a bridge near the royal gate. Here Pulgar stationed six of his followers on guard, bidding them to keep silent and motionless. With the others he made his way up a drain of the stream which passed under a part of the city and opened into the streets. All was dark and silent. Not a soul moved. The renegade, at the command of Pulgar, led the adventurers to the principal mosque. Here the pious cavalier drew from under his cloak a parchment inscribed in large letters with AVE MARIA, and nailed this to the door of the mosque, thus dedicating the heathen temple to the Virgin Mary.

They now hurried to the Alcaiceria, where the combustibles were placed ready to fire. Not until this moment was it discovered that the torch-bearer had carelessly left his torch at the door of the mosque. It was too late to return. Pulgar sought to strike fire with flint and steel, but while doing so the Moorish guard came upon them in its rounds. Drawing his sword and followed by his comrades, the bold Spaniard made a fierce assault upon the astonished Moors, quickly putting them to flight. But the enterprise was at an end. The alarm was given and soldiers were soon hurrying in every direction through the streets. Guided by the renegade, Pulgar and his companions hastened to the drain by which they had entered, plunged into it, and reached their companions under the bridge. Here mounting their horses, they rode back to the camp.

The Moors were at a loss to imagine the purpose of this apparently fruitless enterprise, but wild was their exasperation the next morning when they found the "Ave Maria" on the door of a mosque in the centre of their city. The mosque thus sanctified by Perez del Pulgar was actually converted into a Christian cathedral after the capture of the city.

We have yet to describe the sequel of this exploit. On the succeeding day a powerful train left the Christian camp and advanced towards the city walls. In its centre were the king and queen, the prince and princesses, and the ladies of the court, surrounded by the royal body-guard,—a richly dressed troop, composed of the sons of the most illustrious families of Spain. The Moors gazed with wonder upon this rare pageant, which moved in glittering array across the vega to the sound of martial music; a host brilliant with banners and plumes, shining arms and shimmering silks, for the court and the army moved there hand in hand. Queen Isabella had expressed a wish to see, nearer at hand, a city whose beauty was of world-wide renown, and the Marquis of Cadiz had drawn out this powerful escort that she might be gratified in her desire. The queen had her wish, but hundreds of men died that she might be pleased.

While the royal dame and her ladies were gazing with delight on the red towers of the Alhambra, rising in rich contrast through the green verdure of their groves, a large force of Moorish cavalry poured from the city gates, ready to accept the gage of battle which the Christians seemed to offer. The first to come were a host of richly armed and gayly attired light cavalry, mounted on fleet and fiery Barbary steeds. Heavily armed cavalry followed, and then a strong force of foot-soldiers, until an army was drawn up on the plain. Queen Isabella saw this display with disquiet, and forbade an attack upon the enemy, or even a skirmish, as it would pain her if a single warrior should lose his life through the indulgence of her curiosity.

As a result, though the daring Moorish horsemen rode fleetly along the Christian front, brandishing their lances, and defying the cavaliers to mortal combat, not a Spaniard stirred. The cavaliers were under the eyes of Ferdinand, by whom such duels had been strictly forbidden. At length, however, they were incensed beyond their powers of resistance. Forth from the city rode a stalwart Moorish horseman, clad in steel armor, and bearing a huge buckler and a ponderous lance. His device showed him to be the giant warrior Tarfe, the daring infidel who had flung his lance at the queen's tent. As he rode out he was followed by the shouts and laughter of a mob, and when he came within full view of the Spanish army the cavaliers saw, with indignant horror, tied to his horse's tail and dragging in the dust, the parchment with its inscription of "Ave Maria" which Hernan Perez del Pulgar had nailed to the door of the mosque.

This insult was more than Castilian flesh and blood could bear. Hernan was not present to maintain his deed, but Garcilasso de la Vega, one of the young companions of his exploit, galloped to the king and earnestly begged permission to avenge the degrading insult to their holy faith. The king, who was as indignant as the knight, gave the desired permission, and Garcilasso, closing his visor and grasping his spear, rode out before the ranks and defied the Moor to combat to the death.

Tarfe asked nothing better, and an exciting passage at arms took place on the plain with the two armies as witnesses. Tarfe was the stronger of the two, and the more completely armed. He was skilled in the use of his weapons and dexterous in managing his horse, and the Christians trembled for their champion.

The warriors met in mid career with a furious shock. Their lances were shivered, and Garcilasso was borne back in his saddle. But his horse wheeled away and he was quickly firm in his seat again, sword in hand. Sword against scimitar, the combatants returned to the encounter. The Moor rode a trained horse, that obeyed his every signal. Round the Christian he circled, seeking some opening for a blow. But the smaller size of Garcilasso was made equal by greater agility. Now he parried a blow with his sword, now he received a furious stroke on his shield. Each of the combatants before many minutes felt the edge of the steel, and their blood began to flow.

At length the Moor, thinking his antagonist exhausted, rushed in and grappled with him, using all his force to fling him from his horse. Garcilasso grasped him in return with all his strength, and they fell together to the earth, the Moor uppermost. Placing his knee on the breast of the Spaniard, Tarfe drew his dagger and brandished it above his throat. Terror filled the Christian ranks; a shout of triumph rose from those of the Moors. But suddenly Tarfe was seen to loosen his grasp and roll over in the dust. Garcilasso had shortened his sword and, as Tarfe raised his arm, had struck him to the heart.

The rules of chivalry were rigidly observed. No one interfered on either side. Garcilasso despoiled his victim, raised the inscription " Ave Maria " on the point of his sword, and bore it triumphantly back, amid shouts of triumph from the Christian army.

By this time the passions of the Moors were so excited that they could not be restrained. They made a furious charge upon the Spanish host, driving in its advanced ranks. The word to attack was given the Spaniards in return, the war-cry "Santiago!" rang along the line, and in a short time both armies were locked in furious combat. The affair ended in a repulse of the Moors, the foot-soldiers taking to flight, and the cavalry vainly endeavoring to rally them. They were pursued to the gates of the city, more than two thousand of them being killed, wounded, or taken prisoners in "the queen's skirmish," as the affair came to be called.

THE LAST SIGH OF THE MOOR.

In 1492, nearly eight centuries after the conquest of Spain by the Arabs, their dominion ended in the surrender of the city of Granada by King Boabdil to the army of Ferdinand and Isabella. The empire of the Arab Moors had shrunk, year by year and century by century, before the steady advance of the Christians, until only the small kingdom of Granada remained. This, distracted by anarchy within and assailed by King Ferdinand with all the arts of statecraft and all the strength of arms, gradually decreased in dimensions, city after city, district after district, being lost, until only the single city of Granada remained.

This populous and powerful city would have proved very difficult to take by the ordinary methods of war, and could only have been subdued with great loss of life and expenditure of treasure. Ferdinand assailed it by a less costly and more exasperating method. Granada subsisted on the broad and fertile vega or plain surrounding it, a region marvellously productive in grain and fruits and rich in cattle and sheep. It was a cold-blooded and cruel system adopted by the Spanish monarch. He assailed the city through the vega. Disregarding the city, he marched his army into the plain at the time of harvest and so thoroughly destroyed its growing crops that the smiling and verdant expanse was left a scene of frightful desolation. This was not accomplished without sharp reprisals by the Moors, but the Spaniard persisted until he had converted the fruitful paradise into a hopeless desert, and then marched away, leaving the citizens to a winter of despair.

The next year he came again, encamped his army near the city, destroyed what little verdure remained near its walls, and waited calmly until famine and anarchy should force the citizens to yield. He attempted no siege. It was not necessary. He could safely trust to his terrible allies. The crowded city held out desperately while the summer passed and autumn moved on to winter's verge, and then, with famine stalking through their streets and invading their homes, but one resource remained to the citizens,—surrender.

Ferdinand did not wish to distress too deeply the unhappy people. To obtain possession of the city on any terms was the one thought then in his mind. Harshness could come later, if necessary. Therefore, on the 25th of November, 1492, articles of capitulation were signed, under which the Moors of Granada were to retain all their possessions, be protected in their religious exercises, and governed by their own laws, which were to be administered by their own officials ; the one unwelcome proviso being that they should become subjects of Spain. To Boabdil were secured all his rich estates and the patrimony of the crown, while he was to receive in addition thirty thousand castellanos in gold. Excellent terms, one would say, could Spain have been trusted to live up to them—which Spain only did as long as good faith served her purpose.

On the night preceding the surrender doleful lamentations filled the halls of the Alhambra, for the household of Boabdil were bidding a last farewell to that delightful abode. The most precious effects were hastily packed upon mules, and with tears and wailings the rich hangings and ornaments of the beautiful apartments were removed. Day had not yet dawned when a sorrowful cavalcade moved through an obscure postern gate of the palace and wound through a retired quarter of the city. It was the family of the deposed monarch, which he had sent off thus early to save them from possible scoffs and insults.

The sun had barely risen when three signal-guns boomed from the heights of the Alhambra, and the Christian army began its march across the vega. To spare the feelings of the citizens it was decided that the city should not be entered by its usual gates, and a special road had been opened leading to the Alhambra.

At the head of the procession moved the king and queen, with the prince and princesses and the dignitaries and ladies of the court, attended by the royal guards in their rich array. This cortege halted at the village of Armilla, a league and a half from the city. Meanwhile, Don Pedro Gonzalez de Mendoza, Grand Cardinal of Spain, with an escort of three thousand foot and a troop of cavalry, proceeded towards the Alhambra to take possession of that noblest work of the Moors. At their approach

Boabdil left the palace by a postern gate attended by fifty cavaliers, and advanced to meet the grand cardinal, whom, in words of mournful renunciation, he bade to take possession of the royal fortress of the Moors. Then he passed sadly onward to meet the sovereigns of Spain, who had halted awaiting his approach, while the army stood drawn up on the broad plain.

As the Spaniards waited in anxious hope, all eyes fixed on the Alhambra heights, they saw the silver cross, the great standard of this crusade, rise upon the great watch-tower, where it sparkled in the sunbeams, while beside it floated the pennon of St. James, at sight of which a great shout of "Santiago! Santiago!" rose from the awaiting host. Next rose the royal standard, amid resounding cries of "Castile! Castile! For King Ferdinand and Queen Isabella." The sovereigns sank upon their knees, giving thanks to God for their great victory, the whole army followed their example, and the choristers of the royal chapel broke forth into the solemn anthem of "*Te Deum laudamus.*"

Ferdinand now advanced to a point near the banks of the Xenil, where he was met by the unfortunate Boabdil. As the Moorish king approached he made a movement to dismount, which Ferdinand prevented. He then offered to kiss the king's hand. This homage also, as previously arranged, was declined, whereupon Boabdil leaned forward and kissed the king's right arm. He then with a resigned mien delivered the keys of the city.

"These keys," he said, "are the last relics of the

Arabian empire in Spain. Thine, O king, are our trophies, our kingdom, and our person. Such is the will of God! Receive them with the clemency thou hast promised, and which we look for at thy hands."

"Doubt not our promises," said Ferdinand, kindly, "nor that thou shalt regain from our friendship the prosperity of which the fortune of war has deprived thee."

Then drawing from his finger a gold ring set with a precious stone, Boabdil presented it to the Count of Tendilla, who, he was informed, was to be governor of the city, saying,—

"With this ring Granada has been governed. Take it and govern with it, and God make you more fortunate than I."

He then proceeded to the village of Armilla, where Queen Isabella remained. She received him with the utmost courtesy and graciousness, and delivered to him his son, who had been held as a hostage for the fulfilment of the capitulation. Boabdil pressed the child tenderly to his bosom, and moved on until he had joined his family, from whom and their attendants the shouts and strains of music of the victorious army drew tears and moans.

At length the weeping train reached the summit of an eminence about two leagues distant which commanded the last view of Granada. Here they paused for a look of farewell at the beautiful and beloved city, whose towers and minarets gleamed brightly before them in the sunshine. While they still gazed a peal of artillery, faint with distance, told them that the city was taken possession of and was lost to the Moorish kings forever. Boabdil could no longer contain himself.

"Allah achbar! God is great!" he murmured, tears belicing his words of resignation.

His mother, a woman of intrepid soul, was indignant at this display of weakness.

"You do well," she cried, "to weep like a woman for what you failed to defend like a man."

Others strove to console the king, but his tears were not to be restrained.

"Allah achbar!" he exclaimed again; "when did misfortunes ever equal mine?"

The hill where this took place afterwards became known as Feg Allah Achbar; but the point of view where Boabdil obtained the last prospect of Granada is called by the Spaniards "*El ultimo suspiro del Moro*," or "The last sigh of the Moor."

As Boabdil thus took his last look at beautiful Granada, it behooves us to take a final backward glance at Arabian Spain, from whose history we have drawn so much of interest and romance. In this hospitable realm civilization dwelt when it had fled from all Europe besides. Here luxury reigned while barbarism prevailed in other European lands. We are told that in Cordova a man might walk in a straight line for ten miles by the light of the public lamps, while seven hundred years afterwards there was not a single public lamp in London streets. Its avenues were solidly paved, while centuries afterwards the people of Paris, on rainy days, stepped from their door-sills into mud ankle deep. The dwellings were marked by beauty and luxury, while the people of Europe dwelt in miserable huts, dressed in leather, and lived on the rudest and least nutritive food.

The rulers of France, England, and Germany lived in rude buildings without chimneys or windows, with a hole in the roof for the smoke to escape, at a time when the royal halls of Arabian Spain were visions of grace and beauty. The residences of the Arabs had marble balconies overhanging orange-gardens; their floors and walls were frequently of rich and graceful mosaic; fountains gushed in their courts, quicksilver often taking the place of water, and falling in a glistening spray. In summer cool air was drawn into the apartments through ventilating towers; in winter warm and perfumed air was discharged through hidden passages. From the ceilings, corniced with fretted gold, great chandeliers hung. Here were clusters of frail marble columns, which, in the boudoirs of the sultanas, gave way to verd-antique incrusted with lapis lazuli. The furniture was of sandal- or citron-wood, richly inlaid with gold, silver, or precious minerals. Tapestry hid the walls, Persian carpets covered the floors, pillows and couches of elegant forms were spread about the rooms. Great care was given to bathing and personal cleanliness at a time when such a thought had not dawned upon Christian Europe. Their pleasure-gardens were of unequalled beauty, and were rich with flowers and fruits. In short, in this brief space it is impossible to give more than a bare outline of the marvellous luxury which surrounded this people, recently come from the deserts of Arabia, at a time when the remainder of Europe was plunged into the rudest barbarism.

Much might be said of their libraries, their universities, their scholars and scientists, and the magnificence of their architecture, of which abundant examples still remain in the cities of Spain, the Alhambra of Granada, the palace which Boabdil so reluctantly left, being almost without an equal foi lightness, grace, and architectural beauty in the cities of the world. Well might the dethroned monarch look back with bitter regret upon this rarest monument of the Arabian civilization and give vent, in farewell to its far-seen towers, to "The last sigh of the Moor."

THE RETURN OF COLUMBUS.

In the spring succeeding the fall of Granada there came to Spain a glory and renown that made her the envy of all the nations of Europe. During the year before an Italian mariner, Christopher Columbus by name, after long haunting the camp and court of Ferdinand and Isabella, had been sent out with a meagre expedition in the forlorn hope of discovering new lands beyond the seas. In March, 1493, extraordinary tidings spread through the kingdom and reached the ears of the monarchs at their court in Barcelona. The tidings were that the poor and despised mariner had returned to Palos with wonderful tales of the discovery of a vast, rich realm beyond the seas,—a mighty new empire for Spain.

The marvellous news set the whole kingdom wild with joy. The ringing of bells and solemn thanksgivings welcomed Columbus at the port from which he had set sail. On his journey to the king's court his progress was impeded by the multitudes who thronged to see the suddenly famous man,—the humble mariner who had discovered for Spain what every one already spoke of as a " New World." With him he brought several of the bronze-hued natives of that far land, dressed in their simple island costume, and decorated, as they passed through the principal cities, with collars, bracelets, and other ornaments of gold. He exhibited, also, gold in dust and in shapeless masses, many new plants, some of them of high medicinal value, several animals never before seen in Europe, and birds whose brilliant plumage attracted glances of delight from all eyes.

It was mid-April when Columbus reached Barcelona. The nobility and knights of the court met him in splendid array and escorted him to the royal presence through the admiring throngs that filled the streets. Ferdinand and Isabella, with their son, Prince John, awaited his arrival seated under a superb canopy of state. On the approach of the discoverer they rose and extended their hands to him to kiss, not suffering him to kneel in homage. Instead, they bade him seat himself before them,—a mark of condescension to a person of his rank unknown before in the haughty court of Castile. He was, at that moment, "the man whom the king delighted to honor," and it was the proudest period in his life when, having proved triumphantly all for which he had so long contended, he was honored as the equal of the proud monarchs of Spain.

At the request of the sovereigns Columbus gave them a brief account of his adventures, in a dignified tone, that warmed with enthusiasm as he proceeded. He described the various tropical islands he had landed upon, spoke with favor of their delightful climate and the fertility of their soil, and exhibited the specimens he had brought as examples of their fruitfulness. He dwelt still more fully upon their wealth in the precious metals, of which he had been assured by the natives, and offered the gold he

RECEPTION OF COLUMBUS BY FERDINAND AND ISABELLA.

brought with him as evidence. Lastly, he expatiated on the opportunity offered for the extension of the Christian religion through lands populous with pagans,—a suggestion which appealed strongly to the Spanish heart. When he ceased the king and queen, with all present, threw themselves on their knees and gave thanks to God, while the solemn strains of the *Te Deum* were poured forth by the choir of the royal chapel.

Throughout his residence in Barcelona Columbus continued to receive the most honorable distinction from the Spanish sovereigns. When Ferdinand rode abroad the admiral rode by his side. Isabella, the true promoter of his expedition, treated him with the most gracious consideration. The courtiers, emulating their sovereigns, gave frequent entertainments in his honor, treating him with the punctilious deference usually shown only to a noble of the highest rank. It cannot be said, however, that envy at the high distinction shown this lately obscure and penniless adventurer was quite concealed, and at one of these entertainments is said to have taken place the famous episode of the egg.

A courtier of shallow wit, with the purpose of throwing discredit on the achievement of Columbus, intimated that it was not so great an exploit after all; all that was necessary was to sail west a certain number of days; the lands lay there waiting to be discovered. Were there not other men in Spain, he asked, capable of this?

The response of Columbus was to take an egg and ask those present to make it stand upright on its end.　After they had tried and failed he struck the egg on the table, cracking the shell and giving it a base on which to stand.

"But anybody could do that!" cried the critic.

"Yes; and anybody can become a discoverer when once he has been shown the way," retorted Columbus.　"It is easy to follow in a known track."

By this time all Europe had heard of the brilliant discovery of the Genoese mariner, and everywhere admiration at his achievement and interest in its results were manifested.　Europe had never been so excited by any single event.　The world was found to be larger than had been dreamed of, and it was evident that hundreds of new things remained to be known.　Word came to Barcelona that King John of Portugal was equipping a large armament to obtain a share of the new realms in the west, and all haste was made to anticipate this dangerous rival by sending Columbus again to the New World.

On the 25th of September, 1493, he set sail with a gallant armament, which quite threw into the shade his three humble caravels of the year before.　It consisted of seventeen vessels, some of them of large size for that day, and fifteen hundred souls, including several persons of rank, and members of the royal household.　Many of those that had taken part in the Moorish war, stimulated by the love of adventure, were to win fame in the coming years in the conquest of the alluring realms of the West, and the earliest of these sailed now under the banner of the Great Admiral.

The story of Columbus is too familiar to readers

for more to be said of it here.   It was one in which
the boasted honor of the Spanish court was soon
lost under a cloud of perfidy.   Envy and malice
surrounded the discoverer, and in 1500 he was sent
home in chains by an infamous governor.   The king,
roused by a strong display of public indignation,
disavowed the base act of his agent, and received
Columbus again with a show of favor, but failed to
reinstate him in the office of which he had been un-
justly deprived.   From that time forward the story
of the discoverer was one of neglect and faithless
treatment, he fell into poverty, and died miserable
and neglected at Valladolid in 1506, keeping the
fetters which had been placed on his limbs till the
last, as evidence of the perfidy of Spain.

ABOUT the middle of the year 1365 a formidable
expedition set out from France for the invasion of
Castile. It consisted of the celebrated Free Companies, marauding bands of French and English
knights and archers whose allegiance was to the
sword, and who, having laid waste France, now
sought fresh prey in Spain. Valiant and daring
were these reckless freebooters, bred to war, living
on rapine, battle their delight, revel their relax-
ation. For years the French and English Free
Companies had been enemies. Now a truce existed
between their princes, and they had joined hands
under the leadership of the renowned knight Bertrand du Guesclin, at that time the most famous
soldier of France. Sir Hugh de Calverley headed the
English bands, known as the White Company, and
made up largely of men-at-arms, that is, of heavy
armed horsemen; but with a strong contingent of
the formidable English archers. The total force
comprised more than twelve thousand men.

"You lead the life of robbers," said Du Guesclin
to them. "Every day you risk your lives in forays,
which yield you more blows than booty. I come to
propose an enterprise worthy of gallant knights and

to open to you a new field of action. In Spain both glory and profit await you. You will there find a rich and avaricious king who possesses great treasures, and is the ally of the Saracens; in fact, is half a pagan himself. We propose to conquer his kingdom and to bestow it on the Count of Trastamara, an old comrade of yours, a good lance, as you all know, and a gentle and generous knight, who will share with you his land when you win it for him from the Jews and Moslems of that wicked king, Don Pedro. Come, comrades, let us honor God and shame the devil."

The Free Companies were ready at a word to follow his banner. Among them were many knights of noble birth who valued glory above booty, and looked upon it as a worthy enterprise to dethrone a cruel and wicked king, the murderer of his queen. As for the soldiers, they cared not against whom they fought, if booty was to be had.

"Messire Bertrand," they said, "gives all that he wins to his men-at-arms. He is the father of the soldier. Let us march with him."

And so the bargain was made and the Free Companies marched away, light of heart and strong of hand, with a promising goal before them, and a chance of abundance of fighting before they would see their homes again.

Peter the Cruel, King of Castile and Leon, amply deserved to be dethroned. His reign had been one of massacre. All whom he suspected died by the dagger of the assassin. He bitterly hated his two half-brothers, Fadrique and Henry. Fadrique he enticed to his court by a show of friendship, and then had him brutally murdered at the gate of his palace, the Alcazir of Seville. But his treatment of his queen was what made him specially odious to his people. He married a French princess, Blanche of Bourbon, but deserted her after two days to return to his mistress, Maria de Pedilla. Blanche was taken to Toledo, where she was so closely confined that the people rose and rescued her from the king's guards. Peter marched in anger against the city, but its people defied him and kept the queen. Then the crafty villain pretended sorrow and asked for a reconciliation. The queen consented, went back to him, and was quickly imprisoned in a strong fortress, where she was murdered by his orders in 1361.

It was this shameful act and the murder of his brother Fadrique that roused the people to insurrection. Henry of Trastamara, the remaining brother, headed a revolt against the tyrant and invited the Free Companies to his aid. These were the circumstances that gave rise to the march of Du Guesclin and Calverley and their battle-loving bands.

The adventurers wore crosses on their vests and banners, as though they were a company of crusaders raised in the service of the church. But in truth they were under the ban of excommunication, for they had no more spared the church than the castle or the cottage. Du Guesclin, determined to relieve them from this ban and force the Pope to grant them absolution, directed his march upon Avignon, the papal residence in France. It was not only absolution he wanted. The papal coffers were

HALL OF AMBASSADORS, ALCAZAR OF SEVILLE.

full; his military chest was empty; his soldiers would not remain tractable unless well paid; the church should have the privilege of aiding the army.

It was with dismay that the people of Avignon beheld the White Company encamp before their ramparts, late in the year 1365. The Cardinal of Jerusalem was sent in haste to their camp, with a promise from the Holy Father that he would remove the ban of excommunication if they would evacuate the territory of the Church. The cardinal's mission was a dangerous one, for the fierce Free Companions had no reverence for priest or pope. He had hardly crossed the Rhone before he was confronted by a turbulent band of English archers, who demanded if he had brought money.

"Money?" he asked, in faltering tones.

"Ay, money!" they insolently cried, impeding his passage.

On reaching Du Guesclin's tent he was treated with more politeness, but was met with the same demand.

"We cannot control our troops," said some of the chiefs; "and, as they are ready to hazard their lives for the greater glory of the faith, they well deserve the aid of the Church."

"The Holy Father will incur much danger if he refuses the demand of our men," said Du Guesclin, in smooth but menacing tones. "They have become good Catholics in spite of themselves, and would very readily return to their old trade."

Imminent as the danger was, the Pope resisted, and tried to scare off that flock of reckless warhawks by the thunders of papal condemnation. But he soon learned that appeals and threats alike were wasted on the Free Companies. From the windows of his palace he could see groups of his unruly visitors at work plundering farms and country houses. Fires were here and there kindled. The rich lands of Avignon were in danger of a general ravage.

"What can I do?" said Du Guesclin to the complaints of the people. "My soldiers are excommunicated. The devil is in them, and we are no longer their masters."

Evidently there was but one way to get rid of this irreligious crew. The chiefs agreed to be satisfied with five thousand golden florins. This sum was paid, and the knights companions, laden with plunder and absolved from their sins, set out in the highest spirits, singing the praises of their captain and the joys of war. Such was their farewell to France.

Onward they marched, across the Pyrenees and into Aragon, whose king had joined with Henry of Trastamara in requesting their presence. They were far from welcome to the people of this region of Spain. Pedro IV. of Aragon had agreed to pay them one hundred thousand golden florins on condition that they should pass through his dominions without disorder; but the adventurers, imagining that they were already in the enemy's country, began their usual service of fire and sword. In Barbastro they pillaged the houses, killed the burghers or tortured them to extort ransom, and set fire to a church in which some had taken refuge, burning alive more than two hundred persons.

If such was the course of these freebooting bands in the country of their friends, what would it be in that of their foes? Every effort was made to get them out of the country as soon as possible. Immediate action was needed, for the warlike mountaineers were beginning to revenge the robberies of the adventurers by waylaying their convoys and killing their stragglers. In early March, 1366, the frontier was passed, Sir Hugh de Calverley leading his men against Borja, a town of Aragon which was occupied by soldiers of Castile.

The garrison fled on their approach, and soon the army entered Castile and marched upon Calahorra, a town friendly to Prince Henry, and which opened its gates at sight of their banners. Here an interesting ceremony took place. Du Guesclin and the other leaders of the Free Companies, with as much assurance as if they had already conquered Castile, offered Henry the throne.

"Take the crown," said the burly leader. "You owe this honor to the many noble knights who have elected you their leader in this campaign. Don Pedro, your enemy, has refused to meet you in the battle-field, and thus acknowledges that the throne of Castile is vacant."

Henry held back. He felt that these foreigners had not the crown of Castile in their gift. But when the Castilians present joined in the demand he yielded, and permitted them to place the crown upon his head. His chief captain at once unfurled the royal standard, and passed through the camp, crying, "Castile for King Henry! Long live King

Henry!" Then, amid loud acclamations, he planted the banner on the crest of a hill on the road to Burgos.

We need not delay on the events of this campaign. Everywhere the people of Castile fell away from their cruel king, and Henry's advance was almost unopposed. Soon he was in Burgos, and Don Pedro had become a fugitive without an army and almost without a friend. Henry was now again crowned king, many of the Castilian nobles taking part in the imposing ceremony.

The first acts of the new king were to recompense the men who had raised him to that high office. The money which he found in the treasury served as a rich reward to the followers of Du Guesclin. He gave titles of nobility and grants of land with a free hand to the chiefs of the Free Companies and his other companions in arms. On Du Guesclin he conferred his own countship of Trastamara, and added to it the lordship of Molino, with the domains appertaining to both. Calverley was made Count of Carrion, and received the domains which had formerly been held by the sons-in-law of the Cid. Lesser rewards were given to lesser chiefs, and none had reason to accuse Henry of Castile of want of generosity.

But the Free Companions soon became a sword in the side of the new king. As there was no more fighting to be done, they resumed their old occupation of pillaging, and from every side complaints rained in upon the throne. Henry felt it necessary to get rid of his unruly friends with all despatch.

Retaining Du Guesclin and Calverley in his service, with fifteen hundred lances, mainly French and Breton, he dismissed the remainder, placating them with rich presents and warm thanks. Nothing loath, and gratified that they had avenged the murdered Queen Blanche, they took their way back, finding abundant chance for fighting on their return. The Castilians, the Navarrese, and the Aragonese all rose against them, and everywhere they had to force a passage with their swords. But nothing could stop them. Spain, accustomed to fight with Arabs and Moors, had no warriors fit to face these intrepid and heavily armed veterans. Through the Pyrenees they made their way, and here cut a road with their swords through the main body of a French army which had gathered to oppose their march. Once more they were upon the soil of France.

It was the English and Gascon bands that were principally opposed. It was known that the Black Prince was preparing to invade Spain, and an effort was made to cut off the free lances who might enlist under his banners. This famous knight, son of Edward III. of England, and victor at the battle of Poitiers, where he had taken prisoner the king of France, was a cousin of the fugitive king of Castile, who sought him at Cape Breton, and begged his aid to recover his dominions. The chivalrous prince of Wales knew little of the dastardly deeds of the suppliant. Don Pedro had brought with him his three young maiden daughters, whose helpless state appealed warmly to the generous knight. National policy accorded with the inclination of the prince, for the Castilian revolution had been promoted by France, and the usurper had been in the pay of the French king. These inducements were enough to win for Don Pedro the support of Edward III., and the aid of the Black Prince, who entered upon the enterprise with the passionate enthusiasm which was a part of his nature.

Soon again two armies were in the field, that of King Henry, raised to defend his new dominions, and that of the Prince of Wales, gathered to replace the fugitive Don Pedro upon the throne. With the latter was the White Company, which had aided to drive Pedro from his seat and was now equally ready to replace him there. These bold lancers and archers fought for their own hands, with little care whose cause they backed.

It was through the valley of Roncesvalles, that celebrated pass which was associated with the name of the famous Roland, the chief knight of French romance, that the army of the Black Prince made its way into Spain. Calverley, who was not willing to fight against his liege lord, joined him with his lances, King Henry generously consenting. Du Guesclin, a veteran in the art of war, advised the Castilian king to employ a Fabian policy, harassing the invaders by skirmishes, drawing them deep into the country, and wearing them out with fatigue and hunger. He frankly told him that his men could not face in a pitched battle the English veterans, led by such a soldier as the Black Prince. But the policy suggested would have been hazardous in Castile, divided as it was between two parties. Henry remembered that his rival had lost the kingdom through not daring to risk a battle, and he determined to fight for his throne, trusting his cause to Providence and the strength of his arms.

It was in the month of April, 1367, that the two armies came face to face on a broad plain. They were fairly matched in numbers, and as day broke both marched resolutely to the encounter, amid opposing shouts of " King Henry for Castile" and " St. George and Guyenne." It was a hard, fierce, bitter struggle that followed, in which the onset of Du Guesclin was so impetuous as for a moment to break the English line. But the end was at hand when the Castilian cavalry broke in panic before the charge of an English squadron, which turned Du Guesclin's battalion and took it in flank. The Captal de Buch at the same time fell on the flank of the Castilian vanguard. Thus beset and surrounded, the French and Spanish men-at-arms desperately sought to hold their own against much superior numbers. King Henry fought valiantly, and called on all to rally round his standard. But at length the banner fell, the disorder grew general, the ranks broke, and knights and foot-soldiers joined in a tumultuous retreat.

Their only hope now was the bridge of Najera, over the Najerilla, which stream lay behind their line. Some rushed for the bridge, others leaped into the river, which became instantly red with blood, for the arrows of the archers were poured into the crowded stream. Only the approach of night, the fatigue of the victors, and the temptation to plunder the town and the camp saved the wreck of the Castilian army, which had lost seven thousand foot-soldiers and some six hundred men-at-arms. Du Guesclin's battalion, which alone had made a gallant stand, was half slain. A large number of prisoners were taken, among them the valorous Du Guesclin himself.

Edward the Black Prince now first learned the character of the man whom he had come to aid. Don Pedro galloped excitedly over the plain seeking his rival, and, chancing to meet Lopez de Orozco, one of his former friends, now the prisoner of a Gascon knight, he stabbed him to the heart, despite the efforts of the Gascon in his defence. The report of this murder filled the Black Prince with indignation, which was heightened when Don Pedro offered to ransom all the Castilian prisoners, plainly indicating that he intended to murder them. Prince Edward sternly refused, only consenting to deliver up certain nobles who had been declared traitors before the revolution. These Don Pedro immediately had beheaded before his tent.

The breach between the allies rapidly widened, Don Pedro, as soon as he fairly got possession of the throne, breaking all his engagements with the Black Prince, while he was unable, from the empty state of his treasury, to pay the allied troops. Four months Prince Edward waited, with growing indignation, for redress, while disease was rapidly carrying off his men, and then marched in anger from Spain with scarcely a fifth of the proud array with which he had won the battle of Najera.

The restored king soon justified his title of Peter the Cruel by a series of sanguinary executions, murdering all of the adherents of his rival on whom he could lay his hands. In this thirst for revenge not even women escaped, and at length he committed an act which aroused the indignation of the whole kingdom. Don Alfonso de Guzman had refused to follow the king into exile. He now kept out of his reach, but his mother, Doña Urraca de Osorio, fell into the hands of the monster, and was punished for being the mother of a rebel by being burned alive on the ramparts of Seville.

These excesses of cruelty roused a rebellious sentiment throughout Castile, of which Henry, who had escaped to Aragon from the field of Najera, took advantage. Supplied with money by the king of France, he purchased arms and recruited soldiers, many of the French and Castilians who had been taken prisoners at Najera and been released on parole joining him in hopes of winning the means of paying their ransoms. Crossing the Ebro, he marched upon Calahorra, in which the year before he had been proclaimed king. Here numerous volunteers joined him, and at the head of a considerable force he marched upon Burgos, which surrendered after a faint show of resistance.

During the winter the campaign continued, Leon, Madrid, and other towns being captured, and in the spring of 1368 all northern Castile was in Henry's hands. Don Pedro, whose army was small, had entered into alliance with the Moorish king of Granada, who sent him an army of thirty-five thousand men, with which force a vigorous attack was made on the city of Cordova,—a holy city in the eyes of the Moors. Among its defenders was Don Alfonso de Guzman, whose mother had been burned to death. The defence was obstinate, but the Moors at length made breaches in the walls. They were about to pour into the city when the women, mad with fear, rushed into the streets with cries and moans, now reproaching the men-at-arms with cowardice, now begging them with sobs and tears to make a last effort to save the city from the brutal infidels.

This appeal gave new courage to the Christians. They rushed on the Moors with the fury of despair, drove them from the posts they had taken, hurled them from the ramparts, tore down the black flags which already waved on the towers, and finally expelled them from the breaches and the walls in a panic. The breaches were repaired and the city was saved. In a few days the Moors, thoroughly disheartened by their repulse, dispersed, and Don Pedro lost his allies.

Meanwhile, Henry was engaged in the siege of Toledo, the strongest place in the kingdom, and before which he persistently lay for months, despite all allurements to use his forces in other directions. Here Bertrand du Guesclin, who had been ransomed by the Black Prince, joined him with a force of some six hundred men-at-arms, all picked men; and hither, in March, 1369, Don Pedro marched to the city's relief at the head of a strong army.

Henry, on learning of this movement, at once

gathered all the forces he could spare from the siege, three thousand men-at-arms in all, and hastened to intercept his rival on the march. Not dreaming of such a movement, Don Pedro had halted at Montiel, where his men lay dispersed, in search of food and forage, over a space of several leagues. They were attacked at daybreak, their surprise being so complete that the main body was at once put to flight, while each division was routed as soon as it appeared. Henry's forces suffered almost no loss, and within an hour's time his rival's kingdom was reduced to the castle of Montiel, in which he had taken refuge with a few of his followers.

Leaving the defeated army to take care of itself, Henry devoted himself to the siege of the castle, within whose poorly fortified walls lay the prize for which he fought. Escape was impossible, and the small supply of provisions would soon be exhausted. Don Pedro's only hope was to bribe some of his foes. He sent an agent to Du Guesclin, offering him a rich reward in gold and lands if he would aid in his escape. Du Guesclin asked for time to consider, and immediately informed Henry of the whole transaction. He was at once offered a richer reward than Pedro had promised if he would entice the king out of the castle, and after some hesitation and much persuasion he consented.

On the night of March 23, ten days after the battle, Don Pedro, accompanied by several of his knights, secretly left the fortress, the feet of their horses being bound with cloth to deaden the sound of hoofs. The sentinels, who had been instructed in advance, allowed them to pass, and they approached the camp of the French adventurers, where Du Guesclin was waiting to receive them.

"To horse, Messire Bertrand," said the king, in a low voice; "it is time to set out."

No answer was returned. This silence frightened Don Pedro. He attempted to spring into his saddle, but he was surrounded, and a man-at-arms held the bridle of his horse. An officer asked him to wait in a neighboring tent. Resistance was impossible, and he silently obeyed.

Here he found himself encompassed by a voiceless group, through whose lines, after a few minutes of dread suspense, a man in full armor advanced. It was Henry of Trastamara, who now faced his brother for the first time in fifteen years. He gazed with searching eyes upon Don Pedro and his followers.

"Where is this bastard," he harshly asked, "this Jew who calls himself King of Castile?"

"There stands your enemy," said a French esquire, pointing to Don Pedro.

Henry gazed at him fixedly. So many years had elapsed that he failed to recognize him easily.

"Yes, it is I," exclaimed Don Pedro, "I, the King of Castile. All the world knows that I am the legitimate son of good King Alfonso. It is thou that art the bastard."

At this insult Henry drew his dagger and struck the speaker a light blow in the face. They were in too close a circle to draw their swords, and in mortal fury they seized each other by the waist and struggled furiously, the men around drawing back and no one attempting to interfere.

After a brief period the wrestling brothers fell on a camp bed in a corner of the tent, Don Pedro, who was the stronger, being uppermost. While he felt desperately for a weapon with which to pierce his antagonist, one of those present seized him by the foot and threw him on one side, so that Henry found himself uppermost. Popular tradition says that it was Du Guesclin's hand that did this act, and that he cried, "I neither make nor unmake kings, but I serve my lord;" but Froissart and others say it was the Viscount de Rocaberti, of Aragon.

However that be, Henry at once took advantage of the opportunity, picked up his dagger, lifted the king's coat of mail, and plunged the weapon again and again into his side. Only two of Don Pedro's companions sought to defend him, and they were killed on the spot. Henry had his brother's head at once cut off, and despatched the gruesome relic to Seville.

Thus perished, by an uncalled-for act of treachery on the part of Du Guesclin, for the castle must soon have surrendered, one of the most bloodthirsty kings who ever sat upon a throne. Don Fadrique, his brother, and Blanche of Bourbon, his wife, both of whom he had basely murdered, were at length avenged. Henry ascended the throne as Henry II., and for years reigned over Castile with a mild and just rule that threw still deeper horror upon the bloody career of him who is known in history as Peter the Cruel.

THE GREAT CAPTAIN.

The long and bitter war for the conquest of Granada filled Spain with trained soldiers and skilful leaders, men who had seen service on a hundred fields, grim, daring veterans, without their equals in Europe. The Spanish foot-soldiers of that day were inflexibly resolute, the cavalry were skilled in the brilliant tactics of the Moors, and the leaders were men experienced in all the arts of war. These were the soldiers who in the New World overthrew empires with a handful of adventurers, and within a fraction of a century conquered a continent for Spain. In Europe they were kept actively employed. Charles VIII. of France, moved by ambition and thirst for glory, led an army of invasion into Italy. He was followed in this career of foreign conquest by his successor, Louis XII. The armies of France were opposed by those of Spain, led by the greatest soldier of the age, Gonsalvo de Cordova, a man who had learned the art of war in Granada, but in Italy showed such brilliant and remarkable powers that he gained the distinguishing title of the Great Captain.

These wars were stretched out over years, and the most we can do is to give some of their interesting incidents. In 1502 the Great Captain lay in the far south of Italy, faced by a more powerful French

army under the Duke of Nemours, a young nobleman not wanting in courage, but quite unfit to cope
with the experienced veteran before him. Gonsalvo,
however, was in no condition to try conclusions with
his well-appointed enemy. His little corps was destitute of proper supplies, the men had been so long
unpaid that they were mutinous, he had pleaded for
reinforcements in vain, and the most he could do was
to concentrate his small force in the seaport of Barleta and the neighboring strongholds, and make the
best show he could in the face of his powerful foe.

The war now declined into foraging inroads on
the part of the French, in which they swept the
flocks and herds from the fertile pastures, and into
guerilla operations on the part of the Spanish, who
ambushed and sought to cut off the detached troops
of the enemy. But more romantic encounters occasionally took place. The knights on both sides,
full of the spirit of chivalry, and eager to prove their
prowess, defied one another to jousts and tourneys,
and for the time being brought back a state of warfare then fast passing away.

The most striking of these meetings arose from
the contempt with which the French knights spoke
of the cavalry of their enemy, which they declared to
be far inferior to their own. This insult, when told
to the proud knights of Gonsalvo's army, brought
from them a challenge to the knights of France,
and a warlike meeting between eleven Spanish and
as many French warriors was arranged. A fair
field was offered the combatants in the neutral territory under the walls of the Venetian city of Trani,

and on the appointed day a gallant array of well-armed knights of both parties appeared to guard the lists and maintain the honor of the tournament.

Spectators crowded the roofs and battlements of Trani, while the lists were thronged with French and Spanish cavaliers, who for the time laid aside their enmity in favor of national honor and a fair fight. At the fixed hour the champions rode into the lists, armed at all points, and their horses richly caparisoned and covered with steel panoply. Among those on the Castilian side were Diego de Paredes and Diego de Vera, men who had won renown in the Moorish wars. Most conspicuous on the other side was the good knight Pierre de Bayard, the chevalier "*sans peur et sans reproche*," who was then entering upon his famous career.

At the sound of the signal trumpets the hostile parties rushed to the encounter, meeting in the centre of the lists with a shock that hurled three of the Spaniards from their saddle, while four of their antagonists' horses were slain. The fight, which began at ten in the morning, and was to end at sunset, if not concluded before, was prosecuted with great fury and varied success. Long before the hour of closing all the French were dismounted except the Chevalier Bayard and one of his companions, their horses, at which the Spaniards had specially aimed, being disabled or slain. Seven of the Spaniards were still on horseback, and pressed so hard upon their antagonists that the victory seemed safely theirs.

But Bayard and his comrade bravely held their

own, while the others, intrenched behind their dead horses, defended themselves vigorously with sword and shield, the Spaniards vainly attempting to spur their terrified horses over the barrier. The fight went on in this way until the sun sank below the horizon, when, both parties still holding the field, neither was given the palm of victory, all the combatants being declared to have proved themselves good and valiant knights.

Both parties now met in the centre of the lists, where the combatants embraced as true companions in chivalry, "making good cheer together" before they separated. But the Great Captain did not receive the report of the result with favor.

"We have," said one of his knights, "disproved the taunts of the Frenchmen, and shown ourselves as good horsemen as they."

"I sent you for better," Gonsalvo coldly replied.

A second combat in which the Chevalier Bayard was concerned met with a more tragic termination. A Spanish cavalier, Alonzo de Sotomayor, complained that Bayard had treated him uncourteously while holding him prisoner. Bayard denied the charge, and defied the Spaniard to prove it by force of arms, on horse or on foot, as he preferred. Sotomayor, well knowing Bayard's skill as a horseman, challenged him to a battle on foot *à l'outrance*, or "to the death."

At the appointed time the two combatants entered the lists, armed with sword and dagger and in complete armor, though wearing their visors up. For a few minutes both knelt in silent prayer. They then rose, crossed themselves, and advanced to the combat, "the good knight Bayard," we are told, "moving as light of step as if he were going to lead some fair lady down the dance."

Bayard was the smaller man of the two, and still felt weakness from a fever which had recently prostrated him. The Spaniard, taking advantage of this, sought to crush him by the weight of his blows, or to close with him and bring him to the ground by dint of his superior strength. But the lightness and agility of the French knight enabled him to avoid the Spaniard's grasp, while, by skill with the sword, he parried his enemy's strokes, and dealt him an occasional one in return.

At length, the Spaniard having exposed himself to attack by an ill-directed blow, Bayard got in so sharp a thrust on the gorget that it gave way, and the point of the blade entered his throat. Maddened by the pain of the wound, Sotomayor leaped furiously on his antagonist and grasped him in his arms, both rolling on the ground together. While thus clasped in fierce struggle Bayard, who had kept his poniard in his left hand throughout the fight, while his enemy had left his in his belt, drove the steel home under his eye with such force that it pierced through his brain.

As the victor sprang to his feet, the judges awarded him the honors of the day, and the minstrels began to pour forth triumphant strains in his honor. The good knight, however, bade them desist, as it was no time for gratulation when a good knight lay dead, and, first kneeling and returning grateful thanks for his victory, he walked slowly from the lists, saying that he was sorry for the result of the combat, and wished, since his honor was saved, that his antagonist had lived.

In these passages at arms we discern the fading gleam of the spirit of mediæval chivalry, soon to vanish before the new art of war. Rough and violent as were these displays as compared with the pastimes of later days, the magnificence with which they were conducted, and the manifestations of knightly honor and courtesy which attended them, threw something of grace and softness over an age in which ferocity was the ruling spirit.

Meanwhile, the position of the little garrison of Barleta grew daily worse. No help came, the French gradually occupied the strongholds of the neighboring country, and a French fleet in the Adriatic stood seriously in the way of the arrival of stores and reinforcements. But the Great Captain maintained his cheerfulness through all discouragement, and sought to infuse his spirit into the hearts of his followers. His condition would have been desperate with an able opponent, but he perfectly understood the character of the French commander and patiently bided his time.

The opportunity came. The French, weary of the slow game of blockade, marched from their quarters and appeared before the walls of Barleta, bent on drawing the garrison from the "old den" and deciding the affair in a pitched battle. The Duke of Nemours sent a trumpet into the town to defy the

Great Captain to the encounter, but the latter coolly sent back word,—

"It is my custom to choose my own time and place for fighting, and I would thank the Duc de Nemours to wait till my men have time to shoe their horses and burnish up their arms."

The duke waited a few days, then, finding that he could not decoy his wily foe from the walls, broke camp and marched back, proud of having flaunted a challenge in the face of the enemy. He knew not Gonsalvo. The French had not gone far before the latter opened the gates and sent out his whole force of cavalry, under Diego de Mendoza, with two corps of infantry, in rapid pursuit. Mendoza was so eager that he left the infantry in the rear, and fell on the French before they had got many miles away.

A lively skirmish followed, though of short duration, Mendoza quickly retiring, pursued by the French rear-guard, whose straggling march had detached it from the main body of the army. Mendoza's feigned retreat soon brought him back to the infantry columns, which closed in on the enemy's flanks, while the flying cavalry wheeled in the rapid Moorish style and charged their pursuers boldly in front. All was now confusion in the French ranks. Some resisted, but the greater part, finding themselves entrapped, sought to escape. In the end, nearly all who did not fall on the field were carried prisoners to Barleta, under whose walls Gonsalvo had drawn up his whole army, in readiness to support Mendoza if necessary. The whole affair had passed so quickly that Nemours knew nothing of it until the bulk of his rear-guard were safely lodged within the walls of the Spanish stronghold.

This brilliant success proved the turning-point in the tide of the war. A convoy of transports soon after reached Barleta, bringing in an abundance of provisions, and the Spaniards, restored in health and spirits, looked eagerly for some new enterprise. Nemours having incautiously set out on a distant expedition, Gonsalvo at once fell on the town of Ruvo and took it by storm, in spite of a most obstinate defence. On April 28, 1503, Gonsalvo, strengthened by reinforcements, finally left the stronghold of Barleta, where he and his followers had suffered so severely and shown such indomitable constancy. Reaching Cerignola, about sixteen miles from Barleta, he awaited the advancing army of the French, rapidly intrenching the ground, which was well suited for defence. Before these works were completed, Nemours and his army appeared, and, though it was near nightfall, made an immediate attack. The commander was incited to this by taunts on his courage from some hot-headed subordinates, to whom he weakly gave way, saying, " We will fight to-night, then ; and perhaps those who vaunt the loudest will be found to trust more to their spurs than to their swords,"—a prediction which was to prove true.

Of the battle, it must suffice to say that the trenches dug by the Spaniards fatally checked the French advance, and in the effort to find a passage Nemours fell mortally wounded. Soon the French lines were in confusion, the Spanish arquebusiers pouring a galling fire into their dense masses. Perceiving the situation, Gonsalvo ordered a general advance, and, leaping their intrenchments, the Spaniards rushed in fury on their foes, most of whose leaders had fallen. Panic succeeded, and the flying French were cut down almost without resistance.

The next morning the Great Captain passed over the field of battle, where.lay more than three thousand of the French, half their entire force. The loss of the Spaniards was very small, and all the artillery, the baggage, and most of the colors of the enemy were in their hands. Rarely had so complete a victory been gained in so brief a time, the battle being hardly more than one hour in duration. The body of the unfortunate Duke of Nemours was found under a heap of the slain, much disfigured and bearing the marks of three wounds. Gonsalvo was affected to tears at the sight of the mutilated body of his young and gallant adversary, who, though unfitted to head an army, had always proved himself a valiant knight. During the following month Gonsalvo entered Naples, the main prize of the war, where he was received with acclamations of joy and given the triumph which his brilliant exploits so richly deserved.

The work of the Great Captain was not yet at an end. Finding that his forces were being defeated in every encounter and the cities held by them captured, Louis XII. sent a large army to their relief, and late in the year 1503 the hostile forces came face to face again, Gonsalvo being forced by the exigencies of the campaign to encamp in a deplorable situation, a

GONSALVO DE CORDOVA FINDING THE CORPSE OF THE DUKE OF NEMOURS.

region of swamp, which had been converted by the incessant rains into a mere quagmire. The French occupied higher ground and were much more comfortably situated. But Gonsalvo refused to move. He was playing his old waiting game, knowing that the French dared not attack his intrenched camp, and that time would work steadily in his favor.

" It is indispensable to the public service to maintain our present position," he said to the officers who appealed to him to move; " and be assured, I would sooner march forward two steps, though it would bring me to my grave, than fall back one, to gain a hundred years of life."

After that there were no more appeals. Gonsalvo's usual cheerfulness was maintained, infusing spirit into his men in all the inconveniences of their situation. He had a well-planned object in view. The hardy Spaniards, long used to rough campaigning, bore their trying position with unyielding resolution. The French, on the contrary, largely new recruits, grew weary and mutinous, while sickness broke out in their ranks and increased with alarming rapidity.

At length Gonsalvo's day came. His opponent, not dreaming of an attack, had extended his men over a wide space. On the night of December 28, in darkness and storm, the Spanish army broke camp, marched to the river that divided the forces, silently threw a bridge across the stream, and were soon on its opposite side. Here they fell like a thunderbolt on the unsuspecting and unprepared French, who were soon in disordered retreat, hotly pursued by their foes, their knights vainly attempting

to check the enemy.   Bayard had three horses killed
under him, and was barely rescued from death by a
friend.   So utterly were the French beaten that
their discouraged garrisons gave up town after town
without a blow, and that brilliant night's work not
only ended the control of France over the kingdom
of Naples, but filled Louis XII. with apprehension
of losing all his possessions in Italy.

Such were the most brilliant exploits of the man
who well earned the proud title of the Great Captain.
He was as generous in victory as vigorous in battle,
and as courteous and genial with all he met as if he
had been a courtier instead of a soldier.   In the end,
his striking and unbroken success in war aroused the
envy and jealousy of King Ferdinand, and after the
return of Gonsalvo to Spain the unjust monarch
kept him in retirement till his death, putting smaller
men at the head of his armies rather than permit the
greatest soldier of the century to throw his own
exploits more deeply into the shade.

A KING IN CAPTIVITY.

Two great rivals were on the thrones of France and Spain,—Francis I., who came to power in France in 1515, and Charles I., who became king of Spain in 1516. In 1519 they were rivals for the imperial power in Germany. Charles gained the German throne, being afterwards known as the emperor Charles V., and during the remainder of their reigns these rival monarchs were frequently at war. A league was formed against the French king by Charles V., Henry VIII. of England, and Pope Leo X., as a result of which the French were driven from the territory of Milan, in Italy. In 1524 they were defeated at the battle of Sesia, the famous Chevalier Bayard here falling with a mortal wound; and in 1525 they met with a more disastrous defeat at the battle of Pavia, whose fatal result to the French caused Francis to write to his mother, " *Madame, tout est perdu fors l'honneur*" ("All is lost but honor").

The reason for these words may be briefly given. Francis was besieging Pavia, with hopes of a speedy surrender, when the forces of Charles marched to its relief. The most experienced French generals advised the king to retire, but he refused. He had said he would take Pavia or perish in the attempt, and a romantic notion of honor held him fast. The result was ruinous, as may be expected where sentiment outweighs prudence.   Strongly as the French were intrenched, they were broken and put to rout, and soon there was no resistance except where the king obstinately continued to fight.

Wounded in several places, and thrown from his horse, which was killed under him, Francis defended himself on foot with heroic valor, while the group of brave officers who sought to save his life, one after another, lost their own.   At length, exhausted with his efforts, and barely able to wield his sword, the king was left almost alone, exposed to the fierce assault of some Spanish soldiers, who were enraged by his obstinacy and ignorant of his rank.

At this moment a French gentleman named Pomperant, who had entered the service of Spain, recognized the struggling king and hurried to his aid, helping to keep off the assailants, and begging him to surrender to the Duke of Bourbon, who was close at hand.   Great as was the peril, Francis indignantly refused to surrender to a rebel and traitor, as he held Bourbon to be, and calling to Lannoy, a general in the imperial army who was also near by, he gave up his sword to him.   Lannoy, recognizing his prisoner, received the sword with a show of the deepest respect, and handed the king his own in return, saying,—

" It does not become so great a monarch to remain disarmed in the presence of one of the emperor's subjects."

The lack of prudence in Francis had proved serious not only to himself, but to his troops, ten thousand of whom fell, among them many distinguished nobles who preferred death to dishonor. Numbers of high rank were taken prisoners, among them the king of Navarre. In two weeks not a Frenchman remained in Italy. The gains from years of war had vanished in a single battle.

The tidings of the captivity of the French king filled France with consternation and Spain with delight, while to all Europe it was an event of the deepest concern, for all the nations felt the danger that might arise from the ambition of the powerful emperor of Spain and Germany. Henry VIII. requested that Francis should be delivered to him, as an ally of Spain, though knowing well that such a demand would not gain a moment's consideration. As for Italy, it was in terror lest it should be overrun by the imperial armies.

Francis, whom Lannoy held with great respect, but with the utmost care to prevent an escape, hoped much from the generosity of Charles, whose disposition he judged from his own. He was soon undeceived. Charles refused to set him free unless he would renounce all claims upon Italy, yield the provinces of Provence and Dauphiné to form a kingdom for the Constable Bourbon, and give up Burgundy to Germany. On hearing these severe conditions, Francis, in a transport of rage, drew his dagger, exclaiming,—

"It were better that a king should die thus!"

A by-stander arrested the thrust; but, though Francis soon regained his composure, he declared that he would remain a prisoner for life rather than purchase liberty at such a price to his country.

Thinking that these conditions came from the Spanish council, and not from Charles himself, Francis now became anxious to visit the emperor in Spain, hoping to soften him in a personal interview. He even furnished the galleys for that purpose, Charles at that time being too poor to fit out a squadron, and soon the spectacle was seen of a captive monarch sailing in his own ships past his own dominions, of which he had a distant and sorrowful view, to a land in which he was to suffer the indignities of prison life.

Landing at Barcelona, Francis was taken to Madrid and lodged in the alcazar, under the most vigilant guard. He soon found that he had been far too hasty in trusting to the generosity of his captor. Charles, on learning of his captivity, had made a politic show of sympathy and feeling, but on getting his rival fully into his hands manifested a plain intention of forcing upon him the hardest bargain possible. Instead of treating his prisoner with the courtesy due from one monarch to another, he seemed to seek by rigorous usage to force from him a great ransom.

The captive king was confined in an old castle, under a keeper of such formal austerity of manners as added to the disgust of the high-spirited French monarch. The only exercise allowed him was to ride on a mule, surrounded by armed guards on horseback. Though Francis pressingly solicited an interview, Charles suffered several weeks to pass before going near him. These indignities made so deep an impression on the prisoner that his natural lightness of temper deserted him, and after a period of deep depression he fell into a dangerous fever, in which he bitterly complained of the harshness with which he had been treated, and said that the emperor would now have the satisfaction of having his captive die on his hands.

The physicians at length despaired of his life, and informed Charles that they saw no hope of his recovery unless he was granted the interview he so deeply desired. This news put the emperor into a quandary. If Francis should die, all the advantage gained from the battle of Pavia would be lost. And there were clouds in the sky elsewhere. Henry VIII. had concluded a treaty of alliance with Queen Louise, regent of France, and engaged to use all his efforts for the release of the king. In Italy a dangerous conspiracy had been detected. There was danger of a general European confederacy against him unless he should come to some speedy agreement with the captive king.

Charles, moved by these various considerations, at length visited Francis, and, with a show of respect and affection, gave him such promises of speedy release and princely treatment as greatly cheered the sad heart of the captive. The interview was short; Francis was too ill to bear a long one; but its effect was excellent, and the sick man at once began to recover, soon regaining his former health. Hope had proved a medicine far superior to all the drugs of the doctors.

But the obdurate captor had said more than he meant. Francis was kept as closely confined as ever.

And insult was added to indignity by the emperor's reception of the Constable Bourbon, a traitorous subject of France, whom Charles received with the highest honors which a monarch could show his noblest visitor, and whom he made his general-in-chief in Italy. This act had a most serious result, which may here be briefly described. In 1527 Bourbon made an assault on Rome, with an army largely composed of Lutherans from Germany, and took it by assault, he being killed on the walls. There followed a sack of the great city which had not been surpassed in brutality by the Vandals themselves, and for months Rome lay in the hands of a barbarous soldiery, who plundered and destroyed without stint or mercy.

What Charles mainly insisted upon and Francis most indignantly refused was the cession of Burgundy to the German empire. He was willing to yield on all other points, but bitterly refused to dismember his kingdom. He would yield all claim to territory in Italy and the Netherlands, would pay a large sum in ransom, and would make other concessions, but Burgundy was part of France, and Burgundy he would not give up.

In the end Francis, in deep despair, took steps towards resigning his crown to his son, the dauphin. A plot for his escape was also formed, which filled Charles with the fear that a second effort might succeed. In dread that, through seeking too much, he might lose all, he finally agreed upon a compromise in regard to Burgundy, Francis consenting to yield it, but not until after he was set at liberty. The

FRANCIS I. REFUSING THE DEMANDS OF CHARLES V.

treaty included many other articles, most of them severe and rigorous, while Francis agreed to leave his sons, the dauphin and the Duke of Orleans, in the emperor's hands as hostages for the fulfilment of the treaty. This treaty was signed at Madrid, January 14, 1526. By it Charles believed that he had effectually humbled his rival, and weakened him so that he could never regain any great power. In this the statesmen of the day did not agree with him, as they were not ready to believe that the king of France would live up to conditions of such severity, forced from him under constraint.

The treaty signed, the two monarchs seemed to become at once the best of friends. They often appeared together in public; they had long conferences in private; they travelled in the same litter and joined in the same amusements; the highest confidence and affection seemed to exist between them. Yet this love was all a false show,—Francis still distrusted the emperor, and Charles still had him watched like a prisoner.

In about a month the ratification of the treaty was brought from France, and Francis set out from Madrid with the first true emotions of joy which he had felt for a year. He was escorted by a body of horse under Alarcon, who, when the frontiers of France were reached, guarded him as scrupulously as ever. On arriving at the banks of the Andaye River, which there separated the two kingdoms, Lautrec appeared on the opposite bank, with a guard of horse equal to that of Alarcon. An empty bark was moored in mid-stream. The cavalry drew up

in order on each bank. Lannoy, with eight gentlemen and the king, put off in a boat from the Spanish
side of the stream. Lautrec did the same from the
French side, bringing with him the dauphin and the
Duke of Orleans. The two parties met in the empty
vessel, where in a moment the exchange was made,
Francis embracing his sons and then handing them
over as hostages. Leaping into Lautrec's boat, he
was quickly on the soil of France.

Mounting a Barbary horse which awaited him,
the freed captive waved his hand triumphantly over
his head, shouted joyfully several times, "I am yet
a king!" and galloped away at full speed for Ba-
yonne. He had been held in captivity for a year
and twenty-two days.

Our tale of the captivity of the king ends here,
but the consequences of that captivity must be told.
A league was immediately afterwards formed against
Charles, named the Holy League, from the Pope being at its head. The Pope absolved Francis from
his oath to keep the treaty of Madrid, and the nobles of Burgundy, secretly instigated, refused to be
handed over to the imperial realm. Francis, bewailing his lack of power to do what he had promised
in regard to Burgundy, offered to pay the emperor
two millions of crowns instead. In short, Charles
had overreached himself through his stringency to a
captive rival, and lost all through his eagerness to
obtain too much.

Ten years afterwards the relations between the
two monarchs were in a measure reversed. A rebellion had broken out in Flanders which needed

the immediate presence of Charles, and, for reasons
satisfactory to himself, he wished to go through
France. His counsellors at Madrid looked upon such
a movement as fatally rash; but Charles persisted,
feeling that he knew the character of Francis better
than they. The French king was ready enough to
grant the permission asked, and looked upon the
occasion as an opportunity to show his rival how
kings should deal with their royal neighbors.

Charles was received with an ostentatious welcome, each town entertaining him with all the magnificence it could display. He was presented with
the keys of the gates, the prisoners were set at
liberty, and he was shown all the honor due to the
sovereign of the country itself. The emperor, though
impatient to continue his journey, remained six days
in Paris, where all things possible were done to render his visit a pleasant one. Had Francis listened
to the advice of some of his ministers, he would
have seized and held prisoner the incautious monarch
who had so long kept him in captivity. But the
confidence of the emperor was not misplaced; no
consideration could induce the high-minded French
king to violate his plighted word, or make him believe that Charles would fail to carry out certain
promises he had made. He forgot for the time how
he had dealt with his own compacts, but Charles remembered, and was no sooner out of France than all
his promises faded from his mind, and Francis learned
that he was not the only king who could enter into
engagements which he had no intention to fulfil.

As Italy was invaded by Gonsalvo de Cordova, the Great Captain, so Africa was invaded by Cardinal Ximenes, the Great Churchman, one of the ablest men who ever appeared in Spain, despite the fact that he made a dreadful bonfire of thousands of Arabian manuscripts in the great square of Granada. The greater part of these were copies of the Koran, but many of them were of high scientific and literary value, and impossible to replace. Yet, while thus engaged in a work fitted for an unlettered barbarian, Ximenes was using his large revenues to found the University of Alcala, the greatest educational institution in Spain, and was preparing his famous polyglot Bible, for which the rarest manuscripts were purchased, without regard to cost, that the Scriptures might be shown at one view in their various ancient languages. To indicate the cost of this work, it is said that he paid four thousand golden crowns for seven manuscripts, which came too late to be of use in the work. Such are the results that appear when fanaticism and desire for progress are combined.

. The vast labors undertaken by Ximenes at home did not keep him from enterprises abroad. He was filled with a burning zeal for the propagation of the Catholic faith, formed plans for a crusade to the

192

Holy Land, and organized a remarkably successful expedition against the Moslems of Africa. It is of the latter that we desire to speak.

Soon after the death of Isabella, Mazalquivir, a nest of pirates on the Barbary coast, had been captured by an expedition organized by the energetic Ximenes. He quickly set in train a more difficult enterprise, one directed against Oran, a Moorish city of twenty thousand inhabitants, strongly fortified, with a large commerce, and the haunt of a swarm of piratical cruisers. The Spanish king had no money and little heart for this enterprise, but that did not check the enthusiastic cardinal, who offered to loan all the sums needed, and to take full charge of the expedition, leading it himself, if the king pleased. Ferdinand made no objection to this, being quite willing to make conquests at some one else's expense, and the cardinal set to work.

It is not often that an individual can equip an army, but Ximenes had a great income of his own and had the resources of the Church at his back. By the close of the spring of 1509 he had made ready a fleet of ten galleys and eighty smaller vessels, and assembled an army of four thousand horse and ten thousand foot, fully supplied with provisions and military stores for a four months' campaign. Such was the energy and activity of a man whose life, until a few years before, had been spent in the solitude of the cloister and in the quiet practices of religion, and who was now an infirm invalid of more than seventy years of age.

The nobles thwarted his plans, and mocked at the idea of "a monk fighting the battles of Spain." The soldiers had little taste for fighting under a father of the Church, "while the Great Captain was left to stay at home and count his beads like a hermit." The king threw cold water on the enterprise. But the spirit and enthusiasm of the old monk triumphed over them all, and on the 16th of May the fleet weighed anchor, reaching the port of Mazalquivir on the following day. Oran, the goal of the expedition, lay about a league away.

As soon as the army was landed and drawn up in line, Ximenes mounted his mule and rode along its front, dressed in his priestly robes, but with a sword by his side. A group of friars followed, also with monkish garbs and weapons of war. The cardinal, ascending a rising ground, made an animated address to the soldiers, rousing their indignation by speaking of the devastation of the coast of Spain by the Moslems, and awakening their cupidity by dwelling on the golden spoil to be found in the rich city of Oran. He concluded by saying that he had come to peril his own life in the service of the cross and lead them in person to battle.

The officers now crowded around the warlike old monk and earnestly begged him not to expose his sacred person to the hazards of the fight, saying that his presence would do more harm than good, as the men might be distracted from the work before them by attending to his personal safety. This last argument moved the warlike cardinal, who, with much reluctance, consented to keep in the rear and leave the command of the army to its military leader, Count Pedro Navarro.

The day was now far advanced. Beacon-fires on the hill-tops showed that the country was in alarm. Dark groups of Moorish soldiers could be seen on the summit of the ridge that lay between Oran and Mazalquivir, and which it would be necessary to take before the city could be reached. The men were weary with the labors of landing, and needed rest and refreshment, and Navarro deemed it unsafe to attempt anything more that day; but the energetic prelate bade him "to go forward in God's name," and orders to advance were at once given.

Silently the Spanish troops began to ascend the steep sides of the acclivity. Fortunately for them, a dense mist had arisen, which rolled down the skirts of the hills and filled the valley through which they moved. As soon as they left its cover and were revealed to the Moors a shower of balls and arrows greeted them, followed by a desperate charge down the hill. But the Spanish infantry, with their deep ranks and long pikes, moved on unbroken by the assault, while Navarro opened with a battery of heavy guns on the flank of the enemy.

Thrown into disorder by the deadly volleys, the Moors began to give ground, and, pressed upon heavily by the Spanish spearsmen, soon broke into flight. The Spaniards hotly pursued, breaking rank in their eagerness in a way that might have proved fatal but for the panic of the Moors, who had lost all sense of discipline. The hill-top was reached, and down its opposite slope poured the Spaniards, driving the fleeing Moors. Not far before them rose the walls of Oran. The fleet had anchored before the city and was vigorously cannonading it, being answered with equal spirit by sixty pieces of artillery on the fortifications. Such were the excitement and enthusiasm of the soldiers that they forgot weariness and disregarded obstacles. In swift pursuit they followed the scattering Moors, and in a brief time were close to the walls, defended by a deeply discouraged garrison.

The Spaniards had brought few ladders, but in the intense excitement and energy of the moment no obstacle deterred them. Planting their long pikes against the walls, or thrusting them into the crevices between the stones, they clambered up with remarkable dexterity,—a feat which they were utterly unable to repeat the next day, when they tried it in cold blood.

A weak defence was made, and the ramparts soon swarmed with Spanish soldiers. Sousa, the captain of the cardinal's guard, was the first to gain the summit, where he unfurled the banner of Ximenes, —the cross on one side and the cardinal's arms on the other. Six other banners soon floated from the walls, and the soldiers, leaping down into the streets, gained and threw open the gates. In streamed the army, sweeping all opposition before it. Resistance and flight were alike unavailing. Houses and mosques were tumultuously entered, no mercy being shown, no regard for age or sex, the soldiers abandoning themselves to the brutal license and ferocity common to the religious wars of that epoch.

In vain Navarro sought to check his brutal troops; they were beyond control; the butchery never ceased until, gorged with the food and wine found in the houses, the worn-out soldiers flung themselves down in the streets and squares to sleep. Four thousand Moors had been slain in the brief assault, and perhaps twice that number were taken prisoners. The city of Oran, that morning an opulent and prosperous community, was at night a ruined and captive city, with its ferocious conquerors sleeping amidst their slaughtered victims.

It was an almost incredible victory, considering the rapidity with which it had been achieved. On the morning of the 16th the fleet of transports had set sail from Spain. On the night of the 17th the object of the expedition was fully accomplished, the army being in complete possession of Oran, a strongly manned and fortified city, taken almost without loss. Ximenes, to whose warlike enthusiasm this remarkable victory was wholly due, embarked in his galley the next morning and sailed along the city's margin, his soul swelling with satisfaction at his wonderful success. On landing, the army hailed him as the true victor of Oran, a wave of acclamations following him as he advanced to the alcazar, where the keys of the fortress were put into his hands. A few hours after the surrender of the city a powerful reinforcement arrived for its relief, but on learning of its loss the disconcerted Moors retired. Had the attack been deferred to the next day, as Navarro proposed, it would probably have failed. The people of Spain ascribed the victory to inspiration from heaven; but the only inspiration lay in the impetuous energy and enthusiasm of the cardinal. But the Spaniards of that day were rarely satisfied without their miracle, and it is soberly asserted that the sun stood still for several hours while the action went on, Heaven repeating the miracle of Joshua, and halting the solar orb in its career, that more of the heathen might be slaughtered. The greatest miracle of all would appear to be that the sun stood still nowhere else than over the fated city of Oran.

It may not be amiss to add to this narrative an account of a second expedition against Africa, made by Charles V. some thirty years later, in which Heaven failed to come to the aid of Spain, and whose termination was as disastrous as that of the expedition of Ximenes had been fortunate.

It was the city of Algiers that Charles set out to reduce, and, though the season was late and it was the time of the violent autumnal winds, he persisted in his purpose in spite of the advice of experienced mariners. The expedition consisted of twenty thousand foot and two thousand horse, with a large body of noble volunteers. The storms came as promised and gave the army no small trouble in its voyage, but at length, with much difficulty and danger, the troops were landed on the coast near Algiers and advanced at once upon the town.

Hascan, the Moorish leader, had only about six thousand men to oppose to the large Spanish army, and had little hope of a successful resistance by force of arms. But in this case Heaven—if we admit its interference at all—came to the aid of the Moors. On the second day after landing, and before operations had fairly begun, the clouds gathered and the skies grew threatening. Towards evening rain began to fall and a fierce wind arose. During the night a violent tempest swept the camp, and the soldiers, who were without tents or shelter of any kind, were soon in a deplorable state. Their camp, which was in a low situation, was quickly overflowed by the pouring rains, and the ground became ankle deep in mud. No one could lie down, while the wind blew so furiously that they could only stand by thrusting their spears into the ground and clinging to them. About day-dawn they were attacked by the vigilant Hascan, and a considerable number of them killed before the enemy was forced to retire.

Bad as the night had been, the day proved more disastrous still. The tempest continued, its force increasing, and the sea, roused to its utmost fury by the winds, made sad havoc of the ships. They were torn from their anchorage, flung violently together, beat to pieces on the rocks, and driven ashore, while many sank bodily in the waves. In less than an hour fifteen war-vessels and a hundred and forty transports were wrecked and eight thousand men had perished, those of the crews who reached shore being murdered by the Moors as soon as they touched land.

It was with anguish and astoundment that the emperor witnessed this wreck of all his hopes, the great stores which he had collected for subsistence and military purposes being in one fatal hour buried in the depths of the sea. At length the wind began to fall, and some hopes arose that vessels enough might have escaped to carry the distressed army back to Europe. But darkness was again at hand, and a second night of suspense and misery was passed. In the morning a boat reached land with a messenger from Andrew Doria, the admiral of the fleet, who sent word that in fifty years of maritime life he had never seen so frightful a storm, and that he had been forced to bear away with his shattered ships to Cape Metafuz, whither he advised the emperor to march with all speed, as the skies were still threatening and the tempest might be renewed.

The emperor was now in a fearful quandary. Metafuz was at least three days' march away. All the food that had been brought ashore was consumed. The soldiers, worn out with fatigue, were in no condition for such a journey. Yet it was impossible to stay where they were. There was no need of deliberation; no choice was left; their only hope of safety lay in instant movement.

The sick, wounded, and feeble were placed in the centre, the stronger in front and rear, and the disastrous march began. Some of the men could hardly bear the weight of their arms; others, worn out with toiling through the nearly impassable roads, lay down and died; many perished from hunger and exhaustion, there being no food but roots and berries gathered by the way and the flesh of horses killed by the emperor's order; many were drowned in the streams, swollen by the severe rains; many were killed by the enemy, who followed and harassed them throughout the march. The late gallant army was a bedraggled and miserable fragment when the survivors at length reached Metafuz. Fortunately the storm was at an end, and they were able to obtain from the ships the provisions of which they stood so sorely in need.

The calamities which attended this unluckly expedition were not yet at an end. No sooner had the soldiers embarked than a new storm arose, less violent than the former, but sufficient to scatter the ships to right and left, some making port in Spain, some in Italy, all seeking such harbors of refuge as they could find. The emperor, after passing through great perils, was driven to the port of Bugia in Africa, where contrary winds held him prisoner for several weeks. He at length reached Spain, to find the whole land in dismay at the fate of the gallant expedition, which had set out with such high hopes of success. To the end of his reign Charles V. had no further aspirations for conquest in Africa.

AN EMPEROR RETIRED FROM BUSINESS.

In October of the year 1555 a strange procession passed through a rugged and hilly region of Spain. At its head rode an alcalde with a posse of alguazils. Next came a gouty old man in a horse-litter, like a prisoner in the hands of a convoy of officers of justice. A body of horsemen followed, and in the rear toiled onward a long file of baggage-mules.

As the train advanced into the more settled regions of the country it became evident that the personage thus convoyed was not a prisoner, but a person of the highest consequence. On each side of the road the people assembled to see him pass, with a show of deep respect. At the towns along the route the great lords of the neighborhood gathered in his honor, and in the cities the traveller was greeted by respectful deputations of officials. When Burgos was approached the great constable of Castile, with a strong retinue of attendants, came to meet him, and when he passed through the illuminated streets of that city the bells rang out in merry peals, while enthusiastic people filled the streets.

It was not a prisoner to the law, but a captive to gout, who thus passed in slow procession through the lands and cities of Spain. It was the royal

202

Charles, King of Spain and the Netherlands, Emperor of Germany, and magnate of America, at that time the greatest monarch in Europe, lord of a realm greater than that of Charlemagne, who made his way with this small following and in this simple manner through the heart of his Spanish dominions. He had done what few kings have done before or since, voluntarily thrown off his crown in the height of his power,—weary of reigning, surfeited with greatness,—and retired to spend the remainder of his life in privacy, to dwell far from the pomp of courts in a simple community of monks.

The next principal halting-place of the retired monarch was the city of Valladolid, once the capital of the kingdom and still a rich and splendid place, adorned with stately public buildings and the palaces of great nobles. Here he remained for some time resting from his journey, his house thronged with visitors of distinction. Among these, one day, came the court fool. Charles touched his cap to him.

"Welcome, brother," said the jester; "do you raise your hat to me because you are no longer emperor?"

"No," answered Charles, "but because this sorry courtesy is all I have left to give you."

On quitting Valladolid Charles seemed to turn his back finally on the world, with all its pomps and vanities. Before leaving he took his last dinner in public, and bade an affectionate farewell to his sisters, his daughter, and his grandson, who had accompanied him thus far in his journey. A large train of nobles and cavaliers rode with him to the gates of the city, where he courteously dismissed them, and moved onward attended only by his simple train.

"Heaven be praised!" said the world-weary monarch, as he came nearer his place of retreat; "after this no more visits of ceremony, no more receptions!"

But he was not yet rid of show and ostentation. Spending the night at Medina del Campo, at the house of a rich banker named Rodrigo de Dueñas, the latter, by way of display, warmed the emperor's room with a brazier of pure gold, in which, in place of common fuel, sticks of cinnamon were burned. Neither the perfume nor the ostentation was agreeable to Charles, and on leaving the next morning he punished his over-officious host by refusing to permit him to kiss his hand, and by causing him to be paid for the night's lodging like a common inn-keeper.

This was not the first time that cinnamon had been burned in the emperor's chamber. The same was done by the Fuggers, the famous bankers of Germany, who had loaned Charles large sums for his expedition against Tunis, and entertained him at their house on his return. In this case the emperor was not offended by the odor of cinnamon, since it was modified by a different and more agreeable perfume. The bankers, grateful to Charles for breaking up a pestilent nest of Barbary pirates, threw the receipts for the money they had loaned him into the fire, turning their gold into ashes in his behalf. This was a grateful sacrifice to the emperor, whose warlike enterprises consumed more money than he could readily command.

The vicinity of Yuste was reached late in Novem-

CHARLES V. APPROACHING YUSTE.

ber. Here resided a community of Jeromymite monks, in whose monastery he proposed to pass the remainder of his days. There were two roads by which it could be reached,—one an easy, winding highway, the other a rugged mountain-pass. But by the latter four days would be saved, and Charles, tired of the long journey, determined to take it, difficult as it might prove.

He had been warned against the mountain pathway, and found it fully as formidable as he had been told. A body of hardy rustics were sent ahead, with pikes, shovels, and other implements, to clear the way. But it was choked here and there with fallen stones and trunks of trees which they were unable to move. In some localities the path wound round dizzy precipices, where a false step would have been fatal. To any traveller it would have been very difficult; to the helpless emperor it was frightfully dangerous. The peasants carried the litter; in bad parts of the way the emperor was transferred to his chair; in very perilous places the vigorous peasants carried him in their arms.

Several hours of this hard toil passed before they reached the summit. As they emerged from the dark defiles of the *Puerto Nuevo*—now known as "The Emperor's Pass"—Charles exclaimed, "It is the last pass I shall go through in this world, save that of death."

The descent was much more easy, and soon the gray walls of Yuste, half hidden in chestnut-groves, came in sight. Yet it was three months before the traveller reached there, for the apartments preparing for him were far from ready, and he had to wait throughout the winter in the vicinity, in a castle of the Count of Oropesa, and in the midst of an almost continual downpour of rain, which turned the roads to mire, the country almost to a swamp, and the mountains to vapor-heaps. The threshold of his new home was far from an agreeable one.

Charles V. had long contemplated the step he had thus taken. He was only fifty-five years of age, but he had become an old man at fifty, and was such a victim to the gout as to render his life a constant torment and the duties of royalty too heavy to be borne. So, taking a resolution which few monarchs have taken before or since, he gave up his power and resolved to spend the remainder of his life in such quiet and peace as a retired monastery would give. Spain and its subject lands he transferred to his son Philip, who was to gain both fame and infamy as Philip II. He did his best, also, to transfer the imperial crown of Germany to his fanatical and heartless heir, but his brother Ferdinand, who was in power there, would not consent, and he was obliged to make Ferdinand emperor of Germany, and break in two the vast dominion which he had controlled.

Charles had only himself to thank for his gout. Like many a man in humbler life, he had abused the laws of nature until they had avenged themselves upon him. The pleasures of the table with him far surpassed those of intellectual or business pursuits. He had an extraordinary appetite, equal to that of any royal *gourmand* of whom history speaks, and, while leaving his power behind him, he brought this enemy with him into his retirement.

We are told by a Venetian envoy at his court, in the latter part of his reign, that, while still in bed in the morning, he was served with potted capon, prepared with sugar, milk, and spices, and then went to sleep again. At noon a meal of various dishes was served him, and another after vespers. In the evening he supped heartily on anchovies, of which he was particularly fond, or some other gross and savory food. His cooks were often at their wits' end to devise some new dish, rich and highly seasoned enough to satisfy his appetite, and his perplexed purveyor one day, knowing Charles's passion for timepieces, told him " that he really did not know what new dish he could prepare him, unless it were a *fricassée* of watches."

Charles drank as heartily as he ate. His huge repasts were washed down with potations proportionately large. Iced beer was a favorite beverage, with which he began on rising and kept up during the day. By way of a stronger potation, Rhenish wine was much to his taste. Roger Ascham, who saw him on St. Andrew's day dining at the feast of the Golden Fleece, tells us : " He drank the best that I ever saw. He had his head in the glass five times as long as any of us, and never drank less than a good quart at once of Rhenish."

It was this over-indulgence in the pleasures of the table that brought the emperor to Yuste. His physician warned him in vain. His confessor wasted admonitions on his besetting sin. Sickness and suffering vainly gave him warning to desist. Indigestion troubled him; bilious disorders brought misery to his overworked stomach. At length came gout, the most terrible of his foes. This enemy gave him little rest day or night. The man who had hunted in the mountains for days without fatigue, who had kept the saddle day and night in his campaigns, who had held his own in the lists with the best knights of Europe, was now a miserable cripple, carried, wherever he went, in the litter of an invalid.

One would have thought that, in his monkish retreat, Charles would cease to indulge in gastronomic excesses, but the retired emperor, with little else to think of, gave as much attention to his appetite as ever. Yuste was kept in constant communication with the rest of the world on matters connected with the emperor's table. He was especially fond of fish and all the progeny of the water,—eels, frogs, oysters, and the like. The trout of the neighborhood were too small for his liking, so he had larger ones sent from a distance. Potted fish—anchovies in particular—were favorite viands. Eel pasty appealed strongly to his taste. Soles, lampreys, flounders reached his kitchen from Seville and Portugal. The country around supplied pork, mutton, and game. Sausages were sent him from a distance; olives were brought from afar, as those near at hand were not to his liking. Presents of sweetmeats and confectionery were sent him by ladies who remembered his ancient tastes. In truth, Charles, tortured with gout, did everything he well could to favor its attacks.

The retired emperor, though he made a monastery his abode, had no idea of living like a monk. His apartments were richly furnished and hung with handsome tapestry, and every attention was paid to his personal comfort. Rich carpets, canopies of velvet, sofas and chairs of carved walnut, seats amply garnished with cushions for the ease of his tender joints, gave a luxurious aspect to his retirement. His wardrobe contained no less than sixteen robes of silk and velvet, lined with ermine, eider-down, or the soft hair of the Barbary goat. He could not endure cold weather, and had fireplaces and chimneys constructed in every room, usually keeping his apartments almost at furnace heat, much to the discomfort of his household. With all this, and his wrappings of fur and eider-down, he would often be in a shiver and complain that he was chilled to the bone.

His table was richly provided with plate, its service being of silver, as were also the articles of the toilet, the basins, pitchers, and other utensils of his bed-chamber. With these were articles of pure gold, valuable for their curious workmanship. He had brought with him many jewels of value, and a small but choice collection of paintings, some of them among the noblest masterpieces of art. Among them were eight gems from the hand of Titian. These were hung in rich frames around his rooms. He was no reader, and had brought few books, his whole library comprising but thirty-one volumes, and these mostly religious works, such as psalters, missals, breviaries, and the like. There was some little science and some little history, but the work which chiefly pleased him was a French poem, "*Le Chevalier Délibéré*," then popular, which celebrated the exploits of the house of Burgundy, and especially of Charles the Bold.

And now it comes in place to say something of how Charles employed himself at Yuste, aside from eating and drinking and shivering in his chimney corner. The mode in which a monarch retired from business passes his time cannot be devoid of interest. He by no means gave up his attention to the affairs of the realm, but kept himself well informed in all that was going on, sometimes much to his annoyance, since blunders were made that gave him a passing desire to be again at the head of affairs. In truth, two years after his retirement, the public concerns got into such a snarl that Philip earnestly sought to induce the emperor to leave his retreat and aid him with his ripened experience. This Charles utterly refused to do. He had had his fill of politics. It was much less trouble to run a household than a nation. But he undertook to do what he could to improve the revenues of the crown. Despatches about public affairs were brought to him constantly, and his mental thermometer went up or down as things prospered or the reverse. But he was not to be tempted to plunge again into the turbulent tide of public affairs.

Charles had other and more humble duties to occupy his time. His paroxysms of gout came only at intervals, and in the periods between he kept himself engaged. He had a taste for mechanics, and

among his attendants was an Italian named Torriano, a man of much ingenuity, who afterwards constructed the celebrated hydraulic works at Toledo.
He was a skilful clock-maker, and, as Charles took a
special interest in timepieces, his assistant furnished
his apartments with a series of elaborate clocks.
One of these was so complicated that its construc-
tion occupied more than three years, every detail
of the work being curiously watched by Charles.
Watches were then of recent invention, yet there
were a number of them at Yuste, made by Torriano.

The attempt to make his clocks keep time together
is said to have been one of the daily occupations of
the retired emperor, and the adjustment of his clocks
and watches gave him so much trouble that he is
said to have one day remarked that it was absurd to
try and make men think alike, when, do what he
would, he could not make two of his timepieces agree.

He often amused himself with Torriano in making
little puppets,—soldiers that would go through their
exercises, dancing tambourine-girls, etc. It is even
asserted that they constructed birds that would fly
in and out of the window, a story rather difficult to
accept. The monks began to look upon Torriano as
a professor of magic when he invented a handmill
small enough to be hidden in a friar's sleeve, yet
capable of grinding enough meal in a day to last a
man for a week.

The emperor was very fond of music, particularly
devotional music, and was a devotee in religious exercises, spending much of his time in listening to the
addresses of the chaplains, and observing the fasts

and festivals of the Church. His fondness for fish made the Lenten season anything but a period of penance for him.

He went on, indeed, eating and drinking as he would; and his disease went on growing and deepening, until at length the shadow of death lay heavy on the man whose religion did not include temperance in its precepts. During 1558 he grew steadily weaker, and on the 21st of September the final day came; his eyes quietly closed and life fled from his frame.

Yuste, famous as the abiding-place of Charles in his retirement, remained unmolested in the subsequent history of the country until 1810, when a party of French dragoons, foraging near by, found the murdered body of one of their comrades not far from the monastery gates. Sure in their minds that the monks had killed him, they broke in, dispersed the inmates, and set the buildings on fire. The extensive pile of edifices continued to burn for eight days, no one seeking to quench the flames. On the ninth the ancient monastery was left a heap of ashes, only the church remaining, and, protected by it, the palace of Charles.

In 1820 a body of neighboring insurgents entered and defaced the remaining buildings, carrying off everything they could find of value and turning the church into a stable. Some of the monks returned, but in 1837 came an act suppressing the convents, and the poor Jeromymites were finally turned adrift. To-day the palace of Charles V. presents only desolate and dreary chambers, used as magazines for grain and olives. So passes away the glory of the world.

THE FATE OF A RECKLESS PRINCE.

In 1568 died Don Carlos, Prince of Asturias, the son of Philip II. of Spain ; and in the same year died Isabella of Valois, the young and beautiful queen of the Spanish monarch. Legend has connected the names of Carlos and Isabella, and a mystery hangs over them which research has failed to dispel. Their supposed love, their untimely fate, and the suspicion that their death was due to the jealousy of the king, have proved a prolific theme for fiction, and the story of the supposed unhappy fate of the two has passed from the domain of history into that of romance and the drama, there being more than one fine play based on the loves and misfortunes of Carlos and Isabella. But sober history tells nothing of the kind, and it is with history that we are here concerned.

Carlos, the heir of the throne of Spain, was born in 1545. He was a bold, headstrong boy, reckless in disposition, fond of manly exercises, generous to a fault, fearless of heart, and passionately desirous of a military life. In figure he was deformed, one shoulder being higher and one leg longer than the other, while his chest was flat and his back slightly humped. His features were not unhandsome, though very pale, and he spoke with some difficulty. He was feeble and sickly as a boy, subject to intermittent fever, and wasted away so greatly that it seemed as if he would not live to manhood.

Such were the mental and physical characteristics of the princely youth who while still young was betrothed by treaty to the beautiful French princess Isabella of Valois. The marriage was not destined to take place. Before the treaty was ratified, Queen Mary of England, Philip's wife, died, and his name was substituted for that of his son in the marriage treaty. The wedding ceremony took place at Toledo, in February, 1560, and was celebrated with great splendor. Carlos was present, and may have felt some resentment at being robbed by his father of this beautiful bride. Romantic historians tell us that Isabella felt a tender sentiment for him, a very unlikely statement in view of the fact that he was at that time a sickly, ill-favored boy of only fourteen years of age. Shortly after the marriage Carlos was formally recognized as heir to the crown.

Two years afterwards a serious accident occurred. In descending a flight of stairs the boy slipped and fell headlong, injuring his head so severely that his life was despaired of. His head swelled to an enormous size; he became delirious and totally blind; examination showed that his skull was fractured; a part of the bone was removed, but no relief was obtained. All the arts of the doctors of that day were tried in vain, but the boy got no better. Processions were made to the churches, prayers were offered, and pilgrimages were vowed, all without avail. Then more radical means were tried. The mouldering bones of a holy Franciscan, who had died a hundred years before, were taken from their coffin and laid on the boy's bed, and the cloth that had enclosed the dead man's skull was placed on his forehead. Fortunately for the boy, he was delirious when these gruesome remedies were applied.

That night, we are gravely told, the dead friar came to Carlos in his sleep, bidding him to "be of good cheer, for he would certainly recover." Soon after, the fever subsided, his head shrank back to its natural size, his sight returned. In two months from the date of the accident he was well, and Fray Diego, the worthy friar, was made a saint for the miracle his bones had performed. Possibly youth and nature had their fair share in the cure.

Likely enough the boy was never cured. The blow may have done some permanent injury to his brain. At any rate, he became strikingly eccentric and reckless, giving way to every mad whim that came into his mind. The stories of his wild doings formed the scandal of Madrid. In 1564 one of his habits was to patrol the streets with a number of young nobles as lawless as himself, attacking the passengers with their swords, kissing the women, and using foul language to ladies of the highest rank.

At that time it was the custom for the young gallants of the court to wear very large boots. Carlos increased the size of his, that he might carry in them a pair of small pistols. Fearing mischief, the king ordered the shoemaker to reduce the size of his son's boots; but when the unlucky son of St. Crispin brought them to the palace, the prince flew into a rage, beat him severely, and then ordered the leather to be cut into pieces and stewed, and forced the shoemaker to swallow it on the spot—or as much of it as he could get down.

These are only a sample of his pranks. He beat his governor, attempted to throw his chamberlain out of the window, and threatened to stab Cardinal Espinosa for banishing a favorite actor from the palace.

One anecdote told of him displays a reckless and whimsical humor. Having need of money, Carlos asked of a merchant, named Grimaldo, a loan of fifteen hundred ducats. The money-lender readily consented, thanked the prince for the compliment, and, in the usual grandiloquent vein of Castilian courtesy, told Carlos that all he had was at his disposal.

"I am glad to learn that," answered the prince. "You may make the loan, then, one hundred thousand ducats."

Poor Grimaldo was thunderstruck. He tremblingly protested that it was impossible,—he had not the money. "It would ruin my credit," he declared. "What I said were only words of compliment."

"You have no right to bandy compliments with princes," Don Carlos replied. "I take you at your word. If you do not, in twenty-four hours, pay over the money to the last *real*, you shall have bitter cause to rue it."

The unhappy Grimaldo knew not what to do. Carlos was persistent. It took much negotiation to induce the prince to reduce the sum to sixty thousand ducats, which the merchant raised and paid,—with a malediction on all words of compliment. The money flew like smoke from the prince's hands, he being quite capable of squandering the revenues of a kingdom. He lived in the utmost splendor, and was lavish with all who came near him, saying, in support of his gifts and charities, "Who will give if princes do not?"

The mad excesses of the prince, his wild defiance of decency and decorum, were little to the liking of his father, who surrounded the young man with agents whom he justly looked upon as spies, and became wilder in his conduct in consequence. Offers of marriage were made from abroad. Catharine de Médicis proposed the hand of a younger sister of Isabella. The emperor of Germany pressed for a union with his daughter Anne, the cousin of Carlos. Philip agreed to the latter, but deferred the marriage. He married Anne himself after the death of Carlos, making her his fourth wife. Thus both the princesses intended for the son became the brides of the father.

The trouble between Carlos and his father steadily grew. The prince was now twenty-one years of age, and, in his eagerness for a military life, wished to take charge of affairs in the Netherlands, then in rebellion against Spain. On learning that the Duke of Alva was to be sent thither, Carlos said to him, "You are not to go there; I will go myself."

The efforts of the duke to soothe him only irritated him, and in the end he drew his dagger and exclaimed, "You shall not go; if you do I will kill you."

A struggle followed, the prince making violent efforts to stab the duke. It only ended when a chamberlain came in and rescued Alva. This outrage on his minister doubled the feeling of animosity between father and son, and they grew so hostile that they ceased to speak, though living in the same palace.

The next escapade of Carlos brought matters to a crisis. He determined to fly from Spain and seek a more agreeable home in Germany or the Netherlands. As usual, he had no money, and he tried to obtain funds by demanding loans from different cities,—a reckless process which at once proclaimed that he had some mad design in mind. He went further than this, saying to his confidants that "he wished to kill a man with whom he had a quarrel." This purpose he confessed to a priest, and demanded absolution. The priest refused, and, as the prince persisted, a conclave of sixteen monks were brought together to settle the question of whether they could give absolution to such a penitent.

After a debate on the subject, one of them asked Carlos the name of his enemy, intimating that this might have some effect on their decision. The prince calmly replied,—

"My father is the person. I wish to take his life."

This extraordinary declaration, in which the mad prince persisted, threw the conclave into a state of

THE ROYAL PALACE, MADRID.

the utmost consternation. On breaking up, they sent a messenger to the king, then at the Escorial Palace, and made him acquainted with the whole affair. This story, if it is true, seems to indicate that the prince was insane.

His application to the cities for funds was in a measure successful. By the middle of January, 1568, his agents brought him in a hundred and fifty thousand ducats,—a fourth of the sum he had demanded. On the 17th he sent an order to Don Ramon de Tassis, director-general of the posts, demanding that eight horses should be provided for him that evening. Tassis, suspecting something wrong, sent word that the horses were all out. Carlos repeated his order in a peremptory manner, and the postmaster now sent all the horses out, and proceeded with the news to the king at the Escorial. Philip immediately returned to Madrid, where, the next morning, Carlos attacked his uncle, Don John of Austria, with a drawn sword, because the latter refused to repeat a conversation he had had with the king.

For some time Carlos had slept with the utmost precautions, as if he feared an attack upon his life. His sword and dagger lay ready by his bedside, and he kept a loaded musket within reach. He had also a bolt constructed in such a manner that, by aid of pulleys, he could fasten or unfasten the door of his chamber while in bed. All this was known to Philip, and he ordered the mechanic who had made it to derange the mechanism so that it would not work. To force a way into the chamber of a man like Carlos might not have been safe.

At the hour of eleven that night the king came down-stairs, wearing armor on his body and a helmet on his head. With him were the Duke of Feria, captain of the guard, several other lords, and twelve guardsmen. They quietly entered the chamber of the prince, and the duke, stealing to the bedside, secured the sword, dagger, and musket which lay there.

The noise now wakened Carlos, who sprang up, demanding who was there.

"It is the council of state," answered the duke.

On hearing this the prince leaped from the bed, uttering threats and imprecations, and endeavored to seize his arms. Philip, who had prudently kept in the background until the weapons were secured, now advanced and bade his son to return to bed and keep quiet.

"What does your majesty want of me?" demanded the prince.

"You will soon learn," Philip harshly replied.

He then gave orders that the windows and doors of the room should be strongly secured and the keys brought to him. Every article of furniture, even the andirons, with which violence might have been done, was removed from the room. The king then appointed Feria keeper of the prince, and bade the other nobles to serve him, with due respect, saying that he would hold them as traitors if they permitted him to escape.

"Your majesty had better kill me than keep me a prisoner," exclaimed Carlos. "It will be a great scandal to the kingdom. If you do not kill me I will kill myself."

"You will do no such thing," answered Philip. "That would be the act of a madman."

"Your majesty," replied the prince, "treats me so ill that you drive me to this extremity. I am not mad, but you drive me to despair."

Other words passed, and on the withdrawal of the king the voice of Carlos was so broken by sobs that his words could scarcely be heard. That night the Duke of Feria and two other lords remained in the prince's room,—now his prison. Each succeeding night two of the six appointed lords performed this duty. They were not allowed to wear their swords in the presence of the prince, but his meat was cut up before serving, as no knife was permitted to be used at his meals. A guard was stationed in the passage without, and, as the prince could not look from his barricaded windows, he was from that day dead to the world.

The king immediately summoned his council of state and began a process against the prisoner. Though making a show of deep affliction, he was present at all the meetings and listened to all the testimony, which, when written out, formed a heap of paper half a foot thick.

The news of the arrest of Don Carlos made a great sensation in Spain. The wildest rumors were set afloat. Some said that he had tried to kill his father, others that he was plotting rebellion. Many laid all the blame on the king. "Others, more prudent than their neighbors, laid their fingers on their lips and were silent." The affair created almost as much sensation throughout Europe as in Spain. Philip, in his despatches to other courts, spoke in such vague and mysterious language that it was impossible to tell what he meant, and the most varied surmises were advanced.

Meanwhile, Carlos was kept rigorously confined, so much so that he was not left alone day or night. Of the two nobles in his chamber at night, one was required to keep awake while the other slept. They were permitted to talk with him, but not on political matters nor on the subject of his imprisonment. They were ordered to bring him no messages from without nor receive any from him. No books except devotional ones were allowed him.

If it was the purpose of Philip to end the life of his son by other means than execution he could not have taken better measures. For a young man of his high spirit and fiery temper such strict confinement was maddening. At first he was thrown into a frenzy, and tried more than once to make way with himself. The sullenness of despair succeeded. He grew daily more emaciated, and the malarial fever which had so long affected him now returned in a severe degree. To allay the heat of the fever he would deluge the floor of his chamber with water, and walk for hours with bare feet on the cold floor. He had a warming-pan filled with ice and snow brought him, and kept it for hours at night in his bed. He would drink snow-water in immoderate draughts. In his eating he seemed anxious to break down his strength,—now refusing all food for days together, now devouring a pasty of four partridges at a sitting, washing it down with three gallons or more of iced water.

That he was permitted to indulge in such caprices seems to indicate that Philip wished him to kill himself. No constitution, certainly not so weak a one as that of Carlos, could long withstand these excesses. His stomach refused to perform its duty; severe vomiting attacked him; dysentery set in; his strength rapidly failed. The expected end came on the 24th of July, six months after the date of his imprisonment, death releasing the prince from the misery of his unhappy lot. One writer tells us that it was hastened by a strong purgative dose, administered by his father's orders, and that he was really assassinated. However that be, Philip was certainly quite willing that he should destroy his own life. To one of his austere temperament it was probably an easy solution of a difficult problem.

Less than three months passed after the death of Carlos when Isabella followed him to the grave. She was then but twenty-three years old,—about the same age as himself. The story was soon set afloat that Philip had murdered both his son and his wife, moved thereto by jealousy; and from this has arisen the romantic story of secret love between the two, with the novels and dramas based thereon. In all probability the story is without foundation. Philip is said to have been warmly loved by his wife, and the poison which carried her away seems to have been the heavy doses of medicine with which the doctors of that day sought to cure a passing illness.

SPAIN'S GREATEST VICTORY AT SEA.

On the 16th of September, 1571, there sailed from the harbor of Messina one of the greatest fleets the Mediterranean had ever borne upon its waves. It consisted of more than three hundred vessels, most of them small, but some of great bulk for that day, carrying forty pieces of artillery. On board these ships were eighty thousand men. Of these, less than thirty thousand were soldiers, for in those days, when war-galleys were moved by oars rather than sails, great numbers of oarsmen were needed. At the head of this powerful armament was Don John of Austria, brother of Philip II., and the ablest naval commander that Spain possessed.

At sunrise on the 7th of October the Spanish fleet came in sight, at the entrance to the Bay of Lepanto, on the west of Greece, of the great Turkish armament, consisting of nearly two hundred and fifty royal galleys, with a number of smaller vessels in the rear. On these ships are said to have been not less than one hundred and twenty thousand men. A great battle for the control of the Mediterranean was about to be fought between two of the largest fleets ever seen on its waters.

For more than a century the Turks had been

masters of Constantinople and the Eastern Empire, and had extended their dominion far to the west. The Mediterranean had become a Turkish lake, which the fleets of the Ottoman emperors swept at will. Cyprus had fallen, Malta had sustained a terrible siege, and the coasts of Italy and Spain were exposed to frightful ravages, in which the corsairs of the Barbary states joined hands with the Turks. France only was exempt, its princes having made an alliance with Turkey, in which they gained safety at the cost of honor.

Spain was the leading opponent of this devastating power. For centuries the Spanish people had been engaged in a bitter crusade against the Moslem forces. The conquest of Granada was followed by descents upon the African coast, the most important of which was the conquest of Tunis by Charles the Fifth in 1535, on which occasion ten thousand Christian captives were set free from a dreadful bondage. An expedition against Tripoli in 1559, however, ended in disaster, the Turks and the Moors continued triumphant at sea, and it was not until 1571 that the proud Moslem powers received an effectual check.

The great fleet of which Don John of Austria was admiral-in-chief had not come solely from Spain. Genoa had furnished a large number of galleys, under their famous admiral, Andrew Doria,— a name to make the Moslems tremble. Venice had added its fleet, and the Papal States had sent a strong contingent of ships. Italy had been suffering from the Turkish fleet, fire and sword had turned the Venetian coasts into a smoking desolation, and this was the answer of Christian Europe to the Turkish menace.

The sight of the Turkish fleet on that memorable 7th of October created instant animation in the Christian armament. Don John hoisted his pennon, ordered the great standard of the league, given by the Pope, to be unfurled, and fired a gun in defiance of the Turks. Some of the commanders doubted the wisdom of engaging the enemy in a position where he had the advantage, but the daring young commander curtly cut short the discussion.

"Gentlemen," he said, "this is the time for combat, not for counsel."

Steadily the two fleets approached each other on that quiet sea. The Spanish ships extended over a width of three miles. On the right was Andrew Doria, with sixty-four galleys. The centre, consisting of sixty-three galleys, was commanded by Don John, with Colonna, the captain-general of the Pope, on one flank, and Veniero, the Venetian captain-general, on the other. The left wing, commanded by the noble Venetian Barbarigo, extended as near to the coast of Ætolia as it was deemed safe to venture. The reserve, of thirty-five galleys, was under the Marquis of Santa Cruz. The plan of battle was simple. Don John's orders to his captains were for each to select an adversary, close with him at once, and board as soon as possible.

As the fleet advanced the armament of the Turks came into full view, spread out in half-moon shape over a wider space than that of the allies. The great galleys, with their gilded and brightly painted prows and their myriad of banners and pennons, presented a magnificent spectacle. But the wind, which had thus far favored the Turks, now suddenly shifted and blew in their faces, and the sun, as the day advanced, shone directly in their eyes. The centre of their line was occupied by the huge galley of Ali Pasha, their leader. Their right was commanded by Mahomet Sirocco, viceroy of Egypt; their left by Uluch Ali, dey of Algiers, the most redoubtable of the corsair lords of the sea.

The breeze continued light. It was nearly noon when the fleets came face to face. The sun, now nearing the zenith, shone down from a cloudless sky. As yet it seemed like some grand holiday spectacle rather than the coming of a struggle for life or death.

Suddenly the shrill war-cry of the Turks rang out on the air. Their cannon began to play. The firing ran along the line until the whole fleet was engaged. On the Christian side the trumpets rang defiance and the guns answered the Turkish peals. The *galeazzas*, a number of mammoth war-ships, had been towed a half-mile in advance of the Spanish fleet, and as the Turks came up poured broadsides from their heavy guns with striking effect, doing considerable damage. But Ali Pasha, not caring to engage these monster craft, opened his lines and passed them by. They had done their work, and took no further part, being too unwieldy to enter into close action.

The battle began on the left. Barbarigo, the Venetian admiral, had brought his ships as near the coast as he dared. But Mahomet Sirocco knew the waters better, passed between his ships and the shore, and doubled upon him, bringing the Christian line between two fires. Barbarigo was wounded, eight galleys were sent to the bottom, and several were captured. Yet the Venetians, who hated the Turks with a mortal hatred, fought on with unyielding fury.

Uluch Ali, on the Christian right, tried the same manœuvre. But he had Andrew Doria, the experienced Genoese, to deal with, and his purpose was defeated by a wide extension of the Christian line. It was a trial of skill between the two ablest commanders on the Mediterranean. Doria, by stretching out his line, had weakened his centre, and the corsair captain, with alert decision, fell upon some galleys separated from their companions, sinking several, and carrying off the great Capitana of Malta as a prize.

Thus both on the right and on the left the Christians had the worst of it. The severest struggle was in the centre. Here were the flag-ships of the commanders,—the Real, Don John's vessel, flying the holy banner of the League; Ali Pasha displaying the great Ottoman standard, covered with texts from the Koran in letters of gold, and having the name of Allah written upon it many thousands of times.

Both the commanders, young and ardent, burned with desire to meet in mid battle. The rowers urged forward their vessels with an energy that sent them ahead of the rest of their lines, driving them through the foaming water with such force that the pasha's galley, much the larger and loftier of the two, was hurled upon its opponent until its prow reached the fourth bench of rowers. Both vessels groaned and quivered to their very keels with the shock.

As soon as the vessels could be disengaged the combat began, the pasha opening with a fierce fire of cannon and musketry, which was returned with equal fury and more effect. The Spanish gunners and musketeers were protected by high defences, and much of the Turkish fire went over their heads, while their missiles, poured into the unprotected and crowded crews of Ali's flag-ship, caused terrible loss. But the Turks had much the advantage in numbers, and both sides fought with a courage that made the result a matter of doubt.

The flag-ships were not long left alone. Other vessels quickly gathered round them, and the combat spread fiercely to both sides. The new-comers attacked one another and assailed at every opportunity the two central ships. But the latter, beating off their assailants, clung together with unyielding pertinacity, as if upon them depended the whole issue of the fight.

The complete width of the entrance to the bay of Lepanto was now a scene of mortal combat, though the vessels were so lost under a pall of smoke that none of the combatants could see far to the right or left. The lines, indeed, were broken up into small detachments, each fighting the antagonists in their front, and ignorant of what was going on elsewhere. The battle was in no sense a grand whole, but a series of separate combats in which the galleys grappled and the soldiers and sailors boarded and fought hand to hand. The slaughter was frightful. In the case of some vessels, it is said, every man on board was killed or wounded, while the blood that flowed from the decks stained the waters of the gulf red for miles.

The left wing of the allies, as has been said, was worsted at the beginning of the fight, its commander receiving a wound which proved mortal. But the Venetians fought on with the courage of despair. In the end they drove back their adversaries and themselves became the assailants, taking vessel after vessel from the foe. The vessel of Mahomet Sirocco was sunk, and he was slain after escaping death by drowning. His death ended the resistance of his followers. They turned to fly, many of the vessels being run ashore and abandoned and their crews largely perishing in the water.

While victory in this quarter perched on the Christian banners, the mortal struggle in the centre went on. The flag-ships still clung together, an incessant fire of artillery and musketry sweeping both decks. The Spaniards proved much the better marksmen, but the greater numbers of the Turks, and reinforcements received from an accompanying vessel, balanced this advantage. Twice the Spaniards tried to board and were driven back. A third effort was more successful, and the deck of the Turkish galley was reached. The two commanders cheered on their men, exposing themselves to danger as freely as the meanest soldier. Don John received a wound in the foot,—fortunately a slight one. Ali Pasha led his janizaries boldly against the boarders, but as he did so he was struck in the head by a musket-ball and fell. The loss of his inspiring voice discouraged his men. For a time they continued to struggle, but, borne back by their impetuous assailants, they threw down their arms and asked for quarter.

The deck was covered with the bodies of the dead and wounded. From beneath them the body of Ali was drawn, severely, perhaps mortally, wounded. His rescuers would have killed him on the spot, but he diverted them by pointing out where his money and jewels could be found. The next soldier to come up was one of the galley-slaves, whom Don John had unchained from the oar and supplied with arms. Ali's story of treasure was lost on him. With one blow he severed his head from his shoulders, and carried the gory prize to Don John, laying it at his feet. The generous Spaniard looked at it with a mingling of pity and horror.

"Of what use can such a present be to me?" he coldly asked the slave, who looked for some rich reward; "throw it into the sea."

This was not done. The head was stuck on a pike and raised aloft on the captured galley. At the same time the great Ottoman banner was drawn down, while that of the Cross was elevated with cheers of triumph in its place.

The shouts of "victory!" the sight of the Christian standard at the mast-head of Ali's ship, the news of his death, which spread from ship to ship, gave new courage to the allies and robbed the Turks of spirit. They fought on, but more feebly.

Many of their vessels were boarded and taken. Others were sunk. After four hours of fighting the resistance of the Turkish centre was at an end.

On the right, as related, Andrew Doria had suffered a severe loss by stretching his line too far. He would have suffered still more had not the reserve under Santa Cruz, which had already given aid to Don John, come to his relief. Strengthened by Cardona with the Sicilian squadron, he fell on the Algerine galleys with such fierceness that they were forced to recoil. In their retreat they were hotly assailed by Doria, and Uluch, beset on all sides, was obliged to abandon his prizes and take to flight. Tidings now came to him of the defeat of the centre and the death of Ali, and, hoisting signals for retreat, he stood in all haste to the north, followed by the galleys of his fleet.

With all sail spread and all its oarsmen vigorously at work, the corsair fleet sped rapidly away, followed by Doria and Santa Cruz. Don John joined in the pursuit, hoping to intercept the fugitives in front of a rocky headland which stretched far into the sea. But the skilled Algerine leader weathered this peril, losing a few vessels on the rocks, the remainder, nearly forty in number, bearing boldly onward. Soon they distanced their pursuers, many of whose oarsmen had taken part and been wounded in the fight. Before nightfall the Algerines were vanishing below the horizon.

There being signs of a coming storm, Don John hastened to seek a harbor of refuge, setting fire to such vessels as were damaged beyond usefulness, and

with the remainder of his prizes making all haste
to the neighboring port of Petala, the best harbor
within reach.

The loss of the Turks had been immense, probably not less than twenty-five thousand being killed
and five thousand taken prisoners. To Don John's
prizes may be added twelve thousand Christian captives, chained to the oars by the Turks, who now
came forth, with tears of joy, to bless their deliver-
ers. The allies had lost no more than eight thousand men. This discrepancy was largely due to
their use of fire-arms, while many of the Turks
fought with bows and arrows. Only the forty Algerine ships escaped ; one hundred and thirty vessels
were taken. The Christian loss was but fifteen galleys. The spoils were large and valuable, consisting
in great measure of gold, jewels, and rich brocades.

Of the noble cavaliers who took part in the fight,
we shall speak only of Alexander Farnese, Prince
of Parma, a nephew of Don John, whom he was
destined to succeed in military renown. He began
here his career with a display of courage and daring
unsurpassed on the fleet. Among the combatants
was a common soldier, Cervantes by name, whose
future glory was to throw into the shade that of all
the leaders in the fight. Though confined to bed
with a fever on the morning of the battle, he insisted on taking part, and his courage in the affray
was shown by two wounds on his breast and a third
in his hand which disabled it for life. Fortunately
it was the left hand. The right remained to write
the immortal story of Don Quixote de la Mancha.

Thus ended one of the greatest naval battles of modern times. No important political effect came from it, but it yielded an immense moral result. It had been the opinion of Europe that the Turks were invincible at sea. This victory dispelled that theory, gave new heart to Christendom, and so dispirited the Turks that in the next year they dared not meet the Christians at sea, though they were commanded by the daring dey of Algiers. The beginning of the decline of the Ottoman empire may be said to date from the battle of Lepanto.

THE INVINCIBLE ARMADA.

During almost the whole reign of Philip II. the army of Spain was kept busily engaged, now with the Turks and the Barbary states, now with the revolted Moriscos, or descendants of the Moors of Granada, now in the conquest of Portugal, now with the heretics of the Netherlands. All this was not enough for the ambition of the Spanish king. Elizabeth of England had aided the Netherland rebels and had insulted him in America by sending fleets to plunder his colonies; England, besides, was a nest of enemies of the *true church*, who needed conversion by fire and sword; Philip determined on the conquest of that uncivil and perfidious island and the enforced catholization of its people.

For months all the shipwrights of Spain were kept busy in building vessels of an extraordinary size. Throughout the kingdom stores were actively collected for their equipment. Levies of soldiers were made in Italy, Germany, and the Netherlands, to augment the armies of Spain. What was in view was the secret of the king, but through most of 1587 all Europe resounded with the noise of his preparations.

Philip broached his project to his council of state, but did not gain much support for his enterprise. "England," said one of them, "is surrounded with

a tempestuous ocean and has few harbors. Its navy
is equal to that of any other nation, and if a landing
is made we shall find its coasts defended by a powerful army. It would be better first to subdue the
Netherlands; that done we shall be better able to
chastise the English queen." The Duke of Parma,
Philip's general in chief, was of the same opinion.
Before any success could be hoped for, he said, Spain
should get possession of some large seaport in Zealand, for the accommodation of its fleet.

These prudent counsels were thrown away on the
self-willed king. His armies had lately conquered
Portugal; England could not stand before their valor;
one battle at sea and another on shore would decide
the contest; the fleet he was building would over-
whelm all the ships that England possessed; the
land forces of Elizabeth, undisciplined and unused to
war, could not resist his veteran troops, the heroes
of a hundred battles, and led by the greatest general
of the age. All this he insisted on. Europe should
see what he could do. England should be punished
for its heresy and Elizabeth pay dearly for her dis-
courtesy.

Philip was confirmed in his purpose by the appro-
bation of the Pope. Elizabeth of England was the
greatest enemy of the Catholic faith. She had abol-
ished it throughout her dominions and executed as a
traitor the Catholic Queen Mary of Scotland. For
nearly thirty years she had been the chief support of
the Protestants in Germany, France, and the Netherlands. The interests of the Church demanded that
its arch-enemy should be deprived of power. The

Pope, therefore, encouraged the Spanish king, and he, whose highest ambition was to be considered the guardian of the Church, hastened his preparations for the conquest of the island kingdom.

Elizabeth was not deceived by the falsehoods set afloat by Spain. She did not believe that this great fleet was intended partly for the reduction of Holland, partly for use in America, as Philip declared. Scenting danger afar, she sent Sir Francis Drake with a fleet to the coast of Spain to interrupt these stupendous preparations.

Drake was the man for the work. Dispersing the Spanish fleet sent to oppose him, he entered the harbor of Cadiz, where he destroyed two large galleons and a handsome vessel filled with provisions and naval stores. Then he sailed for the Azores, captured a rich carrack on the way home from the East Indies, and returned to England laden with spoils. He had effectually put an end to Philip's enterprise for that year.

Philip now took steps towards a treaty of peace with England, for the purpose of quieting the suspicions of the queen. She appeared to fall into the snare, pretended to believe that his fleet was intended for Holland and America, and entered into a conference with Spain for the settlement of all disturbing questions. But at the same time she raised an army of eighty thousand men, fortified all exposed ports, and went vigorously to work to equip her fleet. She had then less than thirty ships in her navy, and these much smaller than those of Spain, but the English sailors were the best and boldest in the world, new ships were rapidly built, and pains was taken to increase the abhorrence which the people felt for the tyranny of Spain. Accounts were spread abroad of the barbarities practised in America and in the Netherlands, vivid pictures were drawn of the cruelties of the Inquisition, and the Catholic as well as the Protestant people of England became active in preparing for defence. The whole island was of one mind; loyalty seemed universal; the citizens of London provided thirty ships, and the nobility and gentry of England forty or fifty more. But these were of small size as compared with those of their antagonist, and throughout the island apprehension prevailed.

In the beginning of May, 1588, Philip's strenuous labors were concluded and the great fleet was ready. It was immense as compared with that with which William the Conqueror had invaded and conquered England five centuries before. The Invincible Armada, as the Spaniards called it, consisted of one hundred and fifty ships, many of them of enormous size. They were armed with more than two thousand six hundred great guns, were provisioned for half a year, and contained military stores in a profusion which only the wealth of America and the Indies could have supplied. On them were nearly twenty thousand of the famous troops of Spain, with two thousand volunteers of the most distinguished families, and eight thousand sailors. In addition there was assembled in the coast districts of the Netherlands an army of thirty-four thousand men, for whose transportation to England a great number of flat-bottomed vessels had been procured. These were to venture upon the sea as soon as the Armada was in position for their support.

And now, indeed, "perfidious Albion" had reason to tremble. Never had that nation of islanders been so seriously threatened, not even when the ships of William of Normandy were setting sail for its shores. The great fleet, which lay at Lisbon, then a city of Spain, was to set sail in the early days of May, and no small degree of fear affected the hearts of all Protestant Europe, for the conquest of England by Philip the fanatic would have been a frightful blow to the cause of religious and political liberty.

All had so far gone well with Spain; now all began to go ill. At the very time fixed for sailing the Marquis of Santa Cruz, the admiral of the fleet, was taken violently ill and died, and with him died the Duke of Paliano, the vice-admiral. Santa Cruz's place was not easy to fill. Philip chose to succeed him the Duke of Medina Sidonia, a nobleman totally ignorant of sea affairs, giving him for vice-admiral Martinez de Recaldo, a seaman of much experience. All this caused so much delay that the fleet did not sail till May 29.

Storm succeeded sickness to interfere with Philip's plans. A tempest fell on the fleet on its way to Corunna, where it was to take on some troops and stores. All but four of the ships reached Corunna, but they had been so battered and dishevelled by the winds that several weeks passed before they could again be got ready for sea,—much to the discomfiture of the king, who was eager to become the lord and master of England. He had dwelt there in former years as the husband of Queen Mary; now he was ambitious to set foot there as absolute king.

England, meanwhile, was in an ebullition of joy. Word had reached there that the Spanish fleet was rendered unseaworthy by the storm, and the queen's secretary, in undue haste, ordered Lord Howard, the admiral, to lay up four of his largest ships and discharge their crews, as they would not be needed. But Howard was not so ready to believe a vague report, and begged the queen to let him keep the ships, even if at his own expense, till the truth could be learned. To satisfy himself, he set sail for Corunna, intending to try and destroy the Armada if as much injured as reported. Learning the truth, and finding that a favorable wind for Spain had begun to blow, he returned to Plymouth in all haste, in some dread lest the Armada might precede him to the English coast.

He had not long been back when stirring tidings came. The Armada had been seen upon the seas. Lord Howard at once left harbor with his fleet. The terrible moment of conflict, so long and nervously awaited, was at hand. On the next day—July 30— he came in view of the great Spanish fleet, drawn up in the form of a crescent, with a space of seven miles between its wings. Before this giant fleet his own seemed but a dwarf. Paying no attention to Lord Howard's ships, the Armada moved on with dignity up the Channel, its purpose being to disperse the Dutch and English ships off the Netherland coast and escort to England the Duke of Parma's army, then ready to sail.

Lord Howard deemed it wisest to pursue a guerilla mode of warfare, harassing the Spaniards and taking any advantage that offered. He first attacked the flag-ship of the vice-admiral Recaldo, and with such vigor and dexterity as to excite great alarm in the Spanish fleet. From that time it kept closer order, yet on the same day Howard attacked one of its largest ships. Others hurried to the aid; but in their haste two of them ran afoul, one, a large galleon, having her mast broken. She fell behind and was captured by Sir Francis Drake, who discovered, to his delight, that she had on board a chief part of the Spanish treasure.

Other combats took place, in all of which the English were victorious. The Spaniards proved ignorant of marine evolutions, and the English sailed around them with a velocity which none of their ships could equal, and proved so much better marksmen that nearly every shot told, while the Spanish gunners fired high and wasted their balls in the air. The fight with the Armada seemed a prototype of the much later sea-battles at Manila and Santiago de Cuba.

Finally, after a halt before Calais, the Armada came within sight of Dunkirk, where Parma's army, with its flat-bottomed transports, was waiting to embark. Here a calm fell upon the fleets, and they remained motionless for a whole day. But about midnight a breeze sprang up and Lord Howard put into effect a scheme he had devised the previous day.

He had made a number of fire-ships by filling eight vessels with pitch, sulphur, and other combustibles, and these were now set on fire and sent down the wind against the Spanish fleet.

It was with terror that the Spaniards beheld the coming of these flaming ships. They remembered vividly the havoc occasioned by fire-ships at the siege of Antwerp. The darkness of the night added to their fears, and panic spread from end to end of the fleet. All discipline vanished; self-preservation was the sole thought of each crew. Some took time to weigh their anchors, but others, in wild haste, cut their cables, and soon the ships were driving blindly before the wind, some running afoul of each other and being completely disabled by the shock.

When day dawned Lord Howard saw with the highest satisfaction the results of his stratagem. The Spanish fleet was in the utmost disorder, its ships widely dispersed. His own fleet had just been strengthened, and he at once made an impetuous attack upon the scattered Armada. The battle began at four in the morning and lasted till six in the evening, the Spaniards fighting with great bravery but doing little execution. Many of their ships were greatly damaged, and ten of the largest were sunk, run aground, or captured. The principal galeas, or large galley, manned with three hundred galley slaves and having on board four hundred soldiers, was driven ashore near Calais, and nearly all the Spaniards were killed or drowned in attempting to reach land. The rowers were set at liberty.

The Spanish admiral was greatly dejected by this

series of misfortunes. As yet the English had lost
but one small ship and about one hundred men,
while his losses had been so severe that he began to
dread the destruction of the entire fleet. He could
not without great danger remain where he was.
His ships were too large to approach nearer to the
coast of Flanders. Philip had declined to secure a
suitable harbor in Zealand, as advised. The Armada
was a great and clumsy giant, from which Lord
Howard's much smaller fleet had not fled in terror,
as had been expected, and which now was in such a
condition that there was nothing left for it but to
try and return to Spain.

But the getting there was not easy. A return
through the Channel was hindered by the wind,
which blew strongly from the south. Nor was it a
wise movement in the face of the English fleet.
The admiral, therefore, determined to sail northward
and make the circuit of the British islands.

Unfortunately for Lord Howard, he was in no
condition to pursue. By the neglect of the authori-
ties he had been ill-supplied with gunpowder, and
was forced to return to England for a fresh supply.
But for this deficiency he possibly might, in the distressed condition of the Spanish fleet, have forced a
surrender of the entire Armada. As it was, his return proved fortunate, for the fleets had not far separated when a frightful tempest began, which did
considerable harm to the English ships, but fell with
all its rage on the exposed Armada.

The ships, drawn up in close ranks, were hurled
fiercely together, many being sunk. Driven help-

lessly before the wind, some were dashed to pieces
on the rocks of Norway, others on the Scottish coast
or the shores of the western islands. Some went
down in the open sea. A subsequent storm, which
came from the west, drove more than thirty of them
on the Irish coast. Of these, some got off in a shattered state, others were utterly wrecked and their
crews murdered on reaching the shore. The admiral's ship, which had kept in the open sea, reached
the Spanish coast about the close of September.

Even after reaching harbor in Spain troubles pursued them, two of the galleons taking fire and burning to ashes. Of the delicately reared noble volunteers, great numbers had died from the hardships
of the voyage, and many more died from diseases
contracted at sea. The total loss is not known;
some say that thirty-two, some that more than
eighty, ships were lost, while the loss of life is estimated at from ten thousand to fifteen thousand.
Spain felt the calamity severely. There was hardly
a family of rank that had not some one of its members to mourn, and so universal was the grief that
Philip, to whose ambition the disaster was due, felt
obliged to issue an edict to abridge the time of public
mourning.

In England and Holland, on the contrary, the
event was hailed with universal joy. Days of solemn thanksgiving were appointed, and Elizabeth,
seated in a triumphal chariot and surrounded by her
ministers and nobles, went for this purpose to St.
Paul's Cathedral, the concourse bearing a great number of flags that had been taken from the enemy.

The joy at the destruction of the Armada was not confined to England and Holland. All Europe joined in it. Philip's ambition, in the event of victory over England, might have led him to attempt the subjection of every Protestant state in Europe, while Catholic France, which he afterwards attempted to conquer, had the greatest reason to dread his success.

Thus ended the most threatening enterprise in the religious wars of the sixteenth century, and to Lord Howard and his gallant captains England and Europe owe the deepest debt of gratitude, for the success of the Armada might have proved a calamity whose effects would have been felt to the present day.

THE CAUSES OF SPAIN'S DE-CADENCE.

THE golden age of Spain began in 1492, in which year the conquest of Granada extinguished the Arab dominion, and the discovery of America by Columbus opened a new world to the enterprise of the Spanish cavaliers. It continued during the reigns of Charles I. and Philip II., extending over a period of about a century, during which Spain was the leading power in Europe, and occupied the foremost position in the civilized world. In Europe its possessions included the Netherlands and important regions in Italy, while its king, Charles I., ruled as Charles V. over the German empire, possessing a dominion in Europe only surpassed by that of Charlemagne. Under Philip II. Portugal became a part of the Spanish realm, and with it its colony of Brazil, so that Spain was the unquestioned owner of the whole continent of South America, while much of North America lay under its flag.

Wealth flowed into the coffers of this broad kingdom in steady streams, the riches of America overflowing its treasury; its fleet was the greatest, its army the best trained and most irresistible in Europe; it stood as the bulwark against that mighty Ottoman power before which the other nations

246

trembled, and checked its career of victory at Lepanto; in short, as above said, it was for a brief period the leading power in Europe, and appeared to have in it the promise of a glorious career.

But though the tree was so flourishing at its summit, there was a canker at its root, the eating bane of superstition and bigotry, before whose insidious attacks the far-spreading realm was soon to shrink and decay, and in time to decline into a position of insignificance that would have seemed incredible in the sixteenth century. Spain stood as the right hand of the Church of Rome, the bulwark against the growing flood of reform, and in her strenuous effort to suppress free thought, to make all minds move in the same channel, all men think alike on religious subjects, she at once utterly failed in her purpose and ruined herself in the attempt.

Two methods were adopted in this ruinous effort, the one that of exile of the infidel and heretic, the other that of torture and execution. These were extraordinary methods for the propagation of religious faith, but by them Spain succeeded in suppressing all visible heresy within her confines, and, in her extirpation of free thought, destroyed herself. From being the strongest and most enterprising nation of Europe, she sank into the position of one of the weakest and the least progressive of European kingdoms, her population decreasing within a century or two to nearly one-half, while the demon of dulness and stolid conservatism spread its blasting wings over the entire land.

The first stage in this crusade of fanaticism was

the expulsion of the Jews, a people whose enterprise, progress in science and the arts, and genius
for business had been of immense value to Spain.
Under the Goths the Hebrew race suffered pitiless
persecution, from which they were relieved while
the Arabs ruled in Spain. Favored by the toler-
ant caliphs, the Jews became active agents in the
development of civilization. But the protection
they enjoyed under the Moslems was lost under the
Christians, who had no sooner reconquered Spain
than their ignorant fanaticism led them to a violent
persecution of their Hebrew subjects, who became
objects of scorn and hatred, and in some places were
exposed to pitiless robbery and indiscriminate massacre.

Many of the unfortunate Jews, seeking to escape
persecution, embraced Christianity. But their conversion was doubted, they were subjected to constant
espionage, and the least suspicion of indulging in
their old worship exposed them to the dangerous
charge of heresy, a word of frightful omen in Spain.
It was to punish these delinquent Jews that in 1480
the Inquisition was introduced, and at once began its
frightful work, no less than two thousand "heretics"
being burned alive in 1481, while seventeen thousand were "reconciled," a word of mild meaning elsewhere, but which in Spain signified torture, confiscation of property, loss of citizenship, and frequently
imprisonment for life in the dungeons of the Inquisition. Such was the frightful penalty for daring
to think otherwise on religious subjects than the
Church of Rome said men should and must think.

The year 1492, in which Spain gained glory by the conquest of Granada and the discovery of America, brought her deep dishonor through an act of barbarous cruelty, the expulsion of the Jews. The edict for this was signed by Ferdinand and Isabella at Granada, March 30, 1492, and decreed that all unbaptized Jews, without regard to sex, age, or condition, should leave Spain before the end of the next July, and never return thither under penalty of death and confiscation of property. Every Spaniard was forbidden to give aid in any form to a Jew after the date named. The Jews might sell their property and carry the proceeds with them in bills of exchange or merchandise, but not in gold or silver.

This edict came like a thunderbolt to the Israelites. At a tyrant's word they must go forth as exiles from the land in which they and their forefathers had dwelt for ages, break all their old ties of habit and association, and be cast out helpless and defenceless, marked with a brand of infamy, among nations who held them in hatred and contempt.

Under the unjust terms of the edict they were forced to abandon most of the property which they had spent their lives in gaining. It was impossible to sell their effects in the brief time given, in a market glutted with similar commodities, for more than a tithe of their value. As a result their hard-won wealth was frightfully sacrificed. One chronicler relates that he saw a house exchanged for an ass and a vineyard for a suit of clothes. In Aragon the property of the Jews was confiscated for the benefit of their creditors, with little regard to its value. As for the bills of exchange which they were to take instead of gold and silver, it was impossible to obtain them to the amount required in that age of limited commerce, and here again they were mercilessly robbed.

The migration was one of the most pitiable known in history. As the time fixed for their departure approached the roads of the country swarmed with emigrants, young and old, strong and feeble, sick and well, some on horses or mules, but the great multitude on foot. The largest division, some eighty thousand in number, passed through Portugal, whose monarch taxed them for a free passage through his dominions, but, wiser than Ferdinand, permitted certain skilful artisans among them to settle in his kingdom.

Those who reached Africa and marched towards Fez, where many of their race resided, were attacked by the desert tribes, robbed, slain, and treated with the most shameful barbarity. Many of them, half-dead with famine and in utter despair, returned to the coast, where they consented to be baptized with the hope that they might be permitted to return to their native land.

Those who sought Italy contracted an infectious disease in the crowded and filthy vessels which they were obliged to take; a disorder so malignant that it carried off twenty thousand of the people of Naples during the year, and spread far over the remainder of Italy. As for the Jews, hosts of them perished of hunger and disease, and of the whole number ex-

pelled, estimated at one hundred and sixty thousand,
only a miserable fragment found homes at length
in foreign lands, some seeking Turkey, others gaining refuge and protection in France and England.
As for the effect of the migration on Spain it must
suffice here to quote the remark of a monarch of
that day: "Do they call this Ferdinand a politic
prince, who can thus impoverish his own kingdom
and enrich ours?"

The Jews of Spain thus disposed of, a similar
policy was adopted towards the Moors. The treaty
made with them at the time of the surrender of
Granada was not kept. Ximenes and other bigoted
priests attempted to convert them by force, and drove
them into insurrection. This was suppressed, and
then punishment began. So rigid was the inquiry
that it seemed as if all the people of Granada would
be condemned as guilty, and in mortal dread many
of them made peace by embracing Christianity, while
others sold their estates and migrated to Barbary.
In the end, all who remained escaped persecution
only by consenting to be baptized, the total number
of converts being estimated at fifty thousand. The
name of Moors, which had superseded that of Arabs,
was now changed to that of Moriscos, by which
these unfortunate people were afterwards known.

The ill-faith shown to the Moors of the plain gave
rise to an insurrection in the mountains, in which
the Spaniards suffered a severe defeat. The insurgents, however, were soon subdued, and most of
them, to prevent being driven from their homes,
professed the Christian faith. By the free use of

torture and the sword the kings of Spain had succeeded in adding largely to their Christian subjects.

The Moriscos became the most skilful and industrious agriculturists of Spain, but the bigoted monarchs, instigated by fanatical priests, would not let them alone. Irritating edicts were from time to time issued. In 1560 the Moriscos were forbidden to employ African slaves, for fear that they might make infidels of them. This was a severe annoyance, for the wealthy farmers depended on the labor of these slaves. In 1563 they were forbidden to possess arms except under license. In 1566 still more oppressive edicts were passed. They were no longer to use the Arabic language or wear the Moorish dress, and the women were required to go about with their faces unveiled,—a scandalous thing among Mohammedans. Their weddings were to be conducted in public, after the Christian forms, their national songs and dances were interdicted, and they were even forbidden to indulge in warm baths, bathing being a custom of which the Spaniard of that day appears to have disapproved.

The result of these oppressive edicts was a violent and dangerous insurrection, which involved nearly all the Moriscos of Spain, and continued for more than two years, requiring all the power of Spain for its suppression. Don John of Austria, the victor at Lepanto, led the Spanish troops, but he had a difficult task, the Moriscos, sheltered in their mountain fastnesses, making a desperate and protracted resistance, and showing a warlike energy equal to that which had been displayed in the defence of Granada.

The end of the war was followed by a decree from Philip II. that all the Moors of Granada should be removed into the interior of the country, their lands and houses being forfeited, and nothing left them but their personal effects. This act of confiscation was followed by their reduction to a state of serfdom in their new homes, no one being permitted to change his abode without permission, under a very severe penalty. If found within ten leagues of Granada they were condemned, if between the ages of ten and seventeen, to the galleys for life; if older, to the punishment of death.

The dispersal of the Moriscos of Granada, while cruel to them, proved of the greatest benefit to Spain. Wherever they went the effects of their superior skill and industry were soon manifested. They were skilled not only in husbandry, but in the mechanic arts, and their industry gave a new aspect of prosperity to the provinces to which they were banished, while the valleys and hill-sides of Granada, which had flourished under their cultivation, sank into barrenness under the unskilful hands of their successors.

Enough had not yet been done to satiate Spanish bigotry. The Moriscos were not Spaniards, and could not easily become so while deprived of all civil rights. There was a suspicion that at heart they might still be Moslems. This was a possibility not to be endured in orthodox Spain. Under Philip III., a king as intolerant as his father, and, unlike him, timid and incapable, the final act came. Under priestly influence he was induced to sign an edict for the expulsion of the Moriscos, and this quiet and industrious people, a million in number, were in 1610, like the Jews before them, forced to leave their homes in Spain.

It is not necessary to repeat the story of the suffering which necessarily followed so barbarous an act. What has been said of the circumstances attending the expulsion of the Jews will suffice. That of the Moriscos was not so inhuman in its consequences, but it was serious enough. Fortunately, in view of the intense impolicy and deep intolerance indicated in the act, its evil effects reacted upon its advocates. To the Moriscos the suffering was personal; to Spain it was national. As France half-ruined herself by expelling the Huguenots, the most industrious of her population, Spain did the same in expelling the Moriscos, to whose skill and industry she owed so much of her prosperity. So it ever must be when bigotry is allowed to control the policy of states. France recovered from the evil effects of her mad act. Spain never did. The expulsion of the Moriscos was one of the most prominent causes of her decline, and no indications of a recovery have yet been shown.

The expulsion of the Jews and Moriscos was not sufficient to satisfy the intolerant spirit of Spain. Heresy had made its way even into the minds of Spaniards. Sons of the Church themselves had begun to think in other lines than those laid down for them by the priestly guardians of their minds.

Protestant books were introduced into the ever-faithful land, and a considerable number of converts to Protestantism were made.

Upon these heretics the Inquisition descended with all its frightful force. Philip, in a monstrous edict, condemned all to be burned alive who bought, sold, or read books prohibited by the Church. The result was terrible. The land was filled with spies. Arrests were made on all sides. The instruments of torture were kept busy. In all the principal cities of Spain the monstrous spectacle of the *auto-de-fé* was to be seen, multitudes being burned at the stake for having dared to let what the priests deemed the venom of free thought enter their minds.

The total effect of this horrible system of persecution we can only epitomize. Thousands were burned at the stake, thousands imprisoned for life after terrible torture, thousands robbed of their property, and their children condemned to poverty and opprobrium; and the kingdom of Christ, as the popes of that day estimated it, was established in Spain.

The bigoted kings and fanatical ecclesiastics of Spain had succeeded. Heresy was blotted out from Spain,—and Spain was blotted out from the ranks of enlightened nations. Freedom of thought was at an end. The mind of the Spaniard was put in fetters. Spain, under the sombre shadow of the Inquisition, was shut out from the light which was breaking over the remainder of Europe. Literature moved in narrow channels, philosophy was checked, the domain of science was closed, progress was at an end. Spain stood still while the rest of the world was sweeping onward; and she stands still to-day, her mind in the fifteenth century. The decadence of Spain is due solely to religious bigotry, which manifested itself in the expulsion of the Jews and the Moriscos, the fires of the Inquisition, and that suppression of free thought which, wherever shown, is a fatal barrier to the progress of mankind.

THE LAST OF A ROYAL RACE.

THE rebellion of the Moriscos, due to the oppressive edicts of Philip II., as stated in the preceding tale, was marked by numerous interesting events. Some of these are worth giving in illustration of the final struggle of the Moors in Spain. The insurgents failed in their first effort, that of seizing the city of Granada, still filled with their fellow-countrymen, and restoring as far as possible their old kingdom; and they afterwards confined themselves to the difficult passes and mountain fastnesses of the Sierra Nevada, where they presented a bold front to the power of Spain.

Having proclaimed their independence, and cast off all allegiance to the crown of Spain, their first step was to select a new monarch of their own race. The man selected for this purpose was of royal blood, being descended in a direct line from the ancient family of the Omeyades, caliphs of Damascus, and for nearly four centuries rulers in Spain. This man, who bore the Castilian name of Don Fernando de Valor, but was known by the Moors as Aben-Humeya, was at that time twenty-two years of age, comely in person and engaging in manners, and of a deportment worthy of the princely line from which he had descended. A man of courage and energy, he escaped from Granada and took refuge in the mountains, where he began a war to the knife against Spain.

The early events of the war were unfavorable to the Moors. Their strongholds were invaded by a powerful Spanish force under the Marquis of Mondejar, and their forces soon put to flight. Aben-Humeya was so hotly pursued that he was forced to spring from his horse, cut the hamstrings of the animal to render it useless to his pursuers, and seek refuge in the depths of the sierras, where dozens of hiding-places unknown to his pursuers could be found.

The insurrection was now in a desperate stage. Mondejar was driving the rebels in arms in terror before him; tower and town fell in succession into his hands; everywhere his arms were victorious, and only one thing was wanting to bring all opposition to an end,—the capture of Aben-Humeya, the "little king" of the Alpujarras. This crownless monarch was known to be wandering with a few followers in the wilds of the mountains; but while he lived the insurrection might at any moment blaze out again, and detachments of soldiers were sent to pursue him through the sierras.

The captain of one of these parties learned from a traitor that the fugitive prince remained hidden in the mountains only during the day, finding shelter at night in the house of a kinsman, Aben-Aboo, on the skirts of the sierras. Learning the situation of this mansion, the Spanish captain led his men with the greatest secrecy towards it. Travelling by night, they reached the vicinity of the dwelling under cover of the darkness. In a minute more the house would have been surrounded and its inmates secured; but at this critical moment the arquebuse of one of the Spaniards was accidentally discharged, the report echoing loudly among the hills and warning the lightly sleeping inmates of their danger.

One of them, El Zaguer, the uncle of Aben-Humeya, at once sprang up and leaped from the window of his room, making his way with all haste to the mountains. His nephew was not so fortunate. Running to his window, in the front of the house, he saw the ground occupied by troops. He hastily sought another window, but his foes were there before him. Bewildered and distressed, he knew not where to turn. The house was surrounded; the Spaniards were thundering on the door for admittance; he was like a wolf caught in its lair, and with as little mercy to hope from his captors.

By good fortune the door was well secured. One possible chance for safety occurred to the hunted prince. Hastening down-stairs, he stood behind the portal and noiselessly drew its bolts. The Spaniards, finding the door give way, and supposing that it had yielded to their blows, rushed hastily in and hurried through the house in search of the fugitive who was hidden behind the door. The instant they had all passed he slipped out, and, concealed by the darkness outside, hastened away, soon finding a secure refuge in the mountains.

Aben-Aboo remained in the hands of the assailants, who vainly questioned him as to the haunts of his kinsmen. On his refusal to answer they employed torture, but with no better effect. "I may die," he courageously said, "but my friends will live." So severe and cruel was their treatment, that in the end they left him for dead, returning to camp with the other prisoners they had taken. As it proved, however, the heroic Aben-Aboo did not die, but lived to play a leading part in the war.

With kindly treatment of the Moriscos he would probably have given no more trouble, but the Spanish proved utterly merciless, their soldiers raging through the mountains, and committing the foulest acts of outrage and rapine. In Granada a frightful deed was committed. A large number of the leading Moriscos, about one hundred and fifty in all, had been seized and imprisoned, being held as hostages for the good behavior of their friends. Here, on a night in March, the prison was entered by a body of Spaniards, who assailed the unfortunate captives, arms in hand, and began an indiscriminate massacre. The prisoners seizing what means of defence they could find, fought desperately for their lives, and for two hours the unequal combat continued, not ending while a Morisco remained alive.

This frightful affair, hardly surpassed by the similar massacre of prisoners during the French revolution, and here sanctioned by the government, had its natural effect. The Moriscos were soon in arms again, Aben-Humeya at their head, and the war blazed throughout the length and breadth of the mountains. Even from Barbary came a considerable body of Moors, who entered the service of the Morisco chief. Fierce and intrepid, trained to the military career, and accustomed to a life of wild adventure, these were a most valuable reinforcement to Aben-Humeya's forces, and enabled him to carry on a guerilla warfare which proved highly vexatious to the troops of Spain. He made forays from the mountains into the plain, penetrating into the vega and boldly venturing even to the walls of Granada. The insurrection spread far and wide through the Sierra Nevada, and the Spanish army, now led by Don John of Austria, the king's brother, found itself confronted by a most serious task.

The weak point in the organization of the Moriscos lay in the character of their king. Aben-Humeya, at first popular, soon displayed traits of character which lost him the support of his followers. Surrounded by a strong body-guard, he led a voluptuous life, and struck down without mercy those whom he feared, no less than three hundred and fifty persons falling victims to his jealousy or revenge. His cruelty and injustice at length led to a plot for his death, and his brief reign ended in assassination, his kinsman, Aben-Aboo, being chosen as his successor.

The new king was a very different man from his slain predecessor. He was much the older of the two, a man of high integrity and great decorum of character. While lacking the dash and love of adventure of Aben-Humeya, he had superior judgment in military affairs, and full courage in carrying out his plans. His election was confirmed from Algiers, a large quantity of arms and ammunition was imported from Barbary, reinforcements crossed the Mediterranean, and the new king began his reign under excellent auspices, his first movement being against Orgiba, a fortified place on the road to Granada, which he invested in October with an army of ten thousand men.

The capture of this place, which soon followed, roused the enthusiasm of the Moriscos to the highest pitch. From all sides the warlike peasantry flocked to the standard of their able chief, and a war began resembling that of a century before, when the forces of Ferdinand and Isabella were invading the King-dom of Granada. From peak to peak of the sierras beacon-fires flashed their signals, calling the bold mountaineers to forays on the lands of the enemy. Pouring suddenly down on the lower levels, the daring marauders swept away in triumph to the mountains the flocks and herds of their Christian foes. The vega of Granada became, as in ancient times, the battle-ground of Moorish and Christian cavaliers, the latter having generally the advantage, though occasionally the insurgent bands would break into the suburbs, or even the city of Granada, filling its people with consternation, and causing the great bell of the Alhambra to peal out its tocsin of alarm and call the Spanish chivalry in haste to the fray.

We cannot describe, even in epitome, the varied course of this sanguinary war. As might well have been expected, the greater force of the Spaniards gradually prevailed, and the autumn of 1570 found the insurgents almost everywhere subdued. Only Aben-Aboo, the "little king," remained in arms, a force of four hundred men being all that were left to him of his recent army. But these were men warmly devoted to him, and until the spring of 1571 every effort for his capture proved in vain. Hiding in mountain caves and in inaccessible districts, he defied pursuit, and in a measure kept alive the flame of rebellion.

Treason at length brought his career to an end. One of the few insurgent prisoners who escaped death at the hands of the Spanish executioners revealed the hiding-place of the fugitive king, and named the two persons on whom Aben-Aboo most relied, his secretary, Abou Amer, and a Moorish captain named El Senix.

An effort was made to win over the secretary by one who had formerly known him, a letter being sent him which roused him to intense indignation. El Senix, however, becoming aware of its contents, and having a private grudge against his master, sent word by the messenger that he would undertake, for a suitable recompense, to betray him to the Christians.

An interview soon after took place between the Moor and Barredo, the Spanish agent, some intimation of which came to the ears of Aben-Aboo. The king at once sought a cavern in the neighborhood where El Senix was secreted, and, leaving his followers outside, imprudently entered alone. He found El Senix surrounded by several of his friends, and sternly demanded of him the purpose of his interview with Barredo. Senix, confused by the accusation, faltered out that he had simply been seeking to obtain an amnesty for him. Aben-Aboo listened with a face of scorn, and, turning on his heel with the word "treachery," walked back to the mouth of the cave.

Unluckily, his men, with the exception of two guards stationed at the entrance, had left the spot to visit some near-by friends. Senix, perceiving that his own life was in danger, and that this was his only opportunity for safety, fell with his followers on the guards, one of whom was killed and the other put to flight. Then an attack was made on Aben-Aboo. The latter defended himself desperately, but the odds were too great, and the dastardly El Senix ended the struggle by felling him with the but-end of his musket, when he was quickly despatched.

Thus died the last of the Omeyades, the famous dynasty of Arabian caliphs founded in 660, and established in Spain in 756. Aben-Aboo, the last of this royal race, was given in death a triumphal entrance to Granada, as if he were one whom the Spaniards delighted to honor. The corpse was set astride on a mule, being supported by a wooden frame, which lay hidden beneath flowing robes. On one side rode Barredo; on the other the murderer El Senix bore the scimitar and arquebuse of the dead prince. The kinsmen and friends of the Morisco chief rode in his train, and after them came a regiment of infantry and a troop of horse.

As the procession moved along the street of Zacatin salvos of musketry saluted it, peals of artillery roared from the towers of the Alhambra, and the multitude thronged to gaze with silent curiosity on the ghastly face. Thus the cavalcade proceeded until the great square of Vivarambla was reached. Here were assembled the principal cavaliers and magistrates of the city, and here El Senix dismounted and delivered to Deza, the president of the tribunal before which were tried the insurgent captives, the arms of the murdered prince.

And now this semblance of respect to a brave enemy was followed by a scene of barbarity worthy of the Spain of that day. The ceremony of a public execution was gone through with, the head of the corpse being struck off, after which the body was given to the boys of Granada, who dragged it through the streets and exposed it to every indignity, finally committing it to the flames. The head, enclosed in a cage, was set over the gate that faced towards the Alpujarras. There it remained for a year, seeming to gaze towards the hills which the Morisco chief had loved so well, and which had witnessed his brief and disastrous reign.

Such was the fate of Aben-Aboo, the last of a line of great monarchs, and one of the best of them all; a man of lofty spirit, temperate appetites, and courageous endurance, who, had he lived in more prosperous days, might have ruled in the royal halls of Cordova with a renown equal to that of the most famous caliph of his race.

HENRY MORGAN AND THE BUC-CANEERS.

As the seventeenth century passed on, Spain, under the influence of religious intolerance and bad government, grew weak, both at home and abroad. Its prominent place in Europe was lost. Its vast colonial provinces in America were scenes of persecution and anarchy. There the fortresses were allowed to decay, the soldiers, half-clothed and unpaid, to become beggars or bandits, the treasures to be pilfered, and commerce to become a system of fraud; while the colonists were driven to detest their mother land. This weakness was followed by dire consequences. Bands of outcasts from various nations, who had settled on Spanish territory in the West Indies, at first to forage on the cattle of Hispaniola, organized into pirate crews, and, under the name of buccaneers, became frightful scourges of the commerce of Spain.

These wretches, mainly French, English, and Dutch, deserters and outlaws, the scum of their nations, made the rich merchant and treasure ships of Spain their prey, slaughtering their crews, torturing them for hidden wealth, rioting with profuse prodigality at their lurking-places on land, and turning those fair tropical islands into a pandemonium of outrage, crime, and slaughter. As they troubled

266

little the ships of other nations, these nations rather favored than sought to suppress them, and Spain seemed powerless to bring their ravages to an end. In consequence, as the years went on, they grew bolder and more adventurous. Beginning with a few small, deckless sloops, they in time gained large and well-armed vessels, and created so deep a terror among the Spaniards by their savage attacks that the latter rarely made a strong resistance.

Lurking in forest-hidden creeks and inlets of the West India islands, they kept a keen lookout for the ships that bore to Spain the gold, silver, precious stones, and rich products of the New World, pursued them in their swift barks, boarded them, and killed all who ventured to resist. If the cargo was a rich one, and there had been little effort at defence, the prisoners might be spared their lives; if otherwise, they were flung mercilessly into the sea. Sailing then to their place of rendezvous, the captors indulged in the wildest and most luxurious orgies, their tables groaning with strong liquors and rich provisions; gaming, music, and dancing succeeding; extravagance, debauchery, and profusion of every kind soon dissipating their blood-bought wealth.

Among the pirate leaders several gained prominence for superior boldness or cruelty, among whom we may particularly name L'Olonnois, a Frenchman, of such savage ferocity that all mariners of Spanish birth shuddered with fear at his very name. This wretch suffered the fate he deserved. In an expedition to the Isthmus of Darien he was taken prisoner by a band of savage Indians, who tore him to pieces alive, flung his quivering limbs into the fire, and then scattered the ashes to the air.

Most renowned of all the buccaneers was Henry Morgan, a native of Wales, who ran away from home as a boy, was sold as a slave in Barbadoes, and afterwards joined a pirate crew, in time becoming a leader among the lawless hordes. By this time the raids of the ferocious buccaneers had almost put an end to Spanish commerce with the New World, and the daring freebooters, finding their gains at sea falling off, collected fleets and made attacks on land, plundering rich towns and laying waste thriving settlements. So greatly had Spanish courage degenerated that the pirates with ease put to flight ten times their number of that Spanish soldiery which, a century before, had been the finest in the world.

The first pirate to make such a raid was Lewis Scott, who sacked the town of Campeachy, robbing it of all its wealth, and forcing its inhabitants to pay an enormous ransom. Another named Davies marched inland to Nicaragua, took and plundered that town, and carried off a rich booty in silver and precious stones. He afterwards pillaged the city of St. Augustine, Florida. Others performed similar exploits, but we must confine our attention to the deeds of Morgan, the boldest and most successful of them all.

Morgan's first enterprise was directed against Port au Prince, Cuba, where, however, the Spaniards had received warning and concealed their treasures, so that the buccaneer gained little for his pains. His next expedition was against Porto Bello, on the

Isthmus, one of the richest and best fortified of American cities. Two castles, believed to be impregnable, commanded the entrances to the harbor. When the freebooters learned that their leader proposed to attack so strong a place as this the hearts of the boldest among them shrank. But Morgan, with a few inspiring words, restored their courage.

"What boots it," he exclaimed, "how small our number, if our hearts be great! The fewer we are the closer will be our union and the larger our shares of plunder."

Boldness and secrecy carried the day. One of the castles was taken by surprise, the first knowledge of the attack coming to the people of the town from the concussion when Morgan blew it up. Before the garrison or the citizens could prepare to oppose them the freebooters were in the town. The governor and garrison fled in panic haste to the other castle, while the terrified people threw their treasures into wells and cisterns. The castle made a gallant resistance, but was soon obliged to yield to the impetuous attacks of the pirate crews.

It was no light exploit which Morgan had performed,—to take with five hundred men a fortified city with a large garrison and strengthened by natural obstacles to assault. The ablest general in ordinary war might well have claimed renown for so signal a victory. But the ability of the leader was tarnished by the cruelty of the buccaneer. The people were treated with shocking barbarity, many of them being shut up in convents and churches and burned alive, while the pirates gave themselves up to every excess of debauchery.

The great booty gained by this raid caused numerous pirate captains to enlist under Morgan's flag, and other towns were taken, in which similar orgies of cruelty and debauchery followed. But the impunity of the buccaneers was nearing its end. Their atrocious acts had at length aroused the indignation of the civilized world, and a treaty was concluded between Great Britain and Spain whose chief purpose was to put an end to these sanguinary and ferocious deeds.

The first effect of this treaty was to spur the buccaneers to the performance of some exploit surpassing any they had yet achieved. So high was Morgan's reputation among the pirates that they flocked from all quarters to enlist under his flag, and he soon had a fleet of no fewer than thirty-seven vessels manned by two thousand men. With so large a force an expedition on a greater scale could well be undertaken, and a counsel of the chiefs debated whether they should make an assault upon Vera Cruz, Carthagena, or Panama. Their choice fell upon Panama, as the richest of the three.

The city of Panama at that time (1670) was considered one of the greatest and most opulent in America. It contained two thousand large buildings and five thousand smaller, all of which were three stories high. Many of these were built of stone, others of cedar wood, being elegantly constructed and richly furnished. The city was the emporium for the silver- and gold-mines of New Spain, and its merchants lived in great opulence, their houses rich in articles of gold and silver, adorned with beautiful paintings and other works of art, and full of the luxuries of the age. The churches were magnificent in their decorations, and richly embellished with ornaments in gold and silver. The city presented such a prize to cupidity as freebooters and bandits had rarely conceived of in their wildest dreams.

The daring enterprise began with the capture by four hundred men of the Fort of St. Laurence, at the mouth of the Chagres River. Up this serpentine stream sailed the freebooters, as far as it would bear them, and thence they marched overland, suffering the greatest hardships and overcoming difficulties which would have deterred men of less intrepid spirit. Eight days of this terrible march brought the adventurers within sight of the far-spreading Pacific, and of the spires of the coveted city on its shores.

The people of Panama had been apprised of what was in store for them, and had laid ambuscades for the buccaneers, but Morgan, by taking an indirect route to the town, avoided these. Panama was but partly fortified. In several quarters it lay open to attack. It must be fought for and won or lost on the open plain. Here the Spaniards had assembled to the number of two thousand infantry and four hundred cavalry, well equipped and possessing everything needed but spirit to meet the dreaded foe. They had adopted an expedient sure to prove a dangerous one. A herd of wild bulls, to the number of more than two thousand, was provided, with Indians and negroes to drive them on the pirate horde. The result resembled that in which the Greeks drove elephants upon the Roman legions. Many of the buccaneers were accustomed to the chase of wild cattle, and, by shouts and the waving of colored flags, turned the bulls back upon the Spanish lines, which they threw into disorder.

The buccaneers followed with an impetuous charge which broke the ranks of the defenders of the town, who, after a two hours' combat, were completely routed, the most of them being killed or taken prisoners. The assault was now directed upon the town, which was strongly defended, the pirates being twice repulsed and suffering much from the numerous Spanish guns. But after a three hours' fight they overcame all opposition and the city fell into their hands.

A scene of frightful bloodshed and inhumanity followed. The buccaneers gave no quarter, killing all they met. Lest they should be exposed to a counter assault while intoxicated, Morgan called them together and forbade them to taste the wine of the town, saying that it had been poisoned. Conflagration followed massacre. Fires broke out in several quarters of the city, and great numbers of dwellings, with churches, convents, and numerous warehouses filled with valuable goods were reduced to ashes. These fires continued to burn during most of the month in which the freebooters held the city, and in which they indulged to the full in their accustomed cruelty, rapacity, and licentiousness.

Treasure was found in great quantities in the wells

and caves, where it had been thrown by the terrified people. The vessels taken in the harbor yielded valuable commodities. Detachments were sent into the country to capture and bring back those who had fled for safety, and by torturing these several rich deposits of treasure were discovered in the surrounding forests. A few of the inhabitants escaped with their wealth by sea, seeking shelter in the islands of the bay, and a galleon laden with the king's plate and jewels and other precious articles belonging to the church and the people narrowly escaped after a hot chase by the buccaneers. With these exceptions the rich city was completely looted.

After a month spent among the ruins of Panama Morgan and his villanous followers departed, one hundred and seventy-five mules carrying their more bulky spoil, while with them were six hundred prisoners, some carrying burdens, others held to ransom. Thus laden, they reached again the mouth of the Chagres, where their ships awaited them and where a division of the spoil was to be made.

Treachery followed this stupendous act of piracy, Morgan's later history being an extraordinary one for a man of his infamous record. He was possessed with the demon of cupidity, and a quarrel arose between him and his men concerning the division of the spoil. Morgan ended it by running off with the disputed plunder. On the night preceding the final division, during the hours of deepest slumber, the treacherous chief, with a few of his confidants, set sail for Jamaica, in a vessel deeply laden with spoils. On waking and learning this act of base treachery, the infuriated pirates pursued him, but in vain; he safely reached Jamaica with his ill-gotten wealth.

In this English island the pirate chief gained not only safety, but honors. In some way he won the favor of Charles II., who knighted him as Sir Henry Morgan and placed him on the admiralty court in Jamaica. He subsequently, for a time, acted as deputy governor, and in this office displayed the greatest severity towards his old associates, several of whom were tried before him and executed. One whole crew of buccaneers were sent by him to the Spaniards at Carthagena, in whose hands they were likely to find little favor. He was subsequently arrested, sent to England, and imprisoned for three years under charges from Spain; but this was the sole punishment dealt out to the most notorious of the buccaneers.

The success of Morgan's enterprise stimulated the piratical crews to similar deeds of daring, and the depredations continued, not only in the West Indies and eastern South America, but afterwards along the Pacific, the cities of Leon, in Mexico, New Granada, on the lake of Nicaragua, and Guayaquil, the port of Quito, being taken, sacked, and burned. Finally, France and England joined Spain in efforts for their suppression, the coasts were more strictly guarded, and many of the freebooters settled as planters or became mariners in honest trade. Some of them, however, continued in their old courses, dispersing over all seas as enemies of the shipping of the world; but by the year 1700 their career had fairly come to an end, and the race of buccaneers ceased to exist.

ELIZABETH FARNESE AND AL-BERONI.

In 1714 certain events took place in Spain of sufficient interest to be worth the telling. Philip V., a feeble monarch, like all those for the century preceding him, was on the throne. In his youth he had been the Duke of Anjou, grandson of Louis XIV. of France, and upon the death of that great monarch would be close in the succession to the throne of that kingdom. But, chosen as king of Spain by the will of Charles II., he preferred a sure seat to a doubtful one, and renounced his claim to the French crown, thus bringing to an end the fierce " War of the Succession," which had involved most of the powers of Europe for many years.

Philip, by nature weak and yielding, became in time a confirmed hypochondriac, and on the death of his wife, Maria Louise, in 1714, abandoned himself to grief, refusing to attend to business of any kind, shutting himself up in the strictest seclusion, and leaving the affairs of the kingdom practically in the hands of the Princess Orsini, the governess of his children, and his chief adviser.

Sorrow-stricken as was the bereaved king, affairs were already in train to provide him with a new wife, a plan being laid for that purpose at the very

"

funeral of his queen between the ambitious Princess Orsini and a cunning Italian named Alberoni, while they, with a show of grave decorum, followed Maria Louise to the grave.

The story of Alberoni is an interesting one. This man, destined to become prime minister of Spain, began life as the son of a gardener in the duchy of Parma. While a youth he showed such powers of intellect that the Jesuits took him into their seminary and gave him an education far superior to his station. He assumed holy orders and, by a combination of knowledge and ability with adulation and buffoonery of a shameless character, made his way until he received the appointment of interpreter to the Bishop of St. Domino, who was about to set out on a mission from the Duke of Parma to the Duke of Vendôme, then commander of the French forces in Italy.

The worthy bishop soon grew thoroughly disgusted with Vendôme, who, high as he was in station, displayed a shameless grossness of manner which was more than the pious churchman could endure. The conduct of the affair was therefore left to the interpreter, whose delicacy was not disturbed by the duke's behavior, and who managed to ingratiate himself fully in the good graces of the French general, becoming so great a favorite that in the end he left the service of the Duke of Parma for that of Vendôme.

Subsequently the duke was appointed to a command in Spain, where he employed Alberoni in all his negotiations with the court of Madrid. Here the wily and unscrupulous Italian won the favor of the

Princess Orsini so fully that when, on Vendôme's death, he returned home, the Duke of Parma sent him as his envoy to Spain.

The princess little dreamed the character of the man whom she had taken into confidential relations, and who was plotting to overthrow her influence at court. As the funeral procession of Maria Louise moved slowly onward, the princess spoke to Alberoni of the urgent necessity of finding another bride for the disconsolate king. The shrewd Italian named several eligible princesses, each of whom he dismissed as objectionable for one reason or another. At the end he adroitly introduced the name of Elizabeth Farnese, step-daughter of the Duke of Parma, of whom he spoke carelessly as a good girl, fattened on Parmesan cheese and butter, and so narrowly educated that she had not an idea beyond her embroidery. She might succeed, he hinted, to the throne of Parma, as the duke had no child of his own, in which case there would be a chance for Spain to regain her lost provinces in Italy.

The deluded Princess Orsini was delighted with the suggestion. With such a girl as this for queen she could continue to hold the reins of state. She easily induced Philip to approve the choice; the Duke of Parma was charmed with the offer; and the preliminary steps to the marriage were hurried through with all possible rapidity.

Before the final conclusion of the affair, however, the Princess Orsini discovered in some way that Alberoni had lied, and that the proposed bride was by no means the ignorant and incapable country girl she had been told. Furious at the deception, she at once sent off a courier with orders to stop all further proceedings relating to the marriage. The messenger reached Parma in the morning of the day on which the marriage ceremony was to be performed by proxy. But Alberoni was wide awake to the danger, and managed to have the messenger detained until it was too late. Before he could deliver his despatches Elizabeth Farnese was the legal wife of Philip of Spain.

The new queen had been fully advised of the state of affairs by Alberoni. The Princess Orsini, to whom she owed her elevation, was to be got rid of, at once and permanently. On crossing the frontiers she was met by all her household except the princess, who was with the king, then on his way to meet and espouse his bride. At Alcala the princess left him and hastened to meet the queen, reaching the village of Xadraca in time to receive her as she alighted from her carriage, kiss her hand, and in virtue of her office at court to conduct her to her apartment.

Elizabeth met the princess with a show of graciousness, but on entering her chamber suddenly turned and accused her visitor of insulting her by lack of respect, and by appearing before her in improper attire. The amazed princess, overwhelmed by this accusation, apologized and remonstrated, but the queen refused to listen to her, ordered her from the room, and bade the officer of the guard to arrest and convey her beyond the frontier.

Here was a change in the situation! The officer

hesitated to arrest one who for years had been supreme in Spain.

"Were you not instructed to obey me implicitly?" demanded Elizabeth.

"Yes, your majesty."

"Then do as I have ordered. I assume all responsibility."

"Will your majesty give me a written sanction?"

"Yes," said Elizabeth, in a tone very different from that of the bread-and-butter miss whom Alberoni had represented her.

Calling for pen, ink, and paper, she wrote upon her knee an order for the princess's arrest, and bade the hesitating officer to execute it at once.

He dared no longer object. The princess, in court dress, was hurried into a carriage, with a single female attendant and two officers, being allowed neither a change of clothing, protection against the cold, nor money to procure needed conveniences on the road. In this way a woman of over sixty years of age, whose will a few hours before had been absolute in Spain, was forced to travel throughout an inclement winter night, and continue her journey until she was thrust beyond the limits of Spain, within which she was never again permitted to set foot.

Such was the first act of the docile girl whom the ambitious princess had fully expected to use as a tool for her designs. Schooled by the scheming Italian, and perhaps sanctioned by Philip, who may have wished to get rid of his old favorite, Elizabeth at the start showed a grasp of the situation which she was destined to keep until the end. The feeble-minded monarch at once fell under her influence, and soon all the affairs of the kingdom became subject to her control.

Elizabeth was a woman of restless ambition and impetuous temper, and she managed throughout Philip's reign to keep the kingdom in constant hot water. The objects she kept in view were two: first, to secure to Philip the reversion of the French crown in case of the death of the then Duke of Anjou, despite the fact that he had taken frequent oaths of renunciation; second, to secure for her own children sovereign rule in Italy.

We cannot detail the long story of the intrigues by which the ambitious woman sought to bring about these purposes, but in all of them she found an able ally in Alberoni. Elizabeth did not forget that she owed her high position to this man. They were, besides, congenial in disposition, and she persuaded Philip to trust and consult him, and finally to appoint him prime minister. Not satisfied with this reward to her favorite, she, after a few years, induced the Pope to grant him a cardinal's hat and Philip to make him a grandee of Spain. The gardener's son had, by ability and unscrupulousness, reached the highest summit to which his ambition could aspire.

From the greatest height one may make the most rapid fall. The power of Alberoni was destined quickly to reach its end. Yet it was less his own fault than the ambition of the queen that led to the termination of his career. As a prime minister he proved a marked success, giving Spain an administration far superior to any she had enjoyed for many years. Alberoni was a man of great ability, which he employed in zealous efforts to improve the internal condition of the country, having the wisdom to avail himself of the talents and knowledge of other able men in handling those departments of government with which he was unfamiliar. He seemed inclined to keep Spain at peace, at least until she had regained some of her old power and energy; but the demands of the queen overcame his reluctance, and in the end he entered upon the accomplishment of her purposes with a daring and recklessness in full accordance with the demands of her restless spirit of intrigue.

Louis XIV. died in 1715. Louis XV., his heir, was a sickly child, not yet five years old. Philip would have been regent during his youth, and his heir in case of his death, had he not renounced all claim to the French throne. He was too weak and irresolute in himself to take any steps to gain this position, but his wife spurred him on to ambitious designs, and Alberoni entered eagerly into her projects, beginning a series of intrigues in France with all who were opposed to the Duke of Orleans, the existing regent.

These intrigues led to war. The duke concluded an alliance with England and Germany, the former enemies of France. Philip, exasperated at seeing himself thus thwarted, declared war against the German emperor, despite all that Alberoni could do to prevent, and sent an expedition against Sardinia, which captured that island. Sicily was also invaded.

Alberoni now entered into intrigues for the restoration of the banished Stuarts to the English throne, and took part in a conspiracy in France to seize the Duke of Orleans and appoint Philip to the regency.

Both these plots failed, the war became general, Philip found his armies beaten, and Alberoni was forced to treat for peace. The Spanish minister had made bitter enemies of George I. of England and the Duke of Orleans, who, claiming that he was responsible for disturbing the peace of Europe, demanded his dismissal as a preliminary to peace. His failure had lost him influence with the king, but the queen, the real power behind the throne, supported him, and it was only by promises of the enemies of Alberoni to aid her views for the establishment of her children that she was induced to yield consent to his overthrow.

On the 4th of December, 1719, Alberoni spent the evening transacting affairs of state with the king and queen. Up to that time he remained in full favor and authority, however he may have suspected the intrigues for his overthrow. Their majesties that night left Madrid for their country palace at Pardo, and from there was sent a decree by the hands of a secretary of state, to the all-powerful minister, depriving him of all his offices, and bidding him to quit Madrid within eight days and Spain within three weeks.

Alberoni had long been hated by the people of Spain, and detested by the grandees, who could not be reconciled to the supremacy of a foreigner and his appointment to equality with them in rank. But

this sudden dismissal seemed to change their sentiments, and rouse them to realization of the fact
that Spain was losing its ablest man. Nobles and
clergy flocked to his house in such numbers that the
king became alarmed at this sudden popularity, and
ordered him to shorten the time of his departure.

Alberoni sought refuge in Rome, but here the
enmity of France and England pursued him, and
Philip accused him of misdemeanors in office, for
which he demanded a trial by the Pope and cardinals.
Before these judges the disgraced minister defended
himself so ably that the court brought the investi-
gation to a sudden end by ordering him to retire to
a monastery for three years.

This period the favor of the Pope reduced to one
year, and his chief enemy, the regent of France,
soon after dying, he was permitted to leave the
monastery and pass the remainder of his life free
from persecution. His career was a singular one,
considering the lowness of his origin, and showed
what ability and shrewdness may accomplish even
against the greatest obstacles of fortune.

THE great Mediterranean Sea has its gate-way, nine miles wide, opening into the Atlantic, the gate-posts being the headland of Ceuta, on the African coast, and the famous rock of Gibraltar, in southwestern Spain, two natural fortresses facing each other across the sea. It is a singular fact that the African headland is held by Spain, and the Spanish headland by Great Britain,—this being a result of the wars of the eighteenth century. Gibraltar, in fact, has had a striking history, one worth the telling.

This towering mass of rock rises in solitary grandeur at the extremity of a sandy level, reaching upward to a height of fourteen hundred and eight feet, while it is three miles long and three-fourths of a mile in average width. It forms a stronghold of nature which attracted attention at an early date. To the Greeks it was one of the Pillars of Hercules, —Abyla (now Ceuta) being the other,— and formed the supposed western boundary of the world. Tarik, the Arab, landed here in 711, fortified the rock, and made it his base of operations against Gothic Spain. From him it received its name, Gebel el Tarik (Hill of Tarik), now corrupted into Gibraltar. For seven centuries it remained in Moorish hands, except for a short interval after 1302, when it was taken by Ferdinand II. of Castile. The king of Granada soon

recaptured it; from him it was taken by treachery
by the king of Fez in 1333; Alfonso XI. of Castile
vigorously besieged it, but in vain; the king of
Granada mastered it again in 1410; and it finally
fell into the hands of Spain in 1462.

A formidable attempt was made by the Moors for
its recovery in 1540, it being vigorously attacked by
the pirates of Algiers, who fought fiercely to win the
rock, but were finally repulsed.

For the next event in the history of this much-
coveted rock we must go on to the year 1704, when
the celebrated war of the Succession was in full
play. Louis XIV. of France supported his grandson Philip V. as the successor to the throne of
Spain. The Archduke Charles of Austria was supported by England, Portugal, and Holland, and was
conveyed to the Peninsula and landed at Lisbon by
an English fleet under Admiral Rorke. The admiral,
having disposed of the would-be king, sailed for Barcelona, which he was told was a ripe plum, ready to
fall into his mouth. He was disappointed; Barcelona
was by no means ripe for his purposes, and he sailed
back, ready for any enterprise that might offer itself.

Soon before him towered the rock of Gibraltar,
a handsome prize if it could be captured, and poorly
defended, as he knew. The Spaniards, trusting, as
it seems, in the natural strength of the place, which
they deemed impregnable, had left it with a very
small supply of artillery and ammunition, and with
almost no garrison. Here was a promising opportunity for the disappointed admiral and his associate,
the prince of Hesse Darmstadt, who headed the

foreign troops. A landing was made, siege lines were opened, batteries were erected, and a hot bombardment began, to which the feeble garrison could make but a weak reply. But the most effective work was done by a body of soldiers, who scrambled up a part of the rock that no one dreamed could be ascended, and appeared above the works, filling with terror the hearts of the garrison.

Two days answered for the enterprise. At the end of that time the governor, Don Diego de Salmas, capitulated, and Gibraltar was taken possession of in the name of Queen Anne of England, the prince being left there with a garrison of two thousand men. From that time to this Gibraltar has remained an outpost of Great Britain, with whose outlying strongholds the whole world bristles.

The loss of this strong place proved a bitter draught to the pride of Spain, and strenuous efforts to recapture it were made. In the succeeding year (1705) it was besieged by a strong force of French and Spanish troops, but their efforts were wasted, for the feeble court of Madrid left the army destitute of necessary supplies. By the peace of Utrecht, 1713, Gibraltar was formally made over to Great Britain, a country famous for clinging with a death-grip to any place of which she has once taken hold.

Later efforts were made to win the Rock of Tarik for Spain, one in 1756, but the last and greatest in 1779–82. It is this vigorous effort with which we are here concerned, the siege being one of the most famous of recent times.

The Revolutionary War in the United States stirred up all Europe, and finally brought Great Britian two new foes, the allied kingdoms of France and Spain. The latter country had never lost its irritation at seeing a foreign power in possession of a part of its home territory. Efforts were made to obtain Gibraltar by negotiation, Spain offering her friendly aid to Great Britain in her wars if she would give up Gibraltar. This the British government positively refused to do, and war was declared. A siege of Gibraltar began which lasted for more than three years.

Spain began the work in 1779 with a blockade by sea and an investment by land. Supplies were cut off from the garrison, which was soon in a state of serious distress for food, and strong hopes were entertained that it would be forced to yield. But the British government was alert. Admiral Rodney was sent with a strong fleet to the Mediterranean, the Spanish blockading fleet was defeated, the garrison relieved, provisioned, and reinforced, and Rodney sailed in triumph for the West Indies.

For three years the blockade was continued with varying fortunes, the garrison being now on the verge of starvation, now relieved by British fleets. At the close of the third year it was far stronger than at the beginning. The effort to subdue it by famine was abandoned, and preparations for a vigorous siege were made. France had joined her forces with those of Spain. The island of Minorca, held by the British, had been taken by the allied fleet, and it was thought impossible for Gibraltar to resist the projected assault.

The land force that had so long besieged the rock was greatly strengthened, new batteries were raised, new trenches opened, and a severe fire was begun upon the works. Yet so commanding was the situation and so strong were the defences of the garrison that success from the land side seemed impossible, and it was determined to make the main attack from the sea.

A promising method of attack was devised by a French engineer of the highest reputation for skill in his profession, the Chevalier D'Arçon. The plan offered by him was so original and ingenious as to fill the besiegers with hopes of sure success, and the necessary preparations were diligently made. Ten powerful floating batteries were constructed, which were thought fully adapted to resist fire, throw off shells, and quench red-hot balls. Every effort was made to render them incombustible and incapable of being sunk. These formidable batteries were towed to the bay of Gibraltar and anchored at a suitable distance from the works, D'Arçon himself being in command. Ten ships of the line were sent to co-operate with them, the arrival of reinforcements from France increased the land army to forty thousand men, and Crillon, the conqueror of Minorca, was placed in supreme command. The allied fleets were ordered to cruise in the straits, so as to prevent interference by a British fleet.

These great and scientific preparations filled all hearts with hope. No doubt was entertained that Gibraltar now must fall and Great Britain receive the chastisement she deserved. The nobility of

Spain sought in numbers the scene of action, eager to be present at the triumph of her arms. From Versailles came the French princes, full of expectation of witnessing the humbling of British pride. So confident of success was Charles III., king of Spain, that his first question every morning on waking was, " Is Gibraltar taken ?" All Spain and all France were instinct with hope of seeing the pride of the islanders go down.

Gibraltar was garrisoned by seven thousand troops under General Elliot. These lay behind fortifications on which had been exhausted all the resources of the engineering skill of that day, and in their hearts was the fixed resolve never to surrender. The question had become one of national pride rather than of utility. Gibraltar was not likely to prove of any very important advantage to Great Britain, but the instinct to hold on has always been with that country a national trait, and, however she might have been induced to yield Gibraltar as an act of policy, she was determined not to do so as an act of war.

Early on the 13th of September, 1782, the long-threatened bombardment began from so powerful a park of artillery that its roar is said to have exceeded anything ever before heard. There were defects in the plan. The trenches on land proved to be too far away. The water was rough and the gunboats could not assist. But the work of the batteries came up to the highest expectations. The fire poured by them upon the works was tremendous, while for many hours the shells and red-hot balls of the garrison, fired with the greatest precision, proved of no avail. The batteries seemed invulnerable to fire and shell, and the hopes of the besiegers rose to the highest point, while those of the besieged correspondingly fell.

In the end this powerful assault was defeated by one of those events to which armed bodies of men are always liable,—a sudden and uncalled-for spasm of fear that flew like wildfire through fleet and camp. The day had nearly passed, evening was approaching, the hopes of the allies were at their height, when a red-hot ball from the works lodged in the nearest battery and started a fire, which the crew sought in vain to quench.

In a sudden panic, for which there seems to have been no sufficient cause, the terrified crew wet their powder and ceased to fire on the British works. The panic spread to the other batteries, and from them to the forces on shore, even the commander-in-chief being affected by the causeless fear. At one moment the assailants were enthusiastic with expectation of success. Not many minutes afterwards they were so overcome with unreasoning terror that an insane order was given to burn the batteries, and these were fired with such precipitate haste that the crews were allowed no time to escape. More of the men were saved by their enemies, who came with generous intrepidity to their aid, than by their own terror-stricken friends.

This unfortunate event put a sudden end to the costly and promising effort. The nobles of Spain and the princes of France left the camp in disgust.

Charles III. received word that Gibraltar was not captured, and not likely to be, and the idea of taking the stronghold by force was abandoned, the blockade being resumed.

To keep away British aid the allied fleet was increased until it numbered forty-seven ships of the line, with a considerable number of smaller vessels. Furnaces were prepared to heat shot for the destruction of any transports and store-ships that might enter the harbor. Against this great fleet Lord Howe appeared in October with only thirty sail, and encumbered with a large convoy. The allied leaders seeing this small force, felt sure of victory, and of Gibraltar as their prize.

But again they were doomed to disappointment. The elements came to the British aid. A violent storm drove the allied fleet from its anchorage, dispersed the vessels, injured many of the large ships, and drove the small craft ashore. Lord Howe, whose ships were far better handled, sailed in good order through the straits, and for five days of rough weather offered battle to the disabled enemy, keeping them at a distance while his transports and store-ships entered the harbor and supplied the garrison abundantly with provisions, ammunition, and men. The effort to take Gibraltar was hopelessly defeated. The blockade was still kept up, but merely as a satisfaction to Spanish pride. All hope of taking the fortress was at an end. Gibraltar remains to-day in British hands, and no later attempt to take it has been made.

THE FALL OF A FAVORITE.

THE course of our work now brings us down to
recent times. After the death of Philip II., in 1598,
Spain had little history worth considering. Ruled
by a succession of painfully weak kings, and clasped
in the fetters of a strangling bigotry, the fortunes
of the realm ran steadily downward. From being
the strongest, it became in time one of the weakest
and least considered of European kingdoms; and
from taking the lead in the politics and wars of
Europe, it came to be a plaything of the neighboring
nations,—a catspaw which they used for the advance-
ment of their own ends.

It was in this way that Napoleon treated Spain.
He played with it as a cat plays with a mouse, and
when the proper time came pounced upon it and
gathered it in. Charles IV., the Spanish king of
Napoleon's time, was one of the feeblest of his
weak line,—an imbecile whom the emperor of France
counted no more than a feather in his path. He
sought to deal with him as he had done with the
equally effeminate king of Portugal. When a French
army invaded Portugal in 1807, its weak monarch
cut the knot of the difficulty by taking ship and
crossing the ocean to Brazil, abandoning his old
kingdom and setting up a new one in the New
World. When Spain was in its turn invaded, its
292

king proposed to do the same thing,—to carry the royal court of Spain to America, and leave a kingdom without a head to Napoleon. Such an act would have exactly suited the purposes of the astute conqueror, but the people rose in riot, and Charles IV. remained at home.

The real ruler of Spain at that time was a licentious and insolent favorite of the king and queen, Emanuel Godoy by name, who began life as a soldier, was made Duke of Alcudia by his royal patrons, and was appointed prime minister in 1792. In 1795, having made peace with France after a disastrous war, he received the title of "Prince of the Peace." His administration was very corrupt, and he won the hatred of the nobles, the people, and the heir to the throne. But his influence over the imbecile king and the licentious queen was unbounded, and he could afford to laugh in the face of his foes. But favorites are apt to have a short period of power, and, though Godoy remained long in office, his downfall at length came.

Napoleon had marched his armies through Spain to the conquest of Portugal, no one in Spain having the courage to object. It was stipulated that a second French army should not cross the Pyrenees, but in defiance of this Napoleon filled the north of Spain with his troops in 1808, and sent a third army across the mountains without pretence of their being needed in Portugal. No protest was made against this invasion of a neutral nation. The court of Madrid was helpless with terror, and, with the hope of propitiating Napoleon, admitted his legions into all the cities of Catalonia, Biscay, and Navarre.

Only one thing more was needed to make the French masters of the whole country. They held the towns, but the citadels were in possession of Spanish troops. These could not be expelled by violence while a show of peace was kept up. But Napoleon wanted them, and employed stratagem to get them into his hands.

In two of the towns, St. Sebastian and Figueras, a simple lie sufficed. The officers in command of the French garrisons asked permission to quarter their unruly conscripts in the citadels. As the court had ordered that all the wishes of the emperor's officers should be gratified, this seemingly innocent request was granted. But in place of conscripts the best men of the regiments were sent, and these were gradually increased in numbers until in the end they overpowered the Spanish garrisons and admitted the French.

At Pamplona a similar request was refused by the governor of the citadel, but he permitted sixty unarmed men daily to enter the fortress to receive rations for their respective divisions. Here was the fatal entering wedge. One night the officer in charge, whose quarters were near the citadel gate, secretly filled his house with armed grenadiers. The next morning sixty picked men, with arms hidden under their cloaks, were sent in for rations. The hour was too early, and the French soldiers loitered about under pretence of waiting for the quartermaster. Some sauntered into the Spanish guard-house.

Others, by a sportive scuffle on the drawbridge, prevented its being raised, and occupied the attention of the garrison. Suddenly a signal was given. The men drew their weapons and seized the arms of the Spaniards. The grenadiers rushed from their concealment. The bridge and gate were secured, French troops hastened to the aid of their comrades, and the citadel was won.

At Barcelona a different stratagem was employed. A review of the French forces was held under the walls of the citadel, whose garrison assembled to look on. During the progress of the review the French general, on pretence that he had been ordered from the city, rode with his staff on to the drawbridge with the ostensible purpose of bidding farewell to the Spanish commander. While the Spaniards curiously watched the manœuvres of the troops others of the French quietly gathered on the drawbridge. At a signal this was seized, a rush took place, and the citadel of Barcelona was added to the conquests of France.

The surprise of these fortresses produced an immense sensation in Spain. That country had sunk into a condition of pitiable weakness. Its navy, once powerful, was now reduced to a small number of ships, few of them in condition for service. Its army, once the strongest in Europe, was now but a handful of poorly equipped and half-drilled men. Its finances were in a state of frightful disorganization. The government of a brainless king, a dissolute queen, and an incapable favorite had brought Spain into a condition in which she dared not raise a hand to resist the ambitious French emperor.

In this dilemma Godoy, the so-called "Prince of the Peace," persuaded the king and queen of Spain that nothing was left them but flight. The royal house of Portugal had found a great imperial realm awaiting it in America. Spain possessed there a dominion of continental extent. What better could they do than remove to the New World the seat of their throne and cut loose from their threatened and distracted realm?

The project was concealed under the form of a journey to Andalusia, for the purpose, as announced by Godoy, of inspecting the ports. But the extensive preparations of the court for this journey aroused a suspicion of its true purpose among the people, whose indignation became extreme on finding that they were to be deserted by the royal house, as Portugal had been. The exasperation of all classes —the nobility, the middle class, and the people— against the court grew intense. It was particularly developed in the army, a body which Godoy had badly treated. The army leaders argued that they had better welcome the French than permit this disgrace, and that it was their duty to prevent by force the flight of the king.

But all this did not deter the Prince of the Peace. He had several frigates made ready in the port of Cadiz, the royal carriages were ordered to be in readiness, and relays of horses were provided on the road. The date of departure was fixed for the 15th or 16th of March, 1808.

On the 13th Godoy made his way from Madrid to Aranjuez, a magnificent royal residence on the banks of the Tagus, then occupied by the royal family. This residence, in the Italian style and surrounded by superb grounds and gardens, was fronted by a wide highway, expanding opposite the palace into a spacious place, on which were several fine mansions belonging to courtiers and ministers, one of the finest being occupied by the prime minister. In the vicinity a multitude of small houses, inhabited by tradesmen and shop-keepers, made up the town of Aranjuez.

Godoy, on arriving at Aranjuez, summoned a council of the ministers, the time having arrived to apprise them of what was proposed. One of them, the Marquis of Caballero, kept him waiting, and on his arrival refused to consent, either by word or signature, to the flight of the king.

"I order you to sign," the prime minister angrily exclaimed.

"I take no orders except from the king," haughtily replied the marquis.

A sharp altercation followed, in which the other ministers took part, and the meeting broke up in disorder, nothing being done. On retiring, the irate counsellors, full of agitation, dropped words which were caught up by the public and aroused a commotion that quickly spread throughout the town. Thence it extended into the surrounding country, everywhere arousing the disaffected, and soon strange and sinister faces appeared in the quiet town. The elements of a popular outbreak were gathering.

During the succeeding two days the altercation between the Prince of the Peace and the ministers continued, and the public excitement was added to by words attributed to Ferdinand, the king's son and heir to the throne, who was said to have sought aid against those who proposed to carry him off against his will. On the morning of the 16th, the final day fixed for the journey, the public agitation was so great that the king issued a proclamation, which was posted in the streets, saying that he had no thought of leaving his people. It ended: "Spaniards, be easy; your king will not leave you."

This for the time calmed the people. Yet on the 17th the excitement reappeared. The carriages remained loaded in the palace court-yard; the relays of horses were kept up; all the indications were suspicious. During the day the troops of the garrison of Madrid not on duty, with a large number of the populace, appeared in Aranjuez, having marched a distance of seven or eight leagues. They shouted maledictions on their way against the queen and the Prince of the Peace.

The streets of Aranjuez that night were filled with an excited mob, many of them life-guards from Madrid, who divided into bands and patrolled the vicinity of the palace, determined that no one should leave. About midnight an incident changed the excitement into a riot. A lady left Godoy's residence under escort of a few soldiers. She appeared to be about to enter a carriage. The crowd pressed closely around, and the hussars of the minister, who attended the lady, attempted to force a passage through them. At this moment a gun was fired,—by whom was not known. A frightful tumult at once arose. The life-guards and other soldiers rushed upon the hussars, and a furious mob gathered around the palace, shouting, " Long live the king !" " Death to the Prince of the Peace!"

Soon a rush was made towards the residence of the prince, which the throng surrounded, gazing at it with eyes of anger, yet hesitating to make an attack. As they paused in doubt, a messenger from the palace approached the mansion and sought admission. It was refused from those within. He insisted upon entrance, and a shot came from the guards within. In an instant all hesitation was at an end. The crowd rushed in fury against the doors, broke them in, and swarmed into the building, driving the guards back in dismay.

It was magnificently furnished, but their passion to destroy soon made havoc of its furniture and decorations. Pictures, hangings, costly articles of use and ornament were torn down, dashed to pieces, flung from the windows. The mob ran from room to room, destroying everything of value they met, and eagerly seeking the object of their hatred, with a passionate thirst for his life. The whole night was spent in the search, and, the prince not being found, his house was reduced to a wreck.

Word of what was taking place filled the weak soul of Charles IV. with mortal terror. The prince failed to appear, and, by the advice of the ministers, a decree was issued by the king on the following morning depriving Emanuel Godoy of the offices of grand admiral and generalissimo, and exiling him from the court.

Thus fell this detestable favorite, the people, who blamed him for the degradation of Spain, breaking into a passionate joy, singing, dancing, building bon-fires, and giving every manifestation of delight. In Madrid, when the news reached there, the enthusiasm approached delirium.

Meanwhile, where was the fallen favorite? Despite the close search made by the mob, he remained concealed in his residence. Alarmed by the crash of the breaking doors, he had seized a pistol and a handful of gold, rushed up-stairs, and hid himself in a loft under the roof, rolling himself up in a sort of rush carpet used in Spain. Here he remained during the whole of the 18th and the succeeding night, but on the morning of the 19th, after thirty-six hours' suffering, thirst and hunger forced him to leave his retreat. He presented himself suddenly before a sentry on duty in the palace, offering him his gold. But the man refused the bribe and instantly called the guard. Fortunately the mass of the people were not near by. Some life-guards who just then came up placed the miserable captive between their horses, and conveyed him as rapidly as they could towards their barracks. But these were at some distance, the news of the capture spread like wild-fire, and they had not gone far before the mob began to gather around them, their hearts full of mur-derous rage.

The prince was on foot between two of the mounted guardsmen, leaning for shelter against the pommels of their saddles. Others of the horsemen closed up in front and rear, and did their best to protect him from the fury of the rabble, who struck wildly at him with every weapon they had been able to snatch up. Despite the efforts of the guardsmen some of the blows reached him, and he was finally brought to the barracks with his feet trodden by the horses, a large wound in his thigh, and one eye nearly out of his head. Here he was thrown, covered with blood, upon the straw in the stables, a sad example of what comes of the favor of kings when exercised in defiance of the will of the people. Godoy had begun life as a life-guardsman, and now, after almost sharing the throne, he had thus returned to the barracks and the straw bed of his youth.

We may give in outline the remainder of the story of this fallen favorite. Promise being given that he should have an impartial trial, the mob ceased its efforts to kill him. Napoleon, who had use for him, now came to his rescue, and induced him to sign a deed under which Charles IV. abdicated the throne in favor of his son. His possessions in Spain were confiscated, but Charles, who removed to Rome, was his friend during life. After the death of his protector he went to Paris, where he received a pension from Louis Philippe ; and in 1847, when eighty years of age, he received permission to return to Spain, his titles and most of his property being restored. But he preferred to live in Paris, where he died in 1851.

THE SIEGE OF SARAGOSSA.

On the banks of the Ebro, in northwestern Spain, stands the ancient city of Saragossa, formerly the capital of Aragon, and a place of fame since early Roman days. A noble bridge of seven arches, built nearly five centuries ago, crosses the stream, and a wealth of towers and spires gives the city an imposing appearance. This city is famous for its sieges, of which a celebrated one took place in the twelfth century, when the Christians held it in siege for five years, ending in 1118. In the end the Moors were forced to surrender, or such of them as survived, for a great part of them had died of hunger. In modern times it gained new and high honor from its celebrated resistance to the French in 1808. It is this siege with which we are concerned, one almost without parallel in history.

We have told in the preceding tale how Charles IV. of Spain was forced to yield the throne to his son Ferdinand, who was proclaimed king March 20, 1808. This act by no means agreed with the views of Napoleon, who had plans of his own for Spain, and who sought to end the difficulty by deposing the Bourbon royal family and placing his own brother, Joseph Bonaparte, on the throne.

The imperious emperor of the French had, however, the people as well as the rulers of Spain to

THE CITY OF SARAGOSSA.

deal with. The news of his arbitrary action was received throughout the Peninsula with intense indignation, and suddenly the land blazed into insurrection, and the French garrisons, which had been treacherously introduced into Spain, found themselves besieged. Everywhere the peasants seized arms and took to the field, and a fierce guerilla warfare began which the French found it no easy matter to overcome. At Baylen, a town of Andalusia, which was besieged by the insurgents, the French suffered a serious defeat, an army of eighteen thousand men being forced to surrender as prisoners of war. This was the only important success of the Spanish, but they courageously resisted their foes, and at Saragossa gained an honor unsurpassed in the history of Spain. Never had there been known such a siege and such a defence.

Saragossa was attacked by General Lefebre on June 15, 1808. Thinking that a city protected only by a low brick wall, with peasants and townsmen for its defenders, and few guns in condition for service, could be carried at first assault, the French general made a vigorous attack, but found himself driven back. He had but four or five thousand men, while the town had fifty thousand inhabitants, the commander of the garrison being Joseph Palafox, a man of indomitable spirit.

Lefebre, perceiving that he had been over-confident, now encamped and awaited reinforcements, which arrived on the 29th, increasing his force to twelve thousand men. He was recalled for service elsewhere, General Verdier being left in command,

and during the succeeding two months the siege was vigorously prosecuted, the French being supplied with a large siege train, with which they hotly bombarded the city.

Weak as were the walls of Saragossa, interiorly it was remarkably well adapted for defence. The houses were strongly built, of incombustible material, they being usually of two stories, each story vaulted and practically fireproof. Every house had its garrison, and the massive convents which rose like castles within the circuit of the wall were filled with armed men. Usually when the walls of a city are taken the city falls; but this was by no means the case with Saragossa. The loss of its walls was but the beginning, not the end, of its defence. Each convent, each house, formed a separate fortress. The walls were loop-holed for musketry, ramparts were constructed of sand-bags, and beams were raised endwise against the houses to afford shelter from shells.

It was not until August that the French, now fifteen thousand strong, were able to force their way into the city. But to enter the city was not to capture it. They had to fight their way from street to street and from house to house. At length the assailants penetrated to the Cosso, a public walk formed on the line of the old Moorish ramparts, but here their advance was checked, the citizens defending themselves with the most desperate and unyielding energy.

The singular feature of this defence was that the women of Saragossa took as active a part in it as the men. The Countess Burita, a beautiful young woman of intrepid spirit, took the lead in forming her fellow-women into companies, at whose head were ladies of the highest rank. These, undeterred by the hottest fire and freely braving wounds and death, carried provisions to the combatants, removed the wounded to the hospitals, and were everywhere active in deeds of mercy and daring. One of them, a young woman of low rank but intrepid soul, gained world-wide celebrity by an act of unusual courage and presence of mind.

While engaged one day in her regular duty, that of carrying meat and wine to the defenders of a battery, she found it deserted and the guns abandoned. The French fire had proved so murderous that the men had shrunk back in mortal dread. Snatching a match from the hand of a dead artillery-man, the brave girl fired his gun, and vowed that she would never leave it while a Frenchman remained in Saragossa. Her daring shamed the men, who returned to their guns, but, as the story goes, the brave girl kept her vow, working the gun she had chosen until she had the joy to see the French in full retreat. This took place on the 14th of August, when the populace, expecting nothing but to die amid the ruins of their houses, beheld with delight the enemy in full retreat. The obstinate resistance of the people and reverses to the arms of France elsewhere had forced them to raise the siege.

The deeds of the "Maid of Saragossa" have been celebrated in poetry by Byron and Southey and in art by Wilkie, and she stands high on the roll of heroic women, being given, as some declare, a more elevated position than her exploit deserved.

Saragossa, however, was only reprieved, not abandoned. The French found themselves too busily occupied elsewhere to attend to this centre of Spanish valor until months had passed. At length, after the defeat and retreat of Sir John Moore and the English allies of Spain, a powerful army, thirty-five thousand strong, returned to the city on the Ebro, with a battering train of sixty guns.

Palafox remained in command in the city, which was now much more strongly fortified and better prepared for defence. The garrison was superabundant. From the field of battle at Tudela, where the Spaniards had suffered a severe defeat, a stream of soldiers fled to Saragossa, bringing with them wagons and military stores in abundance. As the fugitives passed, the villagers along the road, moved by terror, joined them, and into the gates of the city poured a flood of soldiers, camp-followers, and peasants, until it was thronged with human beings. Last of all came the French, reaching the city on the 20th of December, and resuming their interrupted siege. And now Saragossa, though destined to fall, was to cover itself with undying glory.

The townsmen, giving up every thought of personal property, devoted all their goods, their houses, and their persons to the war, mingling with the soldiers and the peasants to form one great garrison for the fortress into which the whole city was transformed. In all quarters of the city massive churches and convents rose like citadels, the various large streets running into the broad avenue called the Cosso, and dividing the city into a number of districts, each with its large and massive structures, well capable of defence.

Not only these thick-walled buildings, but all the houses, were converted into forts, the doors and windows being built up, the fronts loop-holed, and openings for communication broken through the party-walls; while the streets were defended by trenches and earthen ramparts mounted with cannon. Never before was there such an instance of a whole city converted into a fortress, the thickness of the ramparts being here practically measured by the whole width of the city.

Saragossa had been a royal depot for saltpetre, and powder-mills near by had taught many of its people the process of manufacture, so no magazines of powder subject to explosion were provided, this indispensable substance being made as it was needed. Outside the walls the trees were cut down and the houses demolished, so that they might not shield the enemy; the public magazines contained six months' provisions, the convents and houses were well stocked, and every preparation was made for a long siege and a vigorous defence.

Again, as before, companies of women were enrolled to attend the wounded in the hospitals and carry food and ammunition to the men, the Countess Burita being once more their commander, and performing her important duty with a heroism and high intelligence worthy of the utmost praise. Not less than fifty thousand combatants within the walls faced the thirty-five thousand French soldiers without, who had before them the gigantic task of overcoming a city in which every dwelling was a fort and every family a garrison.

A month and more passed before the walls were taken. Steadily the French guns played on these defences, breach after breach was made, a number of the encircling convents were entered and held, and by the 1st of February the walls and outer strongholds of the city were lost. Ordinarily, under such circumstances, the city would have fallen, but here the work of the assailants had but fairly begun. The inner defences—the houses with their unyielding garrisons—stood intact, and a terrible task still faced the French.

The war was now in the city streets, the houses nearest the posts held by the enemy were crowded with defenders, in every quarter the alarm-bells called the citizens to their duty, new barricades rose in the streets, mines were sunk in the open spaces, and the internal passages from house to house were increased until the whole city formed a vast labyrinth, throughout which the defenders could move under cover.

Marshall Lannes, the French commander, viewed with dread and doubt the scene before him. Untrained in the art of war as were the bulk of the defenders, courage and passionate patriotism made up for all deficiencies. Men like these, heedless of death in their determined defence, were dangerous to meet in open battle, and the prudent Frenchman resolved to employ the slow but surer process of excavating a passage and fighting his way through house after house until the city should be taken piecemeal.

Mining through the houses was not sufficient. The greater streets divided the city into a number of small districts, the group of dwellings in each of which forming a separate stronghold. To cross these streets it was necessary to construct underground galleries, or build traverses, since a Spanish battery raked each street, and each house had to be fought for and taken separately.

While the Spaniards held the convents and churches the capture of the houses by the French was of little service to them, the defenders making sudden and successful sallies from these strong buildings, and countermining their enemies, their numbers and perseverance often frustrating the superior skill of the French. The latter, therefore, directed their attacks upon these buildings, mining and destroying many of them. On the other hand, the defenders saturated with rosin and pitch the timbers of the buildings they could no longer hold, and interposed a barrier of fire between themselves and their assailants which often delayed them for several days.

Step by step, inch by inch, the French made their way forward, complete destruction alone enabling them to advance. The fighting was incessant. The explosion of mines, the crash of falling buildings, the roar of cannon and musketry, the shouts of the combatants continually filled the air, while a cloud of smoke and dust hung constantly over the city as the terrible scene of warfare continued day after day.

By the 17th of February the Cosso was reached and passed. But the French soldiers had become deeply discouraged by their fifty days of unremitting labor and battle, fighting above and beneath the earth, facing an enemy as bold as themselves and much more numerous, and with half the city still to be conquered. Only the obstinate determination of Marshal Lannes kept them to their work.

By his orders a general assault was made on the 18th. Under the university, a large building in the Cosso, mines containing three thousand pounds of powder were exploded, the walls falling with a terrific crash. Meanwhile, fifty pieces of artillery were playing on the side of the Ebro, where the great convent of St. Lazar was breached and taken, two thousand men being here cut off from the city. On the 19th other mines were exploded, and on the 20th six great mines under the Cosso, loaded with thousands of pounds of powder, whose explosion would have caused immense destruction, were ready for the match, when an offer to surrender brought the terrible struggle to an end.

The case had become one of surrender or death. The bombardment, incessant since the 10th of January, had forced the women and children into the vaults, which were abundant in Saragossa. There the closeness of the air, the constant burning of oil, and the general unsanitary conditions had given rise to a pestilence which threatened to carry off all the inhabitants of the city. Such was the state of the atmosphere that slight wounds became fatal, and many of the defenders of the barricades were fit only for the hospitals. By the 1st of February the death-rate had become enormous. The daily deaths numbered nearly five hundred, and thousands of corpses, which it was impossible to bury, lay in the streets and houses, and in heaps at the doors of the churches, infecting the air with their decay. The French held the suburbs, most of the wall, and one-fourth of the houses, while the bursting of thousands of shells and the explosion of nearly fifty thousand pounds of gunpowder in mines had shaken the city to its foundations. Of the hundred thousand people who had gathered within its walls, more than fifty thousand were dead; thousands of others would soon follow them to the grave; Palafox, their indomitable chief, was sick unto death. Yet despite this there was a strong and energetic party who wished to protract the siege, and the deputies appointed to arrange terms of surrender were in peril of their lives.

The terms granted were that the garrison should march out with the honors of war, to be taken as prisoners to France; the peasants should be sent to their homes; the rights of property and exercise of religion should be guaranteed.

Thus ended one of the most remarkable sieges on record,—remarkable alike for the energy and persistence of the attack and the courage and obstinacy of the defence. Never in all history has any other city stood out so long after its walls had fallen. Rarely has any city been so adapted to a protracted defence. Had not its houses been nearly incombustible it would have been reduced to ashes by the bombardment. Had not its churches and convents possessed the strength of forts it must have quickly yielded. Had not the people been animated by an extraordinary enthusiasm, in which women did the work of men, a host of peasants and citizens could not so long have endured the terrors of assault on the one hand and of pestilence on the other. In the words of General Napier, the historian of the Peninsular War, "When the other events of the Spanish war shall be lost in the obscurity of time, or only traced by disconnected fragments, the story of Zaragoza, like some ancient triumphal pillar standing amidst ruins, will tell a tale of past glory."

Spain for years past has had its double king,—a king in possession and a king in exile, a holder of the throne and an aspirant to the throne. For the greater part of a century one has rarely heard of Spain without hearing of the Carlists, for continually since 1830 there has been a princely claimant named Charles, or Don Carlos, struggling for the crown.

Ferdinand VII., who succeeded to the throne on the abdication of Charles IV. in 1808, made every effort to obtain an heir. Three wives he had without a child, and his brother, Don Carlos, naturally hoped to succeed him. But the persistent king married a fourth time, and this time a daughter was born to him. There was a law excluding females from the throne, but this law had been abrogated by Ferdinand to please his wife, and thus the birth of his daughter robbed Don Carlos of his hopes of becoming king.

Ferdinand died in 1833, and the infant Isabella was proclaimed queen, with her mother as regent. The liberals supported her, the absolutists gathered around Don Carlos, and for years there was a bitter struggle in Spain, the strength of the Carlists being in the Basque provinces and Spanish Navarre,—a land of mountaineers, loyal in nature and conservative by habit.

The dynasty of the pretender has had three successive claimants to the throne. The first Don Carlos abdicated in 1844, and was succeeded by Don Carlos the Second, his son. He died in 1861, and his cousin, Don Carlos the Third, succeeded to the claim, and renewed the struggle for the crown. It was this third of the name that threatened to renew the insurrection during the Spanish-American war of 1898.

This explanation is necessary to make clear what is known by Carlism in Spain. Many as have been the Carlist insurrections, they have had but one leader of ability, one man capable of bringing them success. This was the famous Basque chieftain Zumalacarregui, the renowned "Uncle Tomas" of the Carlists, whose brilliant career alone breaks the dull monotony of Spanish history in the nineteenth century, and who would in all probability have placed Don Carlos on the throne but for his death from a mortal wound in 1835. Since then Carlism has struggled on with little hope of success.

Navarre, the chief seat of the insurrection, borders on the chain of the Pyrenees, and is a wild confusion of mountains and hills, where the traveller is confused in a labyrinth of long and narrow valleys, deep glens, and rugged rocks and cliffs. The mountains are highest in the north, but nowhere can horsemen proceed the day through without dismounting, and in many localities even foot travel is very difficult. In passing from village to village long and winding roads must be traversed, the short cuts across the mountains being such as only a goat or a Navarrese can tread.

Regular troops, in traversing this rugged country, are exhausted by the shortest marches, while the people of the region go straight through wood and ravine, plunging into the thick forests and following narrow paths, through which pursuit is impossible, and where an invading force does not dare to send out detachments for fear of having them cut off by a sudden guerilla attack. It was here and in the Basque provinces to the west, with their population of hardy and daring mountaineers, that the troops of Napoleon found themselves most annoyed by the bold guerilla chiefs, and here the Carlist forces long defied the armies of the crown.

Tomas Zumalacarregui, the "modern Cid," as his chief historian entitles him, was a man of high military genius, rigid in discipline, skilful in administration, and daring in leadership; a stern, grave soldier, to whose face a smile rarely came except when shots were falling thick around him and when his staff appeared as if they would have preferred music of a different kind. To this intrepid chief fear seemed unknown, prudence in battle unthought of, and so many were his acts of rashness that when a bullet at length reached him it seemed a miracle that he had escaped so long. The white charger which he rode became such a mark for the enemy, from its frequent appearance at the head of a charging troop or in rallying a body of skirmishers, that all those of a similar color ridden by members of his staff were successively shot, though his always escaped. On more than one occasion he brought victory out of doubt, or saved his little army in retreat, by an act of hare-brained bravery. Such was the "Uncle Tomas" of the Navarrese, the darling of the mountaineers, the man who would very likely have brought final victory to their cause had not death cut him off in the midst of his career.

Few were the adherents of Don Carlos when this able soldier placed himself at their head,—a feeble remnant hunted like a band of robbers among their native mountains. When he appeared in 1833, escaping from Madrid, where he was known as a brave soldier and an opponent of the queen, he found but the fragment of an insurgent army in Navarre. All he could gather under his banner were about eight hundred half-armed and undisciplined men,—a sorry show with which to face an army of over one hundred and twenty thousand men, many of them veterans of the recent wars. These were thrown in successive waves against Uncle Tomas and his handful of followers, reinforcement following reinforcement, general succeeding general, even the redoubtable Mina among them, each with a new plan to crush the Carlist chief, yet each disastrously failing.

Beginning with eight hundred badly armed peasants and fourteen horses, the gallant leader had at the time of his death a force of twenty-eight thousand well-organized and disciplined infantry and eight hundred horsemen, with twenty-eight pieces of artillery and twelve thousand spare muskets, all won by his good sword from the foe,—his arsenal being, as he expressed it, "in the ranks of the enemy." During these two years of incessant war more than fifty thousand of the army of Spain, including a very large number of officers, had fallen in Navarre, sixteen fortified places had been taken, and the cause of Don Carlos was advancing by leaps and bounds. The road to Madrid lay open to the Carlist hero when, at the siege of Bilboa, a distant and nearly spent shot struck him, inflicting a wound from which he soon died. With the fall of Zumalacarregui fell the Carlist cause. Weak hands seized the helm from which his strong one had been struck, incompetency succeeded genius, and three years more of a weakening struggle brought the contest to an end. In all later revivals of the insurrection it has never gained a hopeful stand, and with the fall of "Uncle Tomas" the Carlist claim to the throne seemingly received its death-blow.

The events of the war between the Navarrese and their opponents were so numerous that it is not easy to select one of special interest from the mass. We shall therefore speak only of the final incidents of Zumalacarregui's career. Among the later events was the siege and capture of Villafranca. Espartero, the Spanish general, led seven thousand men to the relief of this place, marching them across the mountains on a dark and stormy night with the hope of taking the Carlists by surprise. But Uncle Tomas was not the man to be taken unawares, and reversed the surprise, striking Espartero with a small force in the darkness, and driving back his men in confusion and dismay. Eighteen hundred prisoners were taken, and the general himself narrowly escaped. General Mirasol was taken, with all his staff, in a road-side house, from which he made an undignified escape. He was a small man, and by turning up his embroidered cuffs, these being the only marks of the grade of brigadier-general in the Spanish army, he concealed his rank. He told his captors that he was a *tambor*. In their anxiety to capture officers the soldiers considered a drummer too small game, and dismissed the general with a sound kick to the custody of those outside. As these had more prisoners than they could well manage, he easily escaped.

On learning of the defeat of Espartero the city surrendered. The news of the fall of Villafranca had an important effect, the city of Tolosa being abandoned by its garrison and Burgera surrendered, though it was strongly garrisoned. Here Charles V. —as Don Carlos was styled by his party—made a triumphal entry. He was then at the summit of his fortunes and full of aspiring hopes. Eybar was next surrendered, the garrison of Durango fled, and Salvatierra was evacuated.

Victory seemed to have perched upon the banners of the Navarrese, town after town falling in rapid succession into their hands, and the crown of Spain appeared likely soon to change hands. Zumalacarregui proposed next to march upon Vittoria, which had been abandoned with the exception of a few battalions, and thence upon the important city of Burgos, where he would either force the enemy to a battle or move forward upon Madrid. So rapid and signal had been his successes that consternation filled the army of the queen, the soldiers being in such terror that little opposition was feared. Bets ran high in the Carlist army that six weeks would see them in Madrid, and any odds could have been had that they would be there within two months. Such was the promising state of affairs when the impolitic interference of Don Carlos led to a turn in the tide of his fortune and the overthrow of his cause.

What he wanted most was money. His military chest was empty. In the path of the army lay the rich mercantile city of Bilboa. Its capture would furnish a temporary supply. He insisted that the army, instead of crossing the Ebro and taking full advantage of the panic of the enemy, should attack this place. This Zumalacarregui strongly opposed.

" Can you take it ?" asked Carlos.

" I can take it, but it will be at an immense sacrifice, not so much of men as of time, which now is precious," was the reply.

Don Carlos insisted, and the general, sorely against his will, complied. The movement was not only unwise in itself, it led to an accident that brought to an end all the fair promise of success.

The siege was begun. Zumalacarregui, anxious to save time, determined to take the place by storm as soon as a practicable breach should be made, and on the morning of the day he had fixed for the assault he, with his usual daring, stepped into the balcony of a building not far from the walls to inspect the state of affairs with his glass.

On seeing a man thus exposed, evidently a superior officer, to judge from his telescope and the black fur jacket he wore, all the men within that part of the walls opened fire on him. The general soon came out of the balcony limping in a way that at once created alarm, and, unable to conceal his lameness, he admitted that he was wounded. A bullet, glancing from one of the bars of the balcony window, had struck him in the calf of the right leg, fracturing the small bone and dropping two or three inches lower in the flesh.

The wound appeared but trifling,—the slight hurt of a spent ball,—but the surgeons, disputing as to the policy of extracting the ball, did nothing, not even dressing the wound till the next morning. It was of slight importance, they said. He would be on horseback within a month, perhaps in two weeks. The wounded man was not so sanguine.

"The pitcher goes to the well till it breaks at last," . he said. "Two months more and I would not have cared for any sort of wound."

Those two months might have put Don Carlos on the throne and changed the history of Spain. In eleven days the general was dead and a change had come over the spirit of affairs. The operations against Bilboa languished, the garrison regained their courage, the plan of storming the place was set aside, the queen's troops, cheered by tidings of the death of the "terrible Zumalacarregui," took heart again and marched to the relief of the city. Their advance ended in the siege being raised, and in the first encounter after the death of their redoubtable chief the Carlists met with defeat. The decline in

the fortunes of Don Carlos had begun. One man
had lifted them from the lowest ebb almost to the
pinnacle of success. With the fall of Zumalacarregui
Carlism received a death-blow in Spain, for there is
little hope that one of this dynasty of claimants will
ever reach the throne.

MANILA AND SANTIAGO.

THE record of Spain has not been glorious at sea. She has but one great victory, that of Lepanto, to offer in evidence against a number of great defeats, such as those of the Armada, Cape St. Vincent, and Trafalgar. In 1898 two more defeats, those of Manila and Santiago, were added to the list, and with an account of these our series of tales from Spanish history may fitly close.

Exactly three centuries passed from the death of Philip II. (1598) to that of the war with the United States, and during that long period the tide of Spanish affairs moved steadily downward. At its beginning Spain exercised a powerful influence over European politics; at its end she was looked upon with disdainful pity and had no longer a voice in continental affairs. Such was the inevitable result of an attempt to run a great nation on the wheels of bigotry and fanaticism. It could not fail to sink into the slough of ignorance and conservatism at the end.

In her colonial affairs Spain was as intolerant and oppressive as in religious matters at home. When the other nations of Europe were loosening the reins of their colonial policy, Spain kept hers unyieldingly rigid. Colonial revolution was the result, and she lost all her possessions in America but the islands of Cuba and Porto Rico. Yet she had learned no lesson,—she seemed incapable of profiting by experience,—and the old policy of tyranny and rapacity was exercised over these islands until Cuba, the largest of them, was driven into insurrection.

In attempting to suppress this insurrection Spain adopted the cruel methods she had exercised against the Moriscos in the sixteenth century, ignoring the fact that the twentieth century was near its dawn, and that a new standard of humane sympathy and moral obligation had arisen in other nations. Her cruelty towards the insurgent Cubans became so intolerable that the great neighboring republic of the United States bade her, in tones of no uncertain meaning, to bring it to an end. In response Spain adopted her favorite method of procrastination, and the frightful reign of starvation in Cuba was maintained. This was more than the American people could endure, and war was declared. With the general course of that war our readers are familiar, but it embraced two events of signal significance—the naval contests of the war—which are worth telling again as the most striking occurrences in the recent history of Spain.

At early dawn of the 1st of May, 1898, a squadron of United States cruisers appeared before the city of Manila, in the island of Luzon, the largest island of the Philippine archipelago, then a colony of Spain. This squadron, consisting of the cruisers Olympia, Baltimore, Raleigh, and Boston, the gunboats Petrel and Concord, and the despatch-boat McCulloch, had entered the bay of Manila during the night, passing unhurt the batteries at its mouth, and at daybreak swept in proud array past the city front, seeking the Spanish fleet, which lay in the little bay of Cavité, opening into the larger bay.

The Spanish ships consisted of five cruisers and three gunboats, inferior in weight and armament to their enemy, but flanked by shore batteries on each end of the line, and with an exact knowledge of the harbor, while the Americans were ignorant of distances and soundings. These advantages on the side of the Spanish made the two fleets practically equal in strength. The battle about to be fought was one of leading importance in naval affairs. It was the second time in history in which two fleets built under the new ideas in naval architecture and armament had met in battle. The result was looked for with intense interest by the world.

Commodore Dewey, the commander of the American squadron, remained fully exposed on the bridge of his flag-ship, the Olympia, as she stood daringly in, followed in line by the Baltimore, Raleigh, Petrel, Concord, and Boston. As they came up, the shore batteries opened fire, followed by the Spanish ships, while two submarine mines, exploded before the Olympia, tossed a shower of water uselessly into the air.

Heedless of all this, the ships continued their course, their guns remaining silent, while the Spanish fire grew continuous. Plunging shells tore up the waters of the bay to right and left, but not a ship was struck, and not a shot came in return from the frowning muzzles of the American guns. The hour of 5.30 had passed and the sun was pouring its beams brightly over the waters of the bay, when from the forward turret of the Olympia boomed a great gun, and an 8-inch shell rushed screaming in towards the Spanish fleet. Within ten minutes more all the ships were in action, and a steady stream of shells were pouring upon the Spanish ships.

The difference in effect was striking. The American gunners were trained to accurate aiming; the Spanish idea was simply to load and fire. In consequence few shells from the Spanish guns reached their mark, while few of those from American guns went astray. Soon the fair ships of Spain were frightfully torn and rent and many of their men stretched in death, while hardly a sign of damage was visible on an American hull.

Sweeping down parallel to the Spanish line, and pouring in its fire as it went from a distance of forty-five hundred yards, the American squadron swept round in a long ellipse and sailed back, now bringing its starboard batteries into play. Six times it passed over this course, the last two at the distance of two thousand yards. From the great cannon, and from the batteries of smaller rapid-fire guns, a steady stream of projectiles was hurled inward, frightfully rending the Spanish ships, until at the end of the evolutions three of them were burning fiercely, and the others were little more than wrecks.

Admiral Montojo's flag-ship, the Reina Cristina, made a sudden dash from the line in the middle of the combat, with the evident hope of ramming and sinking the Olympia. The attempt was a desperate one, the fire of the entire fleet being concentrated on the single antagonist, until the storm of projectiles grew so terrific that utter annihilation seemed at hand. The Spanish admiral now swung his ship around and started hastily back. Just as she had fairly started in the reverse course an 8-inch shell from the Olympia struck her fairly in the stern and drove inward through every obstruction, wrecking the aft-boiler and blowing up the deck in its explosion. It was a fatal shot. Clouds of white smoke were soon followed by the red glare of flames. For half an hour longer the crew continued to work their guns. At the end of that time the fire was master of the ship.

Two torpedo-boats came out with the same purpose, and met with the same reception. Such a rain of shell poured on them that they hastily turned and ran back. They had not gone far before one of them, torn by a shell, plunged headlong to the bottom of the bay. The other was beached, her crew flying in terror to the shore.

While death and destruction were thus playing havoc with the Spanish ships, the Spanish fire was mainly wasted upon the sea. Shots struck the Olympia, Baltimore, and Boston, but did little damage. One passed just under Commodore Dewey on the bridge and tore a hole in the deck. One ripped up the main deck of the Baltimore, disabled a 6-inch gun, and exploded a box of ammunition, by which eight men were slightly wounded. These were the only men hurt on the American side during the whole battle.

At 7.35 Commodore Dewey withdrew his ships that the men might breakfast. The Spanish ships were in a hopeless state. Shortly after eleven the Americans returned and ranged up again before the ships of Spain, nearly all of which were in flames. For an hour and a quarter longer the blazing ships were pounded with shot and shell, the Spaniards feebly replying. At the end of that time the work was at an end, the batteries being silenced and the ships sunk, their upper works still blazing. Of their crews, nearly a thousand had perished in the fight.

Thus ended one of the most remarkable naval battles in history. For more than three hours the American ships had been targets for a hot fire from the Spanish fleet and forts, and during all that time not a man had been killed and not a ship seriously injured. Meanwhile, the Spanish fleet had ceased to exist. Its burnt remains lay on the bottom of the bay. The forts had been battered into shapeless heaps of earth, their garrisons killed or put to flight. It was an awful example of the difference between accurate gunnery and firing at random.

Two months later a second example of the same character was made. Spain's finest squadron, consisting of the four first-class armored cruisers Maria Teresa, Vizcaya, Almirante Oquendo, and Cristobal Colon, with two torpedo-boat destroyers, lay in the harbor of Santiago de Cuba, blockaded by a powerful American fleet of battle-ships and cruisers under Admiral Sampson. They were held in a close trap. The town was being besieged by land. Sampson's fleet far outnumbered them at sea. They must either surrender with the town or take the forlorn hope of escape by flight.

The latter was decided upon. On the morning of July 3 the lookout on the Brooklyn, Commodore Schley's flag-ship, reported that a ship was coming out of the harbor. The cloud of moving smoke had been seen at the same instant from the battle-ship Iowa, and in an instant the Sunday morning calm on these vessels was replaced by intense excitement.

Mast-head signals told the other ships of what was in view, the men rushed in mad haste to quarters, the guns were made ready for service, ammunition was hoisted, coal hurled into the furnaces, and every man on the alert. It was like a man suddenly awoke from sleep with an alarm cry: at one moment silent and inert, in the next moment thrilling with intense life and activity.

This was not a battle; it was a flight and pursuit. The Spaniards as soon as the harbor was cleared opened a hot fire on the Brooklyn, their nearest antagonist, which they wished to disable through fear of her superior speed. But their gunnery here was like that at Manila, their shells being wasted through unskilful handling. On the other hand the fire from the American ships was frightful, precise, and destructive, the fugitive ships being rapidly torn by such a rain of shells as had rarely been seen before.

Turning down the coast, the fugitive ships drove onward at their utmost speed. After them came the cruiser Brooklyn and the battle-ships Texas, Iowa, Oregon, and Indiana, hurling shells from their great guns in their wake. The New York, Admiral Sampson's flag-ship, was distant several miles up the coast, too far away to take part in the fight.

Such a hail of shot, sent with such accurate aim, could not long be endured. The Maria Teresa, Admiral Cervera's flag-ship, was quickly in flames, while shells were piercing her sides and bursting within. The main steam-pipe was severed, the pump was put out of service, the captain was killed. Lowering her flag, the vessel headed for the shore, where she was quickly beached.

The Almirante Oquendo, equally punished, followed the same example, a mass of flames shrouding her as she rushed for the beach. The Vizcaya was the next to succumb, after a futile effort to ram the Brooklyn. One shell from the cruiser went the entire length of her gun-deck, killing or wounding all the men on it. The Oregon was pouring shells into her hull, and she in turn, burning fiercely, was run ashore. She had made a flight of twenty miles.

Only one of the Spanish cruisers remained,—the Cristobal Colon. She had passed all her consorts, and when the Vizcaya went ashore was six miles ahead of the Brooklyn and more than seven miles from the Oregon. It looked as if she might escape. But she would have to round Cape Cruz by a long detour, and the Brooklyn was headed straight for the cape, while the Oregon kept on the Colon's trail.

An hour, a second hour, passed; the pursuers were gaining mile by mile; the spurt of speed of the Colon was at an end. One of the great 13-inch shells of the Oregon, fired from four miles away, struck the water near the Colon. A second fell beyond her.

An 8-inch shell from the Brooklyn pierced her above her armor-belt. At one o'clock both ships were pounding away at her, an ineffective fire being returned. At 1.20 she hauled down her flag, and, like her consorts, ran ashore. She had made a run of forty-eight miles.

About six hundred men were killed on the Spanish ships; the American loss was one man killed and one wounded. The ships of Spain were blazing wrecks; those of the United States were none the worse for the fight. It was like the victory at Manila repeated. It resembled the latter in another particular, two torpedo-boats taking part in the affair. These were attacked by the Gloucester, a yacht converted into a gunboat, and dealt with so shrewdly that both of them were sunk.

The battle ended, efforts to save on the part of the American ships succeeded the effort to destroy, the Yankee tars showing as much courage and daring in their attempts to rescue the wounded from the decks of the burning ships as they had done in the fight. The ships were blazing fore and aft, their guns were exploding from the heat, at any moment the fire might reach the main magazines. A heavy surf made the work of rescue doubly dangerous; yet no risk could deter the American sailors while the chance to save one of the wounded remained, and they made as proud a record on the decks of the burning ships as they had done behind the guns.

These two signal victories were the great events of the war. Conjoined with one victory on land, they put an end to the conflict. Without a fleet, and with no means of aiding her Cuban troops, Spain was helpless, and the naval victories at Manila and Santiago, in which one man was killed, virtually settled the question of Cuban independence, and taught the nations of Europe that a new and great naval power had arisen, with which they would have to deal when they next sought to settle the destinies of the world. The United States had risen into world-wide prominence upon the ruin of the colonial empire of Spain.

THE END.

By Charles Morris.

Historical Tales.

By Charles Morris.

A History of the United States of America, its People, and its Institutions.

For Advanced Grades.　　Profusely Illustrated.　　School Edition.
Half leather, $1.00.

"Mr. Morris, who is known as the author of several previously written books on American history, gives us here a text-book of noteworthy excellence. It is well written, having a directness and simplicity of narrative especially commendable in a work of this kind, and a cursory examination of the text leads us to judge that the writer has combined the excellence of accuracy and impartiality of statement in an unusual degree. The foot-notes add much to the work, and the illustrations are very good."—*Chicago Inter-Ocean.*

An Elementary History of the United States.

Fully Illustrated, with Maps.　　Price, Exchange, 35 cents;
Introduction, 60 cents.

1. This book is intended as an introduction to the regular school histories in general use, and is adapted to pupils from twelve to fifteen years of age.

2. It is devoted to the leading facts of American history, giving special attention to those relating to the development of the country.

3. These facts are presented in a continuous narrative, showing how the country has developed from the time of Columbus.

4. It not only tells the story of the leaders, but of the people in their home life, manner and customs, progress in invention, and development in the arts and sciences.

5. This book deals not alone with political development, but also with the details of every-day life,—the description of those powerful influences which have made not only America but Americans.

6. The inner story of the American people is set forth in a series of chapters descriptive of city and country life, and various periods of our colonial and national history.

7. Special effort has been made to write this work in a clear, lucid, and simple style, adapting it to the comprehension of the young, and at the same time making it of interest to older readers, so it will be read or studied not only with interest but with delight.

By Charles M. Skinner.

Myths and Legends of Our Own Land.

Fourth Edition. Illustrated with photogravures. Two volumes in box. 12mo. Polished buckram, gilt top, deckle edges, $3.00; half calf or half morocco, $6.00.

"Mr. Skinner certainly has made a remarkable collection of nearly three hundred myths, traditions, and curious stories, out of which novelists, poets, and dramatists might draw excellent material."—*New York Nation.*

"There is a permanent worth in this collection. The subject is a picturesque one, and the author has spared neither time nor trouble in his long and fruitful research."—*New York Bookman.*

"Mr. Skinner is to be congratulated on his idea of collecting these myths and legends."—*New York Critic.*

With Feet to the Earth.

Buckram, ornamental, gilt top, deckle edges, $1.25.

"A sunny, witty, and altogether charming little book of no more than ten short chapters, telling one how to be a gentleman, a scholar, and a vagabond of the roads and fields, even of the streets and by night, and all at the same time. 'With Feet to the Earth' he calls it; while 'with wits keen, heart kind, and eyes everywhere,' is a sub-title not in the book, but which the reader cordially furnishes in his own mind."—*New York Book Buyer.*

J. B. LIPPINCOTT COMPANY, PHILADELPHIA.

By Theodore Wolfe, M.D.

Literary Shrines.

The Haunts of Some Famous American Authors.

A Literary Pilgrimage.

Among the Haunts of Famous British Authors.

Ninth Edition. Two volumes. Illustrated with four photogravures.
12mo. Crushed buckram, gilt top, deckle edges, $1.25;
half calf or half morocco, $3.00 per volume.

"Dr. Theodore F. Wolfe has not only an intense appreciation of belles-lettres, but a mastery inferior to none of those he writes about. His style is perfect, direct, and pointed, yet with every possible grace of expression. Every paragraph, often every sentence, is a pen-picture, but always of something the reader wants to see."
—*New York World.*

"We can heartily commend both this book and its companion for choice merits such as one would look for with confident expectancy in a book of this character. Reading them, one is brought into close and familiar contact with those he chiefly admires and reverences."—*Boston Courier.*

J. B. LIPPINCOTT COMPANY, PHILADELPHIA.